Death Comes Silently

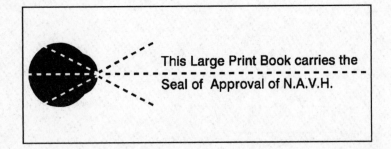

This Large Print Book carries the
Seal of Approval of N.A.V.H.

A DEATH ON DEMAND MYSTERY

DEATH COMES SILENTLY

CAROLYN HART

THORNDIKE PRESS
A part of Gale, Cengage Learning

 GALE
CENGAGE Learning·

Detroit • New York • San Francisco • New Haven, Conn • Waterville, Maine • London

GALE
CENGAGE Learning

LIBRARY OF CONGRESS CATALOGING-IN-PUBLICATION DATA

Hart, Carolyn G.
  Death comes silently / by Carolyn Hart.
    pages ; cm. — (Thorndike Press large print mystery)
  ISBN-13: 978-1-4104-4748-7 (hardcover)
  ISBN-10: 1-4104-4748-0 (hardcover)
  1. Darling, Annie Laurance (Fictitious character)—Fiction. 2. Darling, Max (Fictitious character)—Fiction. 3. Booksellers and bookselling—Fiction. 4. Women detectives—South Carolina—Fiction. 5. Murder—Investigation—Fiction. 6. South Carolina—Fiction. 7. Large type books. I. Title.
  PS3558.A676D4454 2012b
  813'.54—dc22   2012003344

Published in 2012 by arrangement with The Berkley Publishing Group, a member of Penguin Group (USA) Inc.

Printed in the United States of America
1 2 3 4 5 6 7 16 15 14 13 12

To Natalee Rosenstein
in thanks for safe harbor

1

Nicole Hathaway drew the covers over her head to block out the pale winter moonlight. Alone. She felt so alone. How had her life gone so wrong? She stifled a sob. Always, she'd wanted to find the right man. She'd been thrilled when Everett pursued her. He was such a gentleman. Not rough or crude like so many boys she knew. He was older, distinguished. He'd treated her with such courtesy. His manners and cultivated background dazzled her. She'd taken great pride in being Mrs. Everett Hathaway. She wasn't sure when she began to see him for what he was, fussy and pretentious and sometimes not very nice.

She hadn't expected what happened, a man who occupied her every waking thought, a man who brought her ecstasy. By that time, she'd moved to a bedroom of her own, at first with the plea that she had such a cough from her allergies and she would sleep better alone, and then the days continued to pass and they slept apart.

She didn't want to go on this way. Why live a lie? But when she spoke of being together, there were reasons and excuses, and soon her lover didn't meet her as often.

There had to be a way to make it happen . . .

Brad Milton massaged one temple. Another silent migraine. Pretty soon the Coke and Excedrin would take effect. He pushed the spreadsheets away. He couldn't work anymore tonight. It didn't matter how many times he looked, the numbers wouldn't get any better. There was no way out. He glanced at his desk calendar. Fourteen more days and the notes could be called. If only he could have six more months. He was close to lining up two good-sized jobs.

But Everett Hathaway had shrugged and said, "Sorry, old man." Everett had affected a slightly British accent and pseudo upper class attitude ever since he dabbled in art history at a provincial university more than twenty years ago. "Business is business."

Leslie Griffin maintained a bright smile. She tossed her head, a favorite mannerism. Her eyes flicked to the mirror in an art deco frame. As always, she was pleased at her image, long golden hair, creamy complexion, china blue eyes, an image as bright as Jane Lynch on *Glee.* Her cool gaze swung back to the man in the large red leather chair behind the blond wood desk. The chair wasn't suited to his weedy frame, making him look insubstantial. It had been perfect for his burly older brother whose place he'd taken.

Though Leslie's smile never wavered, she dissected him as only the young and arrogant can . . . Reddish hair and eyes like green slime . . . Thinks he's gorgeous in that dorky checked sweater . . . Reminds me of that stupid goat at the stables . . . big, round, dumb eyes . . . All he does is read stupid poetry . . . Looks silly behind Uncle Eddie's desk, like a kid playing grownup . . . Wonder if he knows about Nicole . . . *That would distract him from her, that was for sure . . . Usually* she could get in and out of the agency without dealing with him . . . If she had to listen to him very often, she'd rather be at school, boring as it was . . .

Everett Hathaway cleared his throat, appeared uncomfortable. "I'm deeply disappointed in your behavior, Leslie."

She tried to look bored. But there was something in his voice . . . She clutched her neck in faux distress. "Has that pointy-headed math teacher complained? Honestly" — she heaved an aggrieved sigh — "I don't see any point in algebra."

"This isn't about school, although there is a good deal we might discuss there. Your grades are deplorable. Perhaps your lack of attention to your duties is part of a larger picture." He folded his arms. "I am aware that you did not stay with a friend last Friday night. Instead, you were in Savannah with one Steve Raymond." He spoke the name with distaste.

Leslie made an effort to appear distressed. "Steve and I were just having an adventure." Uncle was such an old sap, maybe he'd believe her. She'd been fooling him for years. "Some of the kids dared me to spend the night with a guy in Savannah." She tried to sound casual, amused, like the old movies where they stood around drinking martinis and smoking and talking smart. "We stayed at a Holiday Inn, but we were kind of like on a scavenger hunt and we went around town getting trinkets to prove we'd stayed and we had the ferry tickets, too, by the time we came back the next morning." She clapped her hands together. "I won the bet and now a bunch of them have to take turns doing whatever I say." She tilted her head. "I'm going to make Margo walk down Main Street in a bikini." For an instant, she wished her fabrication were real. It would be delicious to make tall, skinny, elegant Margo shiver. She was pleased with her invention.

Everett's grim face remained hard. "You spent the night with him in a motel. One of your teachers saw you and called me. You're under age. I understand he's nineteen. If I call the police, he'll go to jail."

Leslie stiffened. "It was a joke. Come on. And I'm almost eighteen." He was a dried-up old stick. No wonder Nicole cheated on him. What was it Mr. Wingate said in English the other day about somebody in a novel? That he was a dunce. She liked that word. That's what Uncle was. A dunce. She wished she could tell him.

Everett glanced at a legal pad on his desk. "Where did you meet him?"

She gave a casual wave of her hand. "On the beach last summer. A bunch of kids hang out together. It's real laid back."

"Where does he live?"

Her shrug was elaborate. "I don't know. We were over at Bunny's" — she was pleased with her casual tone; she could almost believe her own lies — "and the idea came up and he was the one who said, sure,

he'd play along, why not? He's a real joker."
And so good in bed. "But I can't tell you all
that much about him." She had a quick
memory of the shabby cabin where Steve
lived and the fun they had with his dad usually out of town.

Everett's tone was frosty. "The teacher
knew a bit about him. She said he dropped
out of school a couple of years ago. His
mother ran off with a drummer in Savannah. His father's rarely home, always on the
road." His derisive tone dismissed Steve and
his family as undesirables.

Leslie felt a rush of panic. If he kept nosing around, he'd find out about much more
than a single night on the mainland. She
managed a tinkling laugh. "It was just a
joke. I promise I won't do it again." Since
there had been no joke, that wouldn't be a
hard promise to keep.

"You are forbidden to see Steve Raymond
again. And" — he looked at her with that
slimy gaze — "unless you agree, I'll cut your
allowance."

Leslie played a mean hand of poker. She
knew when to fold them. Again she gave a
shrug. "No problem. This was no big deal.
A joke. Steve played along. And don't even
think about going to the cops." There was
an edge to her voice. "That would be sooo

humiliating. I couldn't show my face at school. So let it go and Steve will be history."

As she walked out of his office, she was thinking fast. Would he keep checking? He might. If he did, he might keep his threat to cut her allowance. He didn't live in the real world and he had no idea she had more money than anyone she knew. She had her future planned. As soon as she got out of boring, awful high school, she would rent an apartment in Savannah, maybe take enough classes to keep her uncle agreeable. But she wouldn't be able to do anything without money. Why had their grandfather left a will where she couldn't get her hands on her inheritance until she was twenty-five? Until then, her uncle controlled the checkbook.

Trey Hathaway worked two phones. His round-faced, plump secretary, her expression harried, stood in the doorway flapping a FedEx envelope. He pointed at his desk, continued to talk. "Yeah. Sure. We're about to get that one buttoned down. I'll call you back, first thing in the morning." He put down the landline, picked up his cell, and spoke in a mollifying tone. "Thanks for holding, Regina. There was a mix-up here, but I've straightened everything out." He swung to face his computer, moved the cursor to attach a file, typed an e-mail, tapped send. "I just sent an e-mail with the updated campaign. I'm sorry about the delay. I think you'll be pleased and your project is high priority. I promise it won't happen again." He winced at the edge of anger in the client's reply and the harsh click as the phone slammed down. He put down the receiver and picked up the FedEx envelope. He ripped it open and pulled out a sheet. The words in the second paragraph burned in his mind: Consider our contract with Hathaway Advertising Inc. null and void due to lack of performance . . .

Blood rushed to his head. He pushed up from his desk, strode across the room. Trey was a thin version of his late father, sandy haired, brown eyed, always moving like a man in a hurry. His late father's firm resolve was evident in the tough set of his face. Now was the time for a showdown. His uncle shut him out of everything, made stupid decisions, missed deadlines, and royally screwed up old accounts and new. Trey was eager to take over. He loved planning campaigns. He'd do whatever he needed to do to make the agency tops again, sought out by big companies all over the South. He'd had a great idea for tourist promotion for the Broward's Rock Chamber of Commerce:

Broward's Rock
Jewel of the Sea
Surf, Sand, Sun
Fun for Everyone
Cross the Sound for Island Delight
Dance Away the Night
Lovers' Rendezvous

He'd make the letters big, bright, shiny, maybe emerald green, surround them with a montage of holiday shots, golfing, kayaking, surfing, sunset beach strolls, the island's ferry since Broward's Rock was a good forty minutes from the mainland.

As per usual, all outgoing material passed over Everett's desk. Everett had called him in, advised Trey in his pompous manner that he was glad Trey had some ideas but this sort of thing was better handled by a more mature approach, and the project was shelved.

Trey reached the door, one lean hand on the knob, when he remembered. Everett usually left early on Fridays. He played backgammon at the club in the winter,

15

golfed in good weather.

Trey's thin face hardened. When Everett was in the office, he lounged in his late brother's oversized red leather chair and played with his iPad. A few more months of "work" by Everett would spell an ignominious end for Hathaway Advertising, its reputation shot. It shouldn't be this way. Dad had built a great agency. After his mother's death so long ago, Dad had focused on the agency. Sometimes Trey thought the agency gave his dad something to love after their mom died. He'd worked furiously. When he'd died, Trey wanted more than anything to keep the agency going, keep his dad's dream alive. His cousin, Leslie, thought he was a sap to work. The only reason she came to the office was to get out early from school, claiming an internship at the family business. She did her nails and surfed the Net. Why work when you were rich? Not that either he or Leslie controlled their inheritances yet. Everett was their guardian until they were twenty-five. He paid their bills and provided a monthly stipend. That was infuriating, too. Worst of all had been Everett taking over the house. Until his dad's death, Everett had lived on the mainland. The house ultimately would belong to Trey. Now he had to share it with Everett and his wife and his cousin. There was plenty of room, but the house should have been his. Instead, he had to live like he was a teenager in somebody else's home.

Was Everett taking revenge on his older, handsomer, successful brother, destroying the business Edward Marlow Hathaway II built by sweat and effort? It wasn't about money. There was plenty of money from the estate of Edward M. Hathaway, his grandfather, for Everett and the grandchildren to live on. They didn't need income from the agency, but it wasn't a matter of money for Trey. His dad had been a man with charm and brains and energy. Hathaway Advertising had been the joy of his too-short life.

Trey turned away from the door, jammed his hands in his trouser pockets, walked to the window that overlooked the harbor, and stared moodily out at white-flecked swells. He had to do something. Time was running out for Dad's dream and for his. He couldn't even start a new agency until he had control of his inheritance at twenty-five.

Everett blocked him any way he tried to turn.

■ ■ ■ ■

Sgt. Hyla Harrison, as always, wore a crisp, fresh uniform. Her auburn hair was drawn back in a bun beneath her cap. She zipped her dark blue uniform jacket against the biting chill of the breeze off the Sound as she studied the white fiberglass hull of the empty MasterCraft ProStar 197. She noted the uneven tilt of the boat where it had been run aground. A sweet boat. She liked its name, *Sunny Daze.* The empty boat moved ever so slightly in the rising tide. She pulled a printout from the pocket of her uniform. A bird-watcher found the obviously abandoned craft and notified police, who traced it to owners who were very surprised that it had been taken from its mooring. She gazed at the mushy ground and broken cordgrass where the bow had come to rest.

Hyla knew the island well. This cove abutted a picnic area, deserted on this raw New Year's Day. The boat might have rested here for weeks except for a hardy bird-watcher surveying the area with binoculars because a friend had spotted a rare snowy owl the previous day. The boat had been taken sometime after dark yesterday, according to the owner.

She studied the interior of the boat that was visible from the bank. There appeared to be no damage. She reached into a pocket for a slim digital camera. She worked slowly, always patient, always thorough, taking photographs that made clear the boat's location, then moving nearer for a series of shots. When done, the camera in a zipped pocket of her jacket, she pulled plastic gloves from another pocket, slipped them on, and picked up a black vinyl fingerprint kit.

She reached across a couple of feet of marsh water to the transom and stiff-armed to vault lightly into the boat, the kit in her free hand. She walked slowly forward, eyes scanning the cushions. All were in place. At the front, the key was in the ignition. The owner had been defensive. "Sure the key was in the boat. We've never had a problem. We never worried about the boat." Officer Harrison's smile was sardonic. Broward's Rock wasn't immune to crime.

She placed the kit in the captain's seat, lifted the lid, retrieved powder, and dusted the steering wheel. When the coat had been applied, she stared down in surprise. No fingerprints. None. Not a single whorl or line. Last night the driver might likely have worn gloves as well as a thick jacket to ward off the cold. Even so, there should have been traces of smudged prints. Instead, the grey plastic wheel was clean and shiny. Obviously the wheel had been carefully polished. No gloves? Or simply great care?

The latter seemed out of character for a joy ride.

Joy ride . . .

The police officer's thin, freckled face squeezed in a frown. Kids did nutty things for sure, but a late-night jaunt on a low-forties December night, even colder out on the water with the wind, made no sense. On a hot July night, "borrowed" boats, skinny-dipping, smoking pot behind a sand dune came as no surprise.

Again her probing gaze moved slowly over the boat. No bottles. No trash. If kids took the boat, there should have been some trace. She felt a prickle up her back. Something was off-kilter here. She studied the railing, moved nearer the transom. A scratch on the near gunwale marked the fiberglass. She bent closer, saw a greenish streak. Possibly something metal had struck the fiberglass, left particles of paint. She again used the camera. She almost turned to leave, then stopped. That green streak bothered her. It wouldn't do any harm to get a sample. She picked up the evidence kit. She carefully lifted green paint particles to a transparent rubber-backed gelatin layer. As she removed the layer, she saw a tuft of material adhering to the railing. She methodically finished her task, then used a magnifying glass to look more closely. Her eyes narrowed. The scrap might be black cotton or wool snagged by a cracked spot in the plastic. She visualized a dark figure, moving fast, possibly swinging out of the boat to jump to shore, a gloved hand gripping the rail. Had a jacketed arm grazed the railing and a scrap torn free? She hesitated, then once again used the kit, bagged the scrap, applied a label. Whoever took the boat had tried not to leave a single trace, but that was hard to do in a physical world. Sometimes a tiny scrap would be enough to electrocute a man. Anyway, she'd turn in a complete report. Lou Pirelli would ask when was she going to stop trying to be a super cop, then grin and toss her a jelly donut, like a treat to a retriever. Sure, this wasn't a big-deal heist, no harm done, but she liked to be meticulous. If there was evidence, she would gather every scrap. Never taking anything for granted was her way of keeping a structured world even though she well knew life could turn dangerous in a heartbeat. She swallowed, pushed away a memory that would never leave her, the night she called in from patrol in Miami, *officer down,* as her partner died from gunshots to his chest.

She closed the evidence kit and focused on the slight rock of the boat and the chill breeze, anything to fill her mind.

Jeremiah Young handled the axe easily. He was chunky with big shoulders and sturdy legs. He liked to feel the ripple of his muscles as he chopped kindling. Poor folks in real need of firewood came by Better Tomorrow now that the temperature dipped into the forties at night. Not that a sea island was ever real cold, not like Minnesota. Bad days up there. He swallowed hard. He'd been stupid. Stolen a car and tried to get away when a siren sounded. They told him he was lucky. Two years in jail. His mind shied away like a horse smelling a snake. Lucky . . . He'd never told anybody how bad the nights had been. That guy named . . . His mind shied again. Remembering made him feel sick, made him want to cry. He'd rather die than ever go to jail again. He'd been like a whipped dog when he made it back to the island. His aunt took him in, helped him get the job here at Better Tomorrow. He paused, wiped sweat from his face. Despite the cool day, the chopping made him hot, but he savored the sweat and the freedom. It was good to feel hot, to be outside, free.

An old Chevy rattled up to one side of the shabby frame building and parked in the shade of the lean-to where the mower was stored along with ladders and some of the canned and boxed groceries.

The car door slammed. He knew the driver. Mrs. Burkholt. He called her Mrs. Big-Eyes to himself. She sidled past him with a wide skittery stare like he was going to grab her. He'd opened the back door last week when she was on the phone . . . She spent a lot of time on the phone . . . chatter, chatter, chatter . . . Her high voice had risen and he couldn't help hearing. ". . . supposed to help people who've been in jail, but he's so big and he has such long straggly dirty hair and he always looks sullen. I swear, he scares me to pieces . . ." He'd walked inside, his steps purposefully heavy, and thumped the case of Cokes on a counter by the shelves. He saw a flicker of fear in her eyes as he passed. The old cow. He didn't care about her. She'd be damn lucky if she never really knew what it was like to be scared.

The axe head swung up and crashed down. The log splintered.

On the back steps, Gretchen Burkholt

gasped at the sharp crack. "Oooh. I hate that noise."

Billy Cameron's big broad face, usually genial, was studiously inexpressive. The Broward's Rock police chief sat with his hands planted solidly on his thighs in an office that gleamed with fine woods, a mahogany desk, oak paneling, heart pine floor, and expensive furnishings, an oriental rug, shining gold brocade drapes, a suit of armor on a pedestal. Billy's observant blue eyes never wavered as he gazed across the room. Blond and husky, he was solidly built with massive shoulders and hands. In his crisp khaki uniform, he looked like what he was: a cop's cop, a tough cop, a good cop. He stared impassively at a plump-cheeked, rotund man in a baby blue cashmere sweater who appeared small behind his massive desk.

Only someone who knew Billy well would realize he was coldly angry, unblinking gaze, lines tight at the corners of his full mouth, shoulders braced.

Mayor Cosgrove's green eyes shifted from that steady stare. However, he continued full stride, his high voice penetrating. ". . . expect some accommodation of distinguished visitors. I told that policewoman of yours that I could drive, but she wouldn't listen. She made Buck Troutt get out of the car and treated him like a common criminal. Rude. Uncalled for."

"Sergeant Harrison's actions were appropriate." Billy's tone was even. "The car was driven erratically. Mr. Troutt failed the field sobriety test."

"He's a CEO." The mayor's voice was reverential. "He's thinking of buying the Mansfield property on the beach, developing it. Do you realize what that could mean to the island? The jobs, the people, the growth!" The mayor's voice rose to a squeak. "This matter must be dealt with immediately. None of this should have happened. Why, we just had a few drinks at the club. Nobody was on the road. He had a little trouble seeing in the dark. And there's no reason why that unattractive woman should have had her car parked outside the country club gates." The mayor's eyes slitted. "Let's be clear. If the officer filing the report doesn't appear in court, the charge will be dropped. I expect Sergeant Harrison to be off the island that day."

Billy slowly stood. "Sergeant Harrison will continue to perform her duties."

The mayor bounced to his feet, his penguin-plump face malevolent. "Your contract comes up before the council in three weeks. As police chief, you are expected to make the island attractive to investors."

Billy nodded gravely. "Anyone interested in living on Broward's Rock can be assured that the laws are properly enforced." He turned and walked toward the ornate hand-carved door, a fancy office for a small — but powerful — man.

Annie Darling stopped on the boardwalk and leaned against the railing, drawing a deep breath of chilly sea-scented air. The marina hosted a respectable number of boats even though it was January. A crew-man in a heavy wool jacket hosed down one side of an ocean-going yacht. Chugging out into the Sound was a boat with the unpretentious name *Just Plain Vanilla.* Annie liked unpretentious people and houses and belongings.

As if on cue, she heard a distant throaty rumble and recognized the roar of Max's Maserati. They usually drove separately to the marina shops, she to her mystery book-store and he to Confidential Commissions, his rather unusual office where he offered counsel to people in trouble. Max was quick to insist he wasn't a private detective, which required particular qualifications in the sovereign state of South Carolina. He was comfortable in his job description. He provided advice. If discovering information was essential to serving his clients, that certainly didn't make him a private eye.

The Maserati's engine cut off.

Annie pictured the man in her life swinging out of his red sports car. Max loved his Maserati, but he didn't drive the powerful and swift car because it was expensive. He savored the power and elegance of the ultimate driving machine. Annie was willing to spot everyone an indulgence. The Maserati was Max's. Hers? She possessed an original perfect first-edition — complete with color plate illustrations — of *The Man in Lower Ten* by Mary Roberts Rinehart. Certainly the Maserati was hugely more expensive than the book, but for both of them, the joy was in the object and never in the price.

Annie's smile was wry. Her husband often suggested she was a captive of Calvinistic attitudes, not, he airily continued, a difficulty he'd ever faced. Yes, they were different. Max grew up rich. She and her single mom worried about paying the bills. Annie's home had been in wind-swept Amarillo; Max's in an affluent Connecticut suburb. Annie couldn't imagine life without work; Max firmly believed life was made for pleasure. But one unforgettable night, their eyes had met at a crowded after-theater party in Greenwich Village. She'd thought them too different ever to be together and she'd run away to the little South Carolina sea island of Broward's Rock. Max had followed. Perhaps they weren't suited in some ways, but there was never any doubt that they could not live without each other. What was love? Passion, yes, always, but love meant trust and faith and laughter. To know that Max was in a room with her made that place a haven. They'd known happy days and tough days, but it was always the two of them together.

She crossed her fingers. On both hands. Not, of course, that she was superstitious. But she and Max had come near the unraveling of their lives, and she never ceased to be thankful for their escape. Underneath their cheerful banter, they possessed a sober realization of life's uncertainties.

She turned to look across the boardwalk at the shops that curved in a semicircle facing the marina. Death on Demand, her wonderful mystery bookstore, beckoned her, though she was braced for a frazzling day. She shivered, drew her cheerful peacock blue wool jacket close.

Her cell phone rang.

Annie slipped the cell from the pocket of her wool slacks, glanced at the caller ID, raised an eyebrow. "Hello."

"Don't think she hasn't spotted you." Ingrid spoke in a whisper.

The connection ended. Her clerk was giving her a heads-up. Another day, another encounter with Annie's always unpredictable mother-in-law, Laurel Darling Roethke. Where Max was handsome, Laurel was gorgeous. Silver blond hair framed a fine bone structure. Yet there was more than beauty; there was a hint of rollicking adventure and enthusiasm and eagerness for life. When Laurel walked into a room, everyone suddenly felt touched by magic. Laurel's Nordic blue eyes might sometimes be slightly spacey, but they could also be incredibly perceptive.

Annie moved toward the steps to the shops. Annie had survived Laurel's flirtation with cosmic karma, her delight in saints, most especially the remarkable Teresa of Ávila, and most recently her determination to decorate the bookstore with photographs of exotic cats. Cat photos now hung on the walls among book posters — Harlan Coben's new thriller, Mary Saums's clever new *Thistle and Twigg* — and were adored

29

by customers. Annie enjoyed looking at them as well. As she well knew, cats ruled, especially Agatha, Death on Demand's sleek black resident feline.

Annie reached the front door, thoughts whirling. Laurel was no stranger to the store, but today was challenging, a Beaufort book club arriving for a talk by Emma Clyde and a light lunch. Had the chicken salad been delivered? Emma, the island's famous crime writer, would sign copies of her new Marigold Rembrandt mystery, *The Case of the Convivial Cat.* Woe betide Annie if they ran out of books. Woe betide Annie if she'd ordered too many, making the author feel the signing was a flop.

Annie drew a deep breath. Chicken salad . . . the new books . . . Leave a couple of boxes in the storeroom? She didn't have time for Laurel this morning. It wasn't that she didn't appreciate the charm of Laurel's most recent preoccupation, but she insisted — nicely — upon audience participation. Annie wasn't sure why she objected so strenuously, but she'd always refused to wear silly hats, watch Charlie Chaplin, or draw undue attention to herself.

She stopped with her hand on the knob. Good grief, was she a pompous ass?

What harm would it do to play along? Get

in the spirit?

Annie gave a decided head shake. Responding quickly to a question before she had time to think was too much like a public Rorschach test. She took a deep breath, opened the door, activating the new *Inner Sanctum* door recording that Ingrid's husband, Duane, had installed before Halloween. The satisfying creak of hinges foretold chills and thrills, exactly what readers would find in the finest mystery bookstore north of Florida's Murder on the Beach.

Annie stepped inside, drew another happy breath, this time of books and bindings and coffee.

Slender and intense, her graying hair in a new short cut, Ingrid worked at the front counter, smiling, chatting, and ringing up sales with practiced efficiency. A long line of customers snaked toward the coffee bar. Annie didn't spot her mother-in-law. She smiled in relief. No doubt Laurel was sharing her new vision with one of the ladies from Beaufort. Wonderful. Annie had plenty on her plate. She needed to make sure there was enough chicken salad and help Henny Brawley take orders at the coffee bar. Emma's crusty tone — oh, dear, was she being combative with a reader? — was commandingly audible over the twitter of the club ladies who had arrived way too early and —

"Annie dear!" Her mother-in-law popped from behind the beaded curtain that screened the alcove to the children's mystery section. "Think of the sun!" Laurel beamed. Was it accidental that she was positioned precisely in the glow of a ceiling spotlight? Whatever, her silver gold hair gleamed and her patrician face with deep-set blue eyes, fine bridged nose, and dimpled chin was strikingly lovely.

Annie stared. On anyone else, Laurel's costume would have looked absurd, a pink straw farmer's hat, a red-and-white plaid shirt, sleeves rolled to the elbows, navy denim overalls accented by gold buttons at the straps and pockets, and a pink leather version of farm boots. On Laurel, the result was fetching. The farmer's hat boasted, of course, a sunflower tucked beneath the cerise hat band.

Laurel plucked a two-foot sunflower from a capacious pocket, held the blossom out to Annie with a winning smile. "Sunflower time," she caroled, the pink boots giving a quick Cossack tattoo. "Quick now — five seconds to answer — picture a Sunflower and sweet potatoes. First thought?"

Involuntarily, an obedient mouse in Laurel's mental laboratory, *home* popped into Annie's mind, a memory of a sunflower spoon handle as her mother lifted steaming sugar-streaked candied sweet potatoes to her plate. Annie's lips parted, clamped shut.

"Time's up." Laurel's tone was kind, not chiding. Her manners were exquisite. The five-second limit served two purposes. A quick response was certain to reflect innermost thoughts, but the deadline also afforded an unobtrusive escape hatch for those unwilling to participate. Laurel's smile was approving, whether she received an answer or not. She continued with no hint of irritation, "I'm sure the magic of Sunflowers will be with you now, adding warmth and happiness to your day. Here is a Sunflower just for you." When she spoke, the flower's name was clearly capitalized.

As the days had shortened and the onshore breeze freshened, Laurel had received a bouquet of sunflowers from a new beau. Always seeking the inner meaning of events large and small, she discovered that sunflowers were considered happy flowers, their faces reminiscent of the life-giving warmth of the sun. Ergo, she devised her Sunflower Game, the better, she assured Annie, to encourage happy thoughts that everyone needed, especially in winter.

Annie took the bristly stalk, looked at the flower, noted two opposite spirals, which indicated this was a disk sunflower . . . With an effort, she yanked her mind back toward the work harness. She had learned more about sunflowers in the last few weeks than she'd *ever* wanted to know, and today she didn't have time for extraneous sunflower thoughts.

"It's gorgeous, Laurel." And, of course, it was, the petals as softly gold as summer sunshine. "Thank you." Clutching the stalk, she edged down the congested center aisle, heading for the coffee bar area where the ladies would lunch and, at one side, Emma Clyde would regally hold forth as the Queen of Crime.

Despite her sunflower-be-damned mood, she couldn't help overhearing Laurel confide to a cherubic elderly lady listening with a slightly bemused expression, "Sunflower disk flowers are both male and female and are fertile. Isn't that a happy thought on a cold winter day?"

Fertile. If anyone ever knew about . . . Annie wrenched her mind away from any consideration of her oft-married mother-in-law's romantic proclivities as well as sunflower trivia. There was much to be done . . .

The next hour passed in a frantic blur,

34

food served, spilled iced tea mopped up, a controversy as to seating settled, cell phones hopefully turned off, and finally spiky-haired Emma Clyde in a caftan that looked like a cross between a ship's billowing sail and a flannel nightgown rose majestically to her feet. Stalwart, sturdy, stern-visaged, self-absorbed, and a sponge for attention, Emma looked benignly at her audience. "Marigold Rembrandt and I" — she might have been describing royalty — "have perhaps enjoyed our finest moment —"

Annie watched with a cool gaze. Was Emma grandiose or what?

Emma's knife-sharp blue eyes paused in their sweep of the room.

Annie promptly rearranged her face in what she devoutly hoped would pass as an entranced expression.

"— in *The Case of the Convivial Cat.* Marigold once again takes Inspector Houlihan to task as she insightfully, really quite brilliantly —"

Annie maintained her pleasant expression. Implicit was the premise that Marigold was simply a reflection of the incredible sagacity of author Emma Clyde.

"— follows the cunningly inserted clues —"

Annie's cell phone rang. She'd been

thrilled when Duane Webb had downloaded the Inner Sanctum creak to serve as her ringtone, mirroring the sounds when Death on Demand's front door opened, but the piercing squeal blared in the hushed quiet of the bookstore.

Emma came to a full stop. Her icy blue eyes slitted. She folded her sturdy arms across her chest and gazed at Annie with a stony expression.

Annie fumbled in her pocket. *Cree-aaak* . . . She'd gone from table to table and pled with charm for all cell phones to be turned off. How could she have forgotten her own?

Phone in hand, she flipped it open, whispered, "I can't talk now . . ."

Emma waited, the Empress Dowager contemplating a lower life form.

Some of the ladies turned to stare. A few made disapproving murmurs.

Annie heard a familiar semihysterical voice. "Annie, you have to come . . . Such a fright always . . . I don't think I can stay here with that big hulking brute . . . and" — her voice puffed with self-importance — "I have to decide what to do about that index card that I found . . ."

Annie took a deep breath. Gretchen Burkholt lived in a world of extreme stress, a gentle rain heralded a nor'easter, any stray cat was surely rabid, the potato salad at the picnic might harbor salmonella . . . Annie and Gretchen were among volunteers at Better Tomorrow, the island charity shop, which offered groceries, clothing, job tips, firewood, help with bills, and encouragement to those in a financial bind. Better Tomorrow's client base had swelled during the recent bad times. Gretchen had switched volunteer slots today so Annie could host the luncheon and book event. Therefore, Annie was in no position to be abrupt.

Emma cleared her throat. Emphatically.

Annie heard snatches of Gretchen's increasing frenzied patter. ". . . I always check the clothing, especially when someone's recently deceased . . . family members can be too distraught . . . and everyone was so puzzled that he was out there . . ."

Annie broke in, hating to be rude, but she had to end the distraction before Emma rose and departed with the grace of an offended rhinoceros. "Gretchen, sorry. Have to go. Call back. Leave me a message. As soon as the signing's over" — anything to be free — "I'll do whatever you want." She ended the call, clicked off the phone, dropped it in her pocket.

"I'm very sorry. Unexpected call. I forgot

to turn my phone off." This last in a mumble. "Now I know Emma will forgive me and share with you the wonderful" — great emphasis — "scene where Marigold Rembrandt" — Annie always did her duty and had read the new book even though she loathed the supercilious redheaded sleuth — "realizes in the nick of time that the inverted coffee cup means that Professor Willingham is not what he seems to be."

It was touch and go. Finally, almost graciously, Emma resumed her talk. Fortunately, discussing herself or her work always put Emma in a great good humor.

Peace reigned at Death on Demand. Imperious Emma, pleased by adulation and substantial book sales, had departed. A huge sunflower in a vase on the coffee bar was the only evidence of Laurel's earlier presence. The book club ladies had spilled into the wintry afternoon, clutching filled book bags, ready to cap their island visit by a thorough survey of other marina shops. The tables had been cleared.

Annie lifted a cappuccino in a toast to Henny Brawley, longtime customer and mystery connoisseur. Henny was not only a good friend, she always offered an extra hand at special events. "Thanks, Henny. You were great."

Ingrid nodded in agreement. "To help with cleanup is above and beyond." She also raised her cup, a steaming Kona brew with a dash of raspberry sauce.

"You are very welcome." Henny's well-modulated voice reflected her accomplishments as a valued actress in local theater productions. "You know it's my pleasure. Emma was . . . Emma." Her tone was amused.

The three women exchanged understanding glances. Emma Clyde was a terror.

Henny's smile was wicked. "I wish you could have seen your face, Annie, as you tried to disengage from that call."

Annie sat bolt upright. The phone call . . . "Gretchen subbed for me this afternoon at Better Tomorrow. I told her to call back and leave a message. There've been a couple of calls. I had it on vibrate." As she spoke, Annie retrieved the messages, lifted the phone to listen.

Ingrid murmured to Henny, "It's good that Emma didn't have a dagger!"

Gretchen didn't bother with a salutation in the second call. "Hope you can come pretty soon . . . really awkward . . . Maybe it's better to let sleeping dogs lie . . . Oh, there he is again" — the voice dropped to a whisper — "always clumping in and looking mean . . ." A long silence. "He's gone back out." She spoke normally. "I don't want to be here alone with him any more . . . I'm going to tell Henny. If she doesn't schedule somebody with me, I'm not coming back . . . Anyway, I don't know what to do about the card . . . I heard the police or maybe it was the Coast Guard asked anyone with information to contact them . . . Nobody saw him leave the house . . ."

Annie concentrated. What on earth was Gretchen talking about?

". . . but the card makes it clear . . . No wonder he took the kayak out without telling anyone . . . I don't want to cause trouble, but I think I should let the family know . . . Of course that's what I should do . . ."

The call ended.

Her second message, left twenty-six minutes later, began, "I told the housekeeper." Gretchen sounded disappointed. "It would have been nicer if I could have spoken to Mrs. Hathaway, but the maid said she was out. Anyway, I hope the maid got everything straight. I mentioned the names in the note, but I didn't want to say too much. That wouldn't have been right. I tried to be tactful." She sounded plaintive. "I explained I

40

was going through Mr. Hathaway's clothes and found a very *personal* message in the pocket of a jacket. I told her the card seemed connected to his going out that night in the kayak. Well, obviously it was. There were several names and one of them was in a different handwriting. I don't suppose we'll ever know what that meant. I mean, the card named names, said what was happening 'tonight.' " Her tone put the word in quote marks. "No wonder he went out in the kayak. A scandal really . . ."

Annie now understood Gretchen's mention of the Coast Guard. Two weeks earlier, well-known island resident Everett Hathaway's dead body, buoyed by a life vest, had been found floating not far from his overturned kayak. An autopsy listed drowning due to unconsciousness as a result of hypothermia as the cause of death.

"I know the note to Everett is important because I found it in the pocket of the tweed jacket he wore the day he died. I saw him that last day in the jacket, a blue-flecked tweed with blue leather buttons. You know how he dressed. He always wanted to look like he was a Brit. Anyway, he died that night . . . The note was in the right pocket. Obviously that wasn't what he wore in the kayak. Jeans and a warm jacket probably.

41

Anyway" — Gretchen's tone was bright — "I said the note and some coins and a pocketknife were here and could be picked up anytime. I have them on the table in the sorting room. So, that's that. Oh." Her voice dropped to a whisper. "Here he is again. He scares me. When the signing's over, please come and keep me company."

The connection ended.

Annie gave an exasperated sigh. She took a hearty sip of her now lukewarm cappuccino. "Gretchen's more trouble than she's worth." Her smile at Henny was rueful. "I should have asked you to take my turn, but I wanted you here today." Henny both volunteered and scheduled volunteers at Better Tomorrow. "Gretchen claims she's scared of Jeremiah. I'll admit he's scruffy. That straggly brown hair under a ratty do-rag makes him look like a mean biker, and sometimes he doesn't shave."

Henny looked concerned. "Has Jeremiah done anything to frighten Gretchen?"

"He clumps when he walks inside." Annie's tone was dry.

"Oh, horror." Ingrid was disdainful.

"She wants me to come over." Annie swung down from the coffee bar stool. It would be pleasant to be out in the cool late afternoon. "I don't mind. She did me a favor."

2

Better Tomorrow's location wasn't ideal. A twisting blacktop road led to an old wooden house framed by pines. Island entrepreneur Ben Parotti provided the structure on the north end of the island at no cost. There were no near neighbors, but several paths and a rutted dirt road helped make the property accessible to that impoverished part of the island. The late afternoon sun sank behind the towering loblolly pines, plunging the road into deep shadow. For an instant the Thunderbird's headlights framed a doe before she plunged into the woods.

The house came into view and Annie slowed. Thick woods bounded the small area. Neatly corded firewood was stacked on the north side of a small oyster shell parking lot. Tree limbs waiting to be split were piled to one side of a rattletrap pickup that belonged to the charity. There was room for perhaps a half dozen cars. The only other vehicle was Gretchen's Chevy. Monday was usually a slow day. Clients flooded in toward week's end for food and help with rent money.

Annie parked her red Thunderbird next to the Chevy. She was relieved that Gretchen hadn't deserted her post, though Annie suspected her anxiety about Jeremiah had more to do with self-dramatization than actual fear. In fact, Gretchen had likely enjoyed her afternoon thoroughly, from the discovery of an index card she considered scandalous in Everett Hathaway's jacket to self-induced shivers whenever Jeremiah appeared.

Annie smiled as she crossed the dusty ground toward the front porch. Ben had invested some of his profits from Parotti's Bar and Grill and his ferry to the mainland in island real estate. Ben kept the house in good repair. The porch steps had recently been replaced and a new sink installed in a back workroom.

She paused on the second step. The front door was wide open. She frowned. The house had no central heating, depending upon electric heaters. In December and January volunteers wore heavy wool sweaters and slacks and joked about those who only serve and freeze. Everyone was careful to shut the door firmly, keeping inside the precious warmth.

She opened the screen. A bell clanged, its purpose to alert a volunteer busy in the back of the house that someone had arrived. Annie paused in the open doorway. The lights were turned off. "Gretchen?" She stepped inside, one hand fumbling for the switch.

Light flooded the one-time living room. Filing cabinets and a long trestle table with two donated computers sat to the right. Clothes racks for men, women, and children filled the left side of the room. A hallway led to former bedrooms. One was now a pantry; the second held toys, small appliances, and electronic castoffs; the third served as a sorting room; the fourth as a storeroom.

"Gretchen?" Her voice sounded loud in the stillness. Instead of Gretchen's hurried, twittery voice, there was only silence. "Gretchen?" No response. Not a rustle or a squeak. The quiet was broken only by the distant sounds of pines soughing in the breeze, crows cawing.

Annie stepped slowly forward. The old wooden floor creaked. "Gretchen?"

The landline phone pealed.

Annie stared down the hallway. If Gretchen were in the bathroom, surely she would hear and come.

The phone rang, once, twice, a third time . . .

Annie heard the wobble in her voice as she called out again. "Gretchen? Jeremiah?" Jeremiah should be here, chopping wood, preparing boxes of food, repairing toys.

Annie listened with every fiber of her being. Long ago a policewoman had advised her: Never ignore fear. If you sense danger, get help, run, shout, scream.

Annie felt her body tremble. Something was wrong. The quiet was too intense. She did not sense a human presence. She would know deep inside if someone else were in the silent house. Her hand slipped to her pocket. She pulled out her cell. She could call the police. Mavis Cameron, police chief Billy Cameron's wife, was the dispatcher. Mavis would send a car pronto. Yet Annie had a rock-deep certainty that no one else was near. She was alone in this silent place.

Annie forced herself forward, cell phone in hand. She stiffened each time the floor creaked. She heard the sound of her quick, shallow breaths, recognizing the whistle of fear. She opened the pantry door. Everything was as it should be, foods arranged on shelves, packed boxes stacked to the left of the door. It took only an instant to check the opposite room with small appliances and electronics arranged on several tables. Straight ahead was the bathroom and another hallway to the right. The bathroom door was open. Annie made a right turn, stopped.

A smear of blood stained the worn wooden floor.

She lifted the cell phone.

"Browar —"

"Mavis. Annie Darling." She struggled to talk. "I'm at Better Tomorrow. Blood . . ." The door to the sorting room was ajar. Annie carefully edged past the blood. She never doubted the smudges were blood. The color was too red, too bright to be anything else. In the grip of horror, Annie used her elbow to push the door wide. She had to look. Whatever had happened, Gretchen or someone was hurt. "Send someone." Her voice was quick and harsh. "There's blood . . ." Annie sagged against the doorjamb. There would never be time again for Gretchen Burkholt. "She's dead . . ."

Annie clung to the porch railing, used the support to stay upright. Gretchen had subbed for her . . . Gretchen had subbed for her . . . Gretchen had subbed for her . . .

Sirens shrieked. Two patrol cars jolted to

a stop in the dirt road, short of the parking lot. The forensic van pulled up behind Billy Cameron's unmarked black Ford SUV. Doors opened. Chief Cameron strode toward the house, a forty-five in his hand. In the light streaming from the living room, he looked big and tough, ready for any eventuality.

"Gretchen's dead. The axe . . ." She stopped, shuddered. "I made sure. No pulse. You can't have any pulse when your head . . ." She tried not to remember. She never wanted to remember. She would never forget.

"Any trace of the perp?" His eyes scanned the porch, the woods.

Numbly, Annie shook her head.

Billy turned and gestured to the officers in the yard, several staring hard-faced at the building, ready to serve as backup. Sergeant Harrison, her thin face intent, surveyed the woods, alert and tense, her gun in hand. "Harrison, secure a perimeter, set up spotlights, conduct a ground search. Mavis" — he nodded at his wife, who also headed up the forensic team — "bring Doc inside when he arrives."

Annie concentrated on thinking about police procedure, the search that would begin at the edges of the property, slowly draw in to the structure. The careful survey Billy would make when he walked through Better Tomorrow. He would see what she had seen, but, once he confirmed that the victim was dead, further investigation would await a formal declaration of death by Dr. Burford, the medical examiner. The body could not be moved until Doc arrived.

Billy looked at Annie. "Where did you find her?"

"Down the hall. To the right." Again dreadful images rose. She pressed fingers against her temples, willing the stark pictures away. She focused her mind on Billy, blond hair frosted with white, blunt face etched by good times and bad, observant blue eyes that now, as he worked, looked remote.

"Anyone else here?"

She started to shake her head, stopped. "Jeremiah Young should be here. He's the handyman. I haven't seen him. I called for Gretchen and for him. No one came." Her voice was thin. "He's the one who chops wood. I don't know if that's his axe . . ." She broke off. No one would ever use that axe again.

Billy cupped his free hand to his mouth. "Harrison, check the property for the handyman. Jeremiah Young. He has a record." That was a warning. Step carefully. Possible danger.

Annie looked at Billy in surprise, then wondered at her lack of insight. Billy knew his island. He was a native. He knew the people from the north end to the south. Of course he knew Jeremiah had served time.

He nodded at Annie. "You can wait in your car. We'll get to you as soon as possible." He gestured to Lou Pirelli, and the two men stepped into the living room.

As Annie headed for the Thunderbird, Marian Kenyon's tan Beetle swerved to park behind a patrol car. Marian burst from the car, notepad in hand, Leica hanging from strap. The *Gazette*'s crime reporter, dark hair ruffled by the wind, took one look at the porch, recognized a crime scene off limits to interruption, and bounded toward Annie. "Came over the scanner. How come you're here? What's up?"

Annie folded her arms, wished her jacket were warmer. Marian had the tenacity of a rat terrier. It was easier to tell what she knew. She spoke in short jerky sentences, but confined her remarks to her arrival and what she'd found. "That's all I know, Marian. I'm supposed to wait in my car for Billy."

Marian was already looking past Annie,

51

seeking another source.

Annie was grateful to reach the car. She turned on the motor to warm the car's interior though she didn't feel as if she would ever be warm again. Gretchen had subbed for her . . .

She huddled in the front seat, holding her cell. "Max . . ." The words spilled out and she took strength when he said he was on his way, would soon be there. Doc Burford's dusty black car jolted to a stop. He slammed out the driver's door and walked to the house, face in a glower. Doc loved to deliver babies. He fought death for all his patients and, always, he resented murder.

Max parked behind her.

She tumbled from her car and into his arms, clung to him. "Blood in the hall . . . Gretchen was lying face down . . . The back of her head . . . An axe . . ."

Max's arm was tight around her shoulders. He looked across the yard at freshly chopped wood.

Annie's voice was thin. "There's no axe. Jeremiah chopped the wood." She shuddered. "I'll have to tell Billy."

Max looked at her with worried eyes, smoothed a tendril of hair. "Try not to remember."

All around them the machinery of a

murder investigation unfolded, officers searching, videocams, written notes, low-voiced colloquies.

Annie shuddered. "When I went inside, the silence was dreadful. I knew something was wrong. I called out for Gretchen and for Jeremiah, and no one came. Jeremiah should have been here."

The front door banged and Doc Burford lumbered down the steps, his face folded in a tight frown. Now the police could investigate the sorting room, start their painstaking collection of evidence at the murder scene.

They stood in silence, and Annie clung to his hand. Could she have saved Gretchen?

Portable spotlights turned the dusky yard almost as bright as day. Foot by foot, searchers drew ever nearer the house, checking, collecting, filming, sketching. An ambulance came and technicians wheeled a gurney inside.

A few minutes later, the front door slammed. She didn't look, wouldn't look, but she heard the thud of steps on the wooden porch and knew techs were maneuvering a gurney burdened by a black body bag.

The break room at the police station was

calm and quiet, untenanted except for Annie and Max. Annie appreciated Billy plac-
ing them here rather than in a bleak inter-
rogation room. She took a sip of coffee from
a foam cup. Beyond the closed door, she
was sure the station hummed with intensity,
officers at computers, on phones, all off-
duty officers on hand as well as former chief
Frank Saulter. The Broward's Rock police
had few extra hands, and Frank's island
knowledge and quiet counsel were always
welcomed by Billy Cameron.

"Eat." Max was firm.

Annie wanted to push away the paper
plate even though it held her favorite sandwich in all the world, fried oysters on an
onion bun with dollops of Thousand Island
dressing from Parotti's Bar and Grill just
down the street from the police station. Max
had even ordered cheese fries with a side of
chili in an effort to tempt her. He was right.
She felt the beginning throb of a headache.
Food would help. And caffeine. She un-
wrapped the bun and began to eat.

Max nodded approval.

She managed a smile. Max's presence
gave her strength. Usually they laughed
together, his dark blue eyes gleaming, his
handsome face crinkling in delight, his eyes
telling her she was desirable and his. Now

his steady gaze reassured her. He was beside her, solid and real and strong.

Billy Cameron entered the room with a green folder and a laptop. He settled at the table and handed Annie her cell phone. "We've transcribed the calls from Gretchen Burkholt. She was a volunteer?"

"Yes. I switched with her today." Annie felt a twist of misery. "She was supposed to work Thursday but I needed to be at the store. Henny Brawley schedules the volunteers. My shift — the one Gretchen took — was from noon to four."

"Who worked the first shift?"

Annie picked up her cell, clicked several times. "Verena Rogers."

Billy noted the phone number. He opened the folder, picked up a sheet of paper. "In her calls, Gretchen Burkholt stated four times that she was afraid of Jeremiah Young. At the end of her call —" His eyes dropped to the sheet and he quoted, *"Here he is again. He scares me."*

He didn't repeat Gretchen's final words. There was no need. Annie heard them in her mind, would hear them again and again: *When the signing's over, please come and keep me company.* Annie put down the unfinished sandwich, looked at Billy with anguished eyes. "Gretchen subbed for me.

She was alone and someone killed her. I could have gone the first time she called. I didn't go" — her voice broke — "and Gretchen is dead."

Max's hand shot out, gripped her arm. His voice was stern. "You didn't know she was in danger. Tell Billy about Gretchen." He gave her arm a squeeze and settled back in his chair with his arms folded, his gaze commanding.

Billy pulled a pen from his pocket, drew out a notebook. He gave Annie an encouraging nod.

Annie was hesitant. "I hate to say things about her now."

Billy spoke quietly. "It's important to know whether she had good judgment."

Annie slowly shook her head. "She often exaggerated. She made everything a big deal. She thought every raccoon she saw was going to attack her, every siren meant someone she knew had been hurt in an accident. If some women at a church luncheon stood off in a corner, they were talking about her. That's why I never paid attention when she shivered and whispered that Jeremiah was big and mean-looking. He's not big and mean-looking. I mean, he's big." She looked at her six foot two inch husband and even taller Billy. "Not as big as you and Max, but powerful, like a football player. He's scruffy. Sometimes he doesn't shave. But he never looked mean. He looked pathetic, like a dog that's been kicked."

"Have you worked with him?" Billy watched her closely.

Annie nodded. "Of course. He carries in boxes and bundles and unloads cases of pop and handles big items like refrigerators and TVs."

"Were you ever afraid of him?" Billy's tone was interested.

"Never." She shot back the answer without hesitation. "Honestly, I can't believe he'd hurt anyone, especially not like . . ." She broke off, clutched Max's hand. "Last week somebody dumped a puppy out in front and Jeremiah found him and he made a place for him out back in the shed and got food. When I went back, he was cuddling the puppy, said he'd been crying for his mom. He found a home for him with a family his aunt knows."

"Maybe he was kind to animals" — Billy tapped the transcript of the calls — "but Gretchen Burkholt was afraid of him."

"Gretchen was fine with Jeremiah until she found out he'd been to prison." Annie's voice was sharp. "His sentence came up at the first meeting with the volunteers a few weeks after he was hired and everyone knew he'd stolen a car but he never hurt anyone. Henny hired him because she knows his aunt, and the aunt said he wasn't bad or mean, he made some bad choices and was very sorry. Henny said she checked with you."

Billy's face was somber. "He was part of my Scout troop. He dropped out when he was fourteen. I thought he was a good kid who'd gotten off track, started running with a wild bunch. But so far as I know he was never violent, no fights. Had there been any trouble with him at Better Tomorrow?"

Annie shook her head. "Not so far as I know. I would have heard. He really worked hard. The only person who didn't like him was Gretchen. She treated him like he was a gangster. I don't want to be mean, but she would say anything for attention."

But Gretchen was dead and Jeremiah was missing.

"Billy" — she tried to keep her voice steady — "have you found Jeremiah?"

"No trace so far. He didn't come home from work. His aunt opened the house to Sergeant Harrison. The aunt's upset, shocked, claims he'd never ever hurt anyone. Hyla got a description, six foot one inch, light brown hair, light brown eyes, one hundred and eighty-five pounds, last seen wearing red do-rag, Braves sweatshirt, jeans, work boots, a brown corduroy jacket. Hyla checked the backyard, including some sheds. She walked around the neighborhood. Nobody's seen him. He doesn't have a car. He rode an old black Schwinn that had been donated to Better Tomorrow. The bike's not at Better Tomorrow or at his house. We've got an APB out. Ben Parotti will make sure he doesn't take the ferry. He's bottled up on the island unless he steals a boat. The marinas are alerted. We'll get him. So far as we know, he isn't armed, but we're calling him a person of interest, possibly dangerous. We'll continue to search. The dogs lost his scent at the dirt road behind Better Tomorrow."

Annie looked across the table at Max, saw the sudden stillness in his eyes. She knew that Max remembered confusion and uncertainty and the bay of bloodhounds in pursuit. Neither of them would forget the August days when he was accused of killing a beautiful young woman in a remote cabin on the island.

"Dogs." In her mind she heard their cry.

"Looks like he hopped on his bike and got the hell out." Billy tried to sound matter-of-fact, but his eyes held sadness as he remembered a teenager in a Scout uniform, fresh-faced with no premonition of a troubled future. "That's what looks bad for him. An innocent man doesn't run away."

Max's voice was mild. "Unless you're an ex-con and you find a woman battered to death by the axe you used to chop wood." He met Billy's gaze.

Billy leaned back in his chair, folded his arms. "Except the victim told Annie she was afraid of him and within an hour or so she's dead." His eyes dropped again to the top sheet. "She talked about Jeremiah and about an index card she found in a tweed jacket."

Hope glimmered in Annie's mind. If Gretchen died because of a card she found in a donated jacket, Annie was not at fault for ignoring Gretchen's complaints about Jeremiah. "She said the card was in the jacket Everett Hathaway wore the day he died."

Billy nodded. "Right. We found eight boxes of clothes tagged from the Hathaway house, only one opened. He died two weeks ago. Apparently the family was clearing out his things."

Annie stared at Billy. "Gretchen said the police wondered why Everett Hathaway was out in a kayak that night."

Billy looked mildly surprised. "We asked around. Never discovered much. Strange to

60

take out a kayak on a windy December night, but who's to know? The wife said he hadn't been out in a kayak since the weather turned cold, but obviously he went out that night. His wife said she went to bed around ten. She didn't see him after dinner. They didn't share a room. She was surprised he'd taken the kayak, but the night was clear. Maybe he wanted to look at the stars."

Annie remembered the pleasure in Gretchen's breathy voice. "Gretchen said the note 'named names.' Maybe he went out to meet someone."

"Maybe." Billy was unruffled.

"Why didn't that person come forward when the police asked for help?"

Billy looked sardonic. "Maybe he had a girlfriend and she for sure didn't want to speak up. Maybe he never reached the place where he was going to meet some hypothetical person, and whoever it was kept quiet because it didn't matter after he died. There could be a dozen reasons. Some innocent. Some not so innocent. We checked around. He wasn't a skilled kayaker, he was dumb enough to go out by himself on a cold night, water temperature forty-eight degrees, he capsized, couldn't catch the boat, and was too far from shore to swim to safety before hypothermia got him. As soon as he was unconscious, his face dropped into the water and he drowned. A PFD keeps you afloat. It doesn't keep your head up. It was an accident, Annie." He flipped open his laptop, clicked several times, pushed it toward Annie.

Max leaned forward to look with her at the autopsy report for Everett Morgan Hathaway. It didn't take long to find the pertinent information: Death resulted from drowning, which ensued as a result of hypothermia . . . No evidence of trauma except for abrasions on both hands . . .

Max looked up. "Abrasions on his hands?"

Billy nodded. "Scrapes and scratches. Probably he tried to right the kayak, climb back in." He pulled the laptop back, clicked.

Annie looked hopeful. "Gretchen put the index card on the table in the sorting room. What was written on the card?"

Billy shook his head. "We haven't catalogued everything in the room. We spotted the pocketknife and change that she mentioned but we didn't find an index card. There are a couple of possibilities. We'll check with the Hathaways. There are only four calls on Gretchen's cell. Three to you and one to the Hathaway house. Someone from the family may have come by and picked up the card but left the knife and

62

the coins. If so, she was alive at that point. It would be helpful to find out when Gretchen was last seen. She left the second message on your cell at two fifteen. Your nine-one-one call came in at three nineteen."

Annie remembered the comfortable sense of relaxation at Death on Demand, the coffee she'd shared with Henny and Ingrid while at Better Tomorrow death moved ever nearer Gretchen, who loved to star in her own little dramas, spinning out visions of a dangerous handyman and scandal in the pocket of a dead man's jacket.

"What's the other possibility?"

Billy's face was grim. "We haven't found her purse. Maybe she put the index card in it for safekeeping. The purse is missing. So is Jeremiah Young." Again that flicker of sadness. When had a Scout turned into a thief?

Annie was stricken. "Do you think he killed her to steal her purse?"

Billy looked weary. "Maybe she came in the room and found him in her purse. Maybe he wanted to take a couple of dollars, thought she wouldn't miss them. If she caught him and called the police, he would be back in jail ASAP." His cell rang. Billy unhooked the phone, lifted it, listened. "Right. Good work." He rose, gave Annie and Max a brief nod. "The axe killed her.

63

Trauma to the back of the head. She was struck by the blunt end, not the blade." He pressed his lips together for an instant before he spoke. "Fingerprints on the shaft match Jeremiah Young's."

"I appreciate your coming by." Billy Cameron was a police officer. He was also a Southern gentleman always aware of how to treat a lady. He pulled out a chair at the central table for Henny Brawley.

Henny took her seat. "Of course I came. I'll do everything I can to help. I'm terribly sorry for poor Gretchen. I understand you are looking for Jeremiah? Oh, Billy, are you sure? I can't believe he would hurt anyone."

Billy was somber. "I know. I would have bet that he was going to get straightened out after he came home, but he was at Better Tomorrow when Gretchen left her last voice mail on Annie Darling's cell. She said she was afraid of him. His fingerprints are on the weapon that killed her. He wasn't there when we arrived and his bike is gone. There is no evidence to suggest anyone else visited Better Tomorrow this afternoon. Gretchen made three calls to Annie Darling, and in each one she expressed fear of Jeremiah. She also told Annie that she had called the Everett Hathaway residence to report that she'd found a card and some change and a pocketknife in the pocket of the jacket Hathaway wore the day he died that she thought the family would want to have. We checked with Mrs. Hathaway. She said there wasn't a message from Gretchen on the pad by the main phone but possibly someone may have seen and discarded it, deciding it wasn't important. In any event, so far as Mrs. Hathaway knows, no one from the family came by Better Tomorrow. We'll keep checking to make sure. If one of them dropped by, they might know something useful."

"If someone from the family came, Gretchen should have noted a visitor in a log at the front desk. The volunteer on duty is asked to record the number of visitors every hour." Henny's tone was rueful. "That's what volunteers are supposed to do. A lot of them don't bother or just make a guess at the end of the day."

"Do they get the names?" Billy looked eager.

Henny shook her head. "Not names. Numbers. We end up with a tally of people coming on a given day and the most popular hours. Nothing fancy. Just the usual four lines then a cross bar to make five. Say we averaged nine people on a Wednesday afternoon, thirty-two on a Friday afternoon. It helped me know how many volunteers to schedule. Monday is always slow, so each shift is taken by a single person."

"We still have a crew gathering evidence there." Billy picked up his cell, tapped. "Mavis, look for a notebook on the front desk in the reception area." He raised an eyebrow at Henny.

"A bound spiral notebook on the right back corner of the desk. It should be open to Monday, January sixteen."

Billy described the notebook and the tally system. "What have you got?" He listened, nodded. "Thanks. Take the notebook into evidence." He flicked off the call, looked soberly at Henny. "According to the log, no visitors after one o'clock. She died between two fifteen and three nineteen."

Henny spoke quickly. "It's possible there were visitors and she intended to make the notations before she left." Careless, unmethodical, dramatic Gretchen.

"Possibly." His tone was noncommittal. "We know Jeremiah was there."

Henny understood Billy's focus. Yet she couldn't believe the hangdog young man whose eyes had teared when she offered him the job would commit murder. And why? She didn't believe he'd taken Gretchen's purse. He'd learned his lesson about stealing when he went to prison. Why else commit murder? Gretchen might have treated him unkindly, but murder — violent and ugly — surely required much more reason.

Billy slid his papers together. "I'd like to have a copy of his personnel file."

Henny doubted the file held much that Billy didn't already know, but she nodded. "Tell Mavis she'll find the personnel folders in the middle drawer of the metal file cabinet."

"Thanks." He reached for his cell. "We plan to keep the house closed for a couple of days as a crime scene. You can arrange for a cleanup of the murder room on Thursday. If you think of any other information that might be helpful, give us a call."

Henny was accustomed to the utter darkness that enveloped her home on the marsh, especially on a cloudy winter night. She had no near neighbors. Her one-room weathered gray house on stilts was utterly private. She took great pleasure in her quiet home. She often started and ended her days on the porch that overlooked the ever changing marsh, the cordgrass chartreuse in summer, golden in spring and fall, drab brown in winter. Ducks and cormorants bobbed in the swells of the Sound. Migrating terns often stopped over for weeks. Yesterday she'd spotted a flock of fork-tailed Forster's Terns with their distinctive black eye bars, dusky bills, and yellow feet. Owls hooted deep into the night. She waged a continuing war with an especially wily raccoon who defied her every effort to make the garbage pail lids resistant to his agile fingers.

The house loomed straight ahead. She'd left on the living room light because the front porch light was out. As she turned her old but reliable Dodge into a sandy patch of ground by two palmettos, the headlights swept the fenced area to the right of the steps that contained the garbage pails.

Drat. The gate was ajar. Foiled again, though why Wiley, as she thought of the raccoon, hadn't simply swarmed over the fence was only another puzzle in their relationship. She turned off the car and slammed the door. Sometimes a sharp sound was enough to prompt Wiley's departure. Not tonight.

Shrugging into her winter jacket, she walked toward the enclosure. Clever creature. The wooden bar that latched the gate was upright and the panel ajar. She pushed it wide, stepped into the enclosure, clapping her hands. One foot struck a plastic garbage can lid.

She scarcely had time to realize there was no raccoon crouched atop the pails when she was covered by a thick material, struggling for breath, heart pounding, as strong arms held her in a tight grip.

3

Annie stared into darkness. Their bedroom held a faint radiance from a security light on the end of the second-story verandah. She didn't look toward the digital clock. It had been nearing three when she'd last checked. Tomorrow she would be tired, headachey. She desperately needed to sleep. Sleep would not come. Despite Max's insistence that she could not have prevented Gretchen's death, Annie felt a grim certainty that if she hadn't ignored Gretchen's complaints about Jeremiah, Gretchen's body would not now lie in a mortuary. What if she'd gone to Better Tomorrow as soon as she received Gretchen's first call? Certainly she had been alive then.

All the *what ifs* in the world would not change the fact that Gretchen Burkholt was dead.

Max's strong arm, his warm living arm, pulled her close. "We all do our best." His voice was soft, understanding.

She lay in the comforting circle of his arms, her head on his shoulder. "She was afraid of Jeremiah and I thought she was silly." Annie's voice shook.

His breath was warm against her face. "Why did you think she was silly?"

The words came haltingly. "Jeremiah . . . wasn't mean . . . He was nice to people who came for help."

"You made an honest decision. That's all anyone can do."

An honest decision . . . yes . . . but Gretchen was dead . . .

The gray morning matched Annie's bleak mood. The police station sat on a slight rise near the harbor. Whitecaps rippled across the water. Annie was grateful for her warm wool jacket. A TV camera crew hunkered against the wind a few feet from the front steps. A slender reporter, makeup perfect on a heart-shaped face, blond hair lacquered into submission, stepped toward Annie, held up a mic. "How is this usually bucolic island responding to such a brutal crime?"

Annie's eyes narrowed. How did you answer that kind of question? "As well as can be expected. Excuse me." She tried to brush past.

The reporter kept pace, mic thrust toward Annie. "Did you know the victim? How about the alleged killer?"

Annie pushed past the reporter, pulled open the door, and stepped inside. A chest-high counter separated several desks and filing cabinets from a small waiting area.

Mavis Cameron looked up from the nearest desk, pushed back her chair. Mavis was Billy's wife and the station dispatcher when not doubling as a crime tech. "Thanks for coming in, Annie. Here's your statement. Please look it over and sign and date." She pushed several sheets across the counter, along with a pen.

The door to the station's interior hall opened.

Mavis swung to look, worry evident in her angular face. Mavis had survived an abusive marriage to find happiness in her second marriage to Billy, but her eyes always held a remembrance of bad times.

Mayor Cosgrove bustled through, bleating excitedly, "I'll do the talking."

Billy followed, his square face folded in a frown. "We held a press briefing a half hour ago." He glanced at his watch. "I'm on my way to Better Tomorrow."

The mayor slapped through the wooden gate into the anteroom. "You can spare a

few minutes. I told the TV people to wait."
He was puffed with importance. "I haven't
made my statement. I expect you to be with
me, but I'll handle the questions."

Billy looked grim as he held the front door
and, after an instant's hesitation, followed
the mayor outside.

As the door closed, Annie glanced over
the sheets, signed, pushed the papers toward
Mavis. She jerked a thumb toward outside.
"Why's the mayor here?"

Mavis was laconic. "TV."

Annie nodded and turned away. Mayor
Cosgrove was drawn to media like a shark
to blood. But it might be interesting to hear
what he was going to say. She opened the
door and stepped out into the cold.

The mayor stood in the center of the
sidewalk. Billy remained a pace behind him.
Billy's stance was stiff. Obviously, he wasn't
enjoying the mayor's television appearance.

Annie slipped down the steps and to one
side, determined to remain out of the
camera's range.

Cosgrove stood with his shoulders back,
the better to minimize his rotund physique,
but he still had the shape of a well-dressed
penguin. ". . . wish to reassure island
residents that I am personally overseeing
the investigation into the brutal murder of a

volunteer at a fine local charity. Unfortunately, the suspect — one Jeremiah Young, age twenty-one — remains at large as I speak. Listeners should continue to be suspicious of strangers and to call nine-one-one immediately if in doubt. Unfortunately, the murderer has yet" — the mayor emphasized the adverb, his tone acidic — "to be arrested despite" — more emphasis — "the efforts of the police." There was a clear inference that those efforts must, perforce, have been performed inadequately. "I" — a clarion call — "have insisted upon a large-scale search. If the murderer is not apprehended within the day, I intend to request assistance from county authorities who are perhaps more adept at solving crimes of this nature."

The blond reporter poked the mic forward. "Has the town council lost confidence in Police Chief Cameron?"

"Confidence must be earned." Cosgrove's tone was unctuous. "At the moment, judgment hangs in the balance on Broward's Rock. We shall see what the day brings. Chief Cameron assures me that every possible effort is being made."

The reporter smelled blood. "Chief, is your job in jeopardy?"

Billy was unperturbed. "Mayor Cosgrove

speaks for himself. I can assure islanders that we are seeking Jeremiah Young as a person of interest and encourage him to come forward. There will be a press briefing at four this afternoon. Thank you." With that he turned and headed down the steps.

"Chief, what special efforts will you make now?" The reporter's voice rose above the squawk of sea gulls overhead.

Billy strode past the TV reporters without a word.

"Mayor Cosgrove, are you and the police chief on bad terms?" The reporter's voice was piercing.

Annie walked fast, head down, toward her car. She ignored the mayor. She and Max and the mayor had an unhappy history. The mayor had resented Max's success in winning town council support for funds for the Haven, the island's youth recreation center. As Annie well knew, the mayor never forgot an enmity. Cosgrove had taken great delight when Max was a murder suspect. Now the mayor obviously had his knife out for Billy. Cosgrove was contemptible, but that didn't make him any less dangerous as an opponent. As she slid behind the wheel of the Thunderbird, she pulled out her cell. Max didn't answer, so she left a message describing the scurrilous news conference. Her mind churned with resentment all the way to Death on Demand.

It was only when she stood in Death on Demand, a terribly quiet and empty place this gray Tuesday morning, that she faced again the unalterable fact that yesterday she'd traded places with Gretchen and Gretchen had died as a result.

She wandered disconsolately down the central corridor. She'd thought she might find solace in routine, but all she could think about was the cheer of yesterday, the store bustling with customers, Emma at her most entertaining, a successful luncheon, many books sold. What did that matter now? She wished mightily for someone to talk to, but in January, Ingrid only came in for special events and toward the end of the week. She had called early this morning and said brightly that there were a few odds and ends she hadn't finished yesterday and she'd be by. Annie knew Ingrid and her husband, Duane, had planned an outing to an art show in Savannah. Annie had managed to sound equally bright and careless, assuring Ingrid that everything was fine.

Everything wasn't fine.

Annie usually enjoyed solitary time in the bookstore because she never really felt alone, not when surrounded by books that she knew and a cat who reveled in having Annie all to herself.

In fact, at this very moment, Agatha padded ahead of Annie down the central corridor toward the coffee bar. The silky black cat looked over her shoulder, golden eyes gleaming. She might as well have said aloud, "What's keeping you? I'm here. Pet me."

Agatha jumped onto the coffee bar and waited expectantly.

Annie took a moment to light the logs in the fireplace, then stepped to the coffee bar and stroked sleek fur. "You're beautiful."

Agatha stood very still, tail held high.

Annie wanted to gather Agatha in her arms and bury her face in sweet-smelling fur, but she knew very well that Agatha was intent upon continued adulation. The beauty of her cat and the warmth from the fire crackling in the grate gave Annie comfort.

Comfort from searing memories of the hallway in an old frame house . . . Annie knew she must not obsessively rerun that dreadful moment. She had to turn her thoughts to the present, remember that the world also held goodness that touched the heart and infused the spirit with joy. That was the comfort of mysteries. Bad things happened, but good people tried to make things better. She looked at a tall jade vase at the end of the coffee bar and smiled at the blooms of a half dozen fresh sunflowers. Obviously, Laurel had dropped by, using the key she'd retained ever since she and Henny and Emma once kept the store going.

Annie walked to the coffee bar, noted a small white card propped at the foot of the vase with the inscription: Velvet Queens. She smiled. A perfect name for opulent six-inch copper blooms with chocolate-colored centers. She lifted the dangling card and read in Laurel's elegant cursive writing: Monarch butterflies enjoy the nectar of sunflowers during their fall migration. Think Monarchs.

Obediently Annie envisioned monarchs, glorious in their tawny colors, flying south.

In a quick tribute to her mother-in-law's effort to bring cheer, Annie pretended she was playing Laurel's Sunflower Game. She said, "Monarchs," and quickly replied, "Santa Cruz," and remembered a sky filled with glorious monarchs on a beautiful October day, swirling among six-foot-tall sunflowers as she and Max watched, hand in hand.

The phone rang. Annie answered, "Death on —"

Emma Clyde was gruff. "Be glad to drop by. I could" — an almost startled pause — "unpack books."

Annie was truly touched. The empress dowager of crime fiction was accustomed to others taking care of life's mundane details. Moreover, Annie knew that Emma was in midbook, a period when her ice blue eyes were often glazed in thought and the world around her a pale shadow of the reality of Marigold Rembrandt. "Emma, that's very kind, but I know you're trying to figure out how Inspector Houlihan is going to escape from that attic. Maybe he can use his suspenders as a rope."

Silence on the line.

Annie pictured Emma yanked back into her book, mind racing. "Suspenders . . . something heavy . . . maybe catapult a note . . ." A chortle. "Marigold will love it. Caught with his pants down. Oh. That's good. Got to go."

Annie brewed a cappuccino and sat at the coffee bar, alternately sipping the coffee and petting Agatha. She tried to think about anything but yesterday. Determinedly, she looked at the watercolors hanging above the fireplace. She always took pleasure in admiring the paintings in the monthly mystery contest. Each painting represented a mystery that Annie had enjoyed reading. The first customer to correctly identify the paintings by title and author received a month of free coffee.

In the first painting, a blue spot illuminated a makeshift stage in an old cemetery. Weathered and canted headstones were dimly visible. A young woman with curly auburn hair watched as a white-haired man staggered through the open curtains onto the stage.

In the second painting, a once beautiful young woman with glossy blond hair lay dead, her neck twisted, on the stone floor of a small, windowless cell accessible only by rope. She wore an elegant white dress. One black heel lay a few feet away. Candlelight provided the only illumination.

In the third painting, sun flooded the bedroom, but the coppery-haired young woman seated on the edge of the bed had an air of great sorrow, her face pale, her eyes red-rimmed. A tanned blonde looked at her gravely and pointed at the younger woman's distinctive wedding band, a circle of mamo feathers carved in gold.

In the fourth painting, a tall, thin woman faced a pink dressing table crowded with lotions and bottles and cosmetics. Costume jewelry dangled from the mirror. She held a small wooden box in one hand. Across the small, dark bedroom, an attractive honey blonde pulled a long white envelope from the third drawer of a battered mahogany dresser. The single bed was unmade. A coverlet was pulled over a pillow to mimic a sleeping form. Clothes were piled on the single chair.

In the fifth painting, the battlements of a mosque rose on one side of a square. A well-built, tanned man stood in the open door-way of a carpet shop as merchants gathered up their wares from the sidewalk. The observer wore a tarboosh with his linen suit and could have passed for a Levantine. He looked at an open car stopped before a huge crowd of young men in black gowns. The stockily built, fair-haired passenger stood in the back, staring out at the milling throng. He possessed an air of authority. A troop of mounted police approached at a trot. Each man held a long pickaxe handle tied to his right wrist by a leather thong.

Although the contest was open to anyone who visited the store, in reality it was usually a neck-and-neck race between Emma Clyde and Henny Brawley. Annie knew a great deal about mysteries. She could talk knowledgeably about John Buchan's gallant Richard Hannay (the musical parody offended her), Michael Innes's contemplative John Appleby, Lucille Kallen's independent Maggie Rome, John Marquand's exceedingly polite Mr. Moto, and Mary Roberts Rinehart's rollicking Tish Carberry, but she was quick to admit that Emma and Henny were the true experts.

Emma loved to toss back a rum and Coke and quote Charlie Chan. Among her favorites:

All foxes come at last to fur store.

Cannot tell where path lead until reach end of road.

Theory like mist on eyeglasses — obscures facts.

As for Henny, she was a connoisseur, treasuring books as elegantly devised as an astrophysicist's explication: *It's Different Abroad* by Henry Calvin, *Going Nowhere Fast* by Gar Anthony Haywood, *The Franchise Affair* by Josephine Tey, *The Light of Day* by Eric Ambler, *The Bone Chamber* by Robin Burcell.

Since Emma was immersed in writing, Henny likely would once again claim the prize.

Annie put down her mug, her gaze caught by the paintings. Henny had already identified the third painting. The long-ago book was the third in a wonderful series that had been reprinted by Rue Morgue Press. Henny often dropped by on these winter mornings for a strong Kenya coffee brewed with cloves and cinnamon sticks.

Henny . . . If there was anyone she might have expected to call her this morning, Henny topped the list. Henny was the volunteer coordinator at Better Tomorrow. Certainly she would by now be aware of Gretchen Burkholt's murder there and she would very likely know that Annie had discovered her body. Certainly she knew Gretchen had taken Annie's place Monday.

Annie stood so quickly that Agatha came to her feet and stared, golden eyes wary. "Agatha, I'm an idiot. All I've thought about is myself. If I'm upset, think how Henny feels. She hired Jeremiah. I should have called her first thing this morning. That's why she hasn't called me. She's blaming herself."

Annie grabbed the phone, pressed familiar numbers.

Henny finally answered on the fourth ring. "Hello." Her voice sounded stiff and strange.

Annie was apologetic. "I should have called sooner. Henny, don't blame yourself for hiring Jeremiah. He never acted in a way

83

anyone could have considered dangerous. He didn't go to prison for a violent crime. You couldn't have known. Of course, you hired him. Better Tomorrow offers people a second chance." That was what mattered. Henny must realize and accept that her choices had been reasonable . . .

Annie felt a tiny jolt of discovery. That was exactly what Max had told her. She plunged ahead into the well of silence between them. "You and I couldn't possibly have expected what happened. I never felt Jeremiah was dangerous. Never."

"I'm glad you didn't." Again Henny's voice sounded distant. "Thanks for calling."

Annie realized the call was going to be ended, then and there. "Henny, I'll be right over."

"No." The retort was quick, decisive.

Again there was a well of silence between them.

Henny cleared her throat. "I appreciate your thinking of me. Obviously, we're all distressed about Gretchen. I understand that you found her. I'm sorry." A pause. "Did you see anyone?"

"No one was there. Only Gretchen." Annie knew her voice was thin.

"The police have requested that the house remain closed until Thursday. I agreed, of course." Henny sounded as if her mind were far away.

"I'll bring you a clove and cinnamon coffee, and I found of box of really old Patricia Wentworths at a flea market in Savannah, an original *Devil's Wind* —"

"Not today. I'll come by tomorrow."

The connection ended.

Annie stared at the receiver. Abrupt. Distant. Uninterested in a highly collectible Patricia Wentworth title. Annie replaced the receiver, whirled, and headed for the storeroom. She grabbed her jacket and purse, pulled out her car keys, placed the Back Soon sign in the window, and slammed out the front door, head down against a gusting wind. She tossed her purse in the trunk of her car, climbed in, turned the key, and the bright red car jolted out of the marina parking lot.

Annie passed only two cars on Sand Dollar Road before she reached the exit from the island's gated area. A quarter mile past the gate, she turned left onto a narrow dirt road that meandered eastward to the marsh and the solitary wooden house. She drove a little too fast, trying to reassure herself that Henny was fine, she was simply struggling to cope.

She felt a rush of relief when she saw Henny's car and lights in the house, shining brightly against January grayness. She parked and walked fast. She wished she'd taken time to brew the special coffee. After all, she'd offered to bring Henny's favorite coffee.

Henny stepped out onto the porch, closing her front door firmly behind her. Even Henny's casual clothes always seemed elegant. This morning's loose red-and-black plaid jacket, gray wool slacks, and suede boots provided warmth as well as style.

Annie raised a hand in greeting. "I'm glad I caught you."

Henny shrugged into a red corduroy car coat as she came down the steps. She held car keys in a gloved hand. "I'm sorry, Annie, I'm on my way to the police station. Billy has some more questions. I don't want to keep him waiting." The words came glibly.

Annie felt puzzled. A short time ago Billy had told the mayor he was on his way to Better Tomorrow. She looked into Henny's face, always intelligent, strong, and vivid. This morning Henny was pale, emphasizing the purplish patches beneath her dark eyes, the deep lines around her mouth, the sag of fatigue in her cheeks.

"I'm sorry you came all this way for nothing." Henny smoothly took Annie's elbow, gently turning her. They walked away from the house. "I'll be in touch as soon as I can." She moved toward her car, stood by the driver's door.

Annie walked back to her car, slid behind the wheel. She turned on the motor, backed into the dirt road, and drove slowly away. In her rearview mirror, she watched Henny settle in the driver's seat, heard the rumble as the old car's motor revved.

Annie drove around the curve. She drove slowly, but she didn't see Henny's Dodge in the rearview mirror. She drove a quarter mile. An old logging trail with narrow ruts cut into the woods to the south. Annie passed the gap, slowed, stopped.

No sign of Henny's car.

There could be many reasons why the Dodge had yet to appear.

Perhaps Henny had received a call on her cell and was waiting to drive after she finished the conversation. Perhaps she was simply sitting there, thinking, possibly dreading a visit to the police station. Perhaps . . .

Perhaps she wanted Annie to leave, did not want Annie to come into her house.

Annie waited for a slow minute, counting the seconds, one and two and three and . . .

The road lay quiet behind her.

Annie put the car in reverse, maneuvered until she had backed into the logging trail. She waited with the nose of her car not quite in the road. She would see Henny pass. If Henny looked to her right, she would spot Annie's car, but surely her thoughts would be focused on Billy and Jeremiah.

Annie waited five minutes, minutes that felt unending, heavy, quiet, ominous minutes.

The Dodge didn't appear.

Annie had a funny constricted feeling in her chest. She eased the Thunderbird farther back until the road was no longer visible. She turned off the motor. She walked carefully to avoid twisting an ankle in the uneven ruts. She brushed aside tendrils of dead vines that swayed like seaweed in the soggy breeze.

At the road, she stopped to listen. There was no sound of a car motor. She began to feel foolish. Perhaps Henny had spoken imprecisely. Maybe Billy had called from Better Tomorrow and asked Henny to go to the station. Perhaps there was some information an officer would show her, another question would be asked. She heard Henny's voice, distant and stiff: *Billy has some*

more questions. I don't want to keep him wait-
ing.

Whatever Henny might be — acidulous, clever, cogent, brisk — she was never imprecise. If she said Billy, she meant Billy.

Had she lied?

Annie moved swiftly, though she stepped lightly, always ready at the sound of a motor to dart into the woods, thick here with undergrowth and rotted tree limbs. At least the day was cold and damp and she wouldn't be likely to disturb a den of rattlesnakes if she dashed for cover. Whatever happened, she didn't want Henny to see her. What Henny chose to do or not to do was certainly her own affair. Yet, Annie felt there had been a touch of desperation in Henny's determination to send Annie away.

A crow cawed. Live oak leaves rustled in a stiff breeze. A faint mist made the cold air penetrating, unpleasant. Annie hesitated. If Henny saw her, she would have every right to be offended. But the memory of Henny's face drove her forward. She promised herself she'd take a quick look, be sure Henny was all right, then she would slip away unseen. Henny had every right to order her day any way she pleased, but Annie felt seized by uneasiness that verged on fear.

Why had Henny been determined that Annie not come inside?

Why had she lied about Billy?

Why had she started her car and yet the car never came up the road, the only way it could come?

Annie reached the last curve. She left the road, stepped cautiously beneath the limbs of an old live oak. She stood in the deep shadow of the tree and watched, eyes widening, breaths coming quickly.

Henny stood at the end of her pier. Her boat, an old Sea Ray 160, bobbed in the swells. She bent forward, handing a Coleman stove to Jeremiah Young. He stowed the stove, turned back to grab a folded tent. Next came a cooler, a box, a small hatchet.

Annie's breath caught in her throat as Jeremiah took the hatchet.

He turned and added the tool to the growing pile stacked behind the seats. After a final transfer of what looked like folded blankets, Jeremiah offered a hand to Henny as she stepped into the boat.

Annie leaned forward. There was no weapon in evidence. The hatchet had joined the other goods behind the seats. Jeremiah's demeanor wasn't threatening nor did Henny appear threatened. She moved into the captain's seat, the motor rumbled. As the boat edged away from the pier, Jeremiah stood with his back to Henny, coiling the mooring line.

Jeremiah was a fugitive. Authorities were looking for him on the island and the mainland. Description: white male, twenty-one, approximately six feet tall, muscular, unkempt shoulder-length light brown hair often beneath a do-rag, rounded face, light brown eyes, occasionally unshaven, no distinguishing marks. Last seen wearing Braves sweatshirt, jeans, work boots, brown corduroy jacket. Wanted on suspicion of murder. Considered dangerous.

Henny expertly steered through channels toward more open water.

The mist was heavier now. Whitecaps indicated rough water in the Sound.

Annie was bewildered. Surely Henny wasn't taking Jeremiah to the mainland. She would make herself guilty of aiding and abetting a fugitive, an accessory after the fact.

The boat was perhaps thirty yards from shore now. The boat curved around a small hammock and turned south, nosing into a wide channel between thick cordgrass.

The mainland was due west.

The boat headed straight for one of the largest hammocks in the bay, a hump of land densely covered with trees, a wildlife sanctuary, and absolutely inaccessible except by boat. Jeremiah would need the hatchet to hack through tangled vines and limbs of salt myrtle, Southern bayberry, and yaupon holly that thrived beneath a canopy of live oaks.

The boat disappeared on the far side of the hammock.

Annie felt frantic. The boat was out of sight, Henny alone with a man wanted for murder. What was Henny thinking? Jeremiah could easily overpower her.

To call for help, Annie would have to run to her car, retrieve her purse from the trunk.

Henny didn't want help.

The thought came instantly with the hard glint of unvarnished truth.

If Henny had needed or wanted help, she would have given some indication to Annie when they stood on the porch. If Jeremiah was a threat, she could have whispered quickly, "Leave, get help, Jeremiah in the house." Henny had stood with her back to the door. Jeremiah could not have seen what she did or heard what she said.

Henny didn't want help.

The conclusion seemed inescapable, yet

Annie felt desperately unsure. She stood, riveted, staring across the marsh, watching, hoping. Minutes crawled past. Her thoughts raced. Should she turn and run, call Billy Cameron?

Not unless she felt Henny was in danger.

At this moment, she wouldn't even address the idea of right or wrong. At this moment, all that mattered was Henny's safety.

There had been no hint of coercion. Unless Annie had completely misread the actions of Henny and Jeremiah, they were working together. Henny wasn't frightened or under duress.

The only possible conclusion was that Henny had decided to help Jeremiah hide. Henny would have made that decision gravely, understanding that her actions were unlawful. To break the law, Henny must have a powerful motive.

Obviously, Henny had decided Jeremiah was innocent.

Innocent.

Annie felt as though a boulder had rolled from her shoulders. If Jeremiah was innocent, Gretchen had not died because Annie had been slow in coming to Better Tomorrow.

The relief that buoyed her was short lived. Was Jeremiah innocent? Henny couldn't be sure. She would have taken his word on faith. Perhaps he'd spun a tale, convinced her to help him hide. If that were true, the boat might not return to the island.

Annie stood with her hands clenched, her shoulders hunched. Faintly, she heard the rumble of the motor. She swallowed hard. Would Henny be in the captain's seat? Or would the boat curve toward the mainland with a killer at the wheel? Dear Henny, her stalwart friend, generous, thoughtful, smart, capable, acerbic, a woman who faced life with grace and courage, one of the famed women in their flying machines, a pilot in the WASPs who flew during World War II. Her husband died in a bombing raid over Berlin. She spent a lifetime as a teacher, retired to the island, found a late love that was lost because of a good man's honor.

The old boat chugged from the channel, turned east to head toward the bank and the pier.

Annie felt a wave of relief when she saw Henny's red-and-black plaid jacket. She was alone in the boat.

When the boat slid next to the pier, Henny climbed the ladder, tied the line, walked swiftly on the pier.

Annie almost stepped from the shadow of the live oak, then stopped. If she confronted

Henny, told her what she had seen, that she knew Jeremiah was encamped on the hammock free from discovery, both she and Henny would have to face the consequences.

Either Annie would have to join Henny in protecting Jeremiah or she would have to inform Billy Cameron.

Annie felt a rush of understanding. Henny sent her away because she did not want to draw Annie into a criminal conspiracy.

Why take the horrendous chance of hiding a fugitive? If Henny had decided that Jeremiah was innocent, she should have persuaded him to turn himself in, assured him that Billy Cameron would listen and act fairly, offered to contact a first-rate lawyer.

There had to be a compelling reason that Henny had chosen instead to provide sanctuary.

Henny strode swiftly toward her house, her face etched in grim lines.

Annie drew back into deeper shadow. She had no right to be here. If she hadn't parked and walked up the road, she would have no knowledge of the boat's departure and return.

Henny clattered up the stairs, was inside the house and out again in scarcely a minute, her purse over her shoulder. She slammed into her car. The old motor roared.

Annie waited until the Dodge was out of sight. As she walked to the logging trail, she knew she, too, had made a fateful choice.

As Annie poured a cappuccino, she looked into the golden eyes of her elegant bookstore cat. "What would you do?"

Agatha lifted a paw, daintily licked, smoothed her fur.

"Whatever made you feel good, right?" Annie knew her cat.

What would it be like to be a cat, self-absorbed yet attuned to environment with a thoughtful gaze, superior hearing, and clear grasp of cause and effect? "You don't have to make moral judgments."

Agatha's ears flattened. Clearly she'd heard the sound of remonstrance in Annie's voice.

Quickly Annie spoke softly, sweetly. "Gorgeous, that's what you are. Gorgeous and perfect."

Agatha's expression became benign.

Annie smiled as she turned away. Anyone who described cats as inscrutable never lived with a cat. Cats made their hopes, desires, intentions, irritations, judgments, and appraisals unmistakably clear.

Annie settled at a table, sipped the frothy coffee. "Moral judgments." She spoke aloud. Given the circumstances, the words sounded ominous. Black, white. Either, or. Legal, illegal.

Annie drew a deep breath. She had made a choice. She'd chosen to remain silent. Henny was not to know what Annie had seen. But that didn't absolve Annie of responsibility.

Annie popped up, retrieved a yellow legal pad and a pen, returned to the table, wrote, paused, scratched out, added. Finally she nodded.

1. Henny believes Jeremiah Young is innocent.
2. If she's right, Gretchen Burkholt was killed by a person or persons unknown.
3. Gretchen made four calls on her cell phone Monday afternoon from Better Tomorrow. She spoke to me and left two messages for me. She called the Hathaway house.
4. Gretchen found an index card in the tweed jacket worn by Everett Hathaway the day he died.
5. Gretchen left a message with the

Hathaway maid.
6. Gretchen spoke of "scandal."

Agatha flowed to the top of the table, settled atop the legal pad.

Annie looked into observant, watchful eyes. "You want attention and I may no longer write."

A faint purr indicated pleasure.

Annie put down the pen. She petted Agatha and thought about a card in a dead man's pocket. Was it possible that the discovery of the card signed a death warrant for Gretchen?

Why?

According to Gretchen, the card explained why Everett Hathaway had gone out in a kayak on a cold winter night. Was the explanation so incriminating that Gretchen had to die to keep the contents of the card secret?

Everett had drowned in winter-cold water.

What was incriminating about the reason he went out in the kayak?

Slowly, an idea took shape.

What if Everett Hathaway's death was not an accident?

Agatha rubbed her cheek against Annie's hand.

Annie looked into golden eyes. "Agatha,

I'd think I was nuts except Gretchen's dead and the only thing different about her day at Better Tomorrow was finding the index card in Everett's pocket. Gretchen whining about Jeremiah wasn't new. She complained every time she saw him. No, what was new was the card."

Cause and effect, card found, call made, woman dead.

Annie knew everything seemed clear to her. Would anyone else believe her, most especially Billy Cameron?

She reached into her pocket for her cell phone.

4

Billy Cameron answered his cell. "Yo, Annie." His tone held faint inquiry.

She plunged straight to her point. "I've been thinking over everything Gretchen said, and I'm sure Gretchen was acting just as usual about Jeremiah and that he's innocent. She wasn't really frightened of him."

"I heard the calls." Billy spoke in a level voice. "She sounded scared. Her purse is gone. He's gone. No trace of him. We have to deal with the facts as they are. I wish they were different. So we'll look for him until we find him. I'm leaving now for a search near the bluffs."

The bluffs were an eroding end of the island between the open sea and the Sound where heavy currents pulled at crumbling shoreline, a wild and uninhabited area and a good distance from Henny's marsh.

Annie was careful to keep the relief from her voice. "Has someone sighted him?"

"We've had some reports."

As she'd expected, Billy was totally focused on Jeremiah Young. She picked her way as delicately as a cat through dewy grass. "Billy, what about the Hathaways? Gretchen was sure she'd found something shocking in the pocket of Everett's jacket."

"From what you've told me" — his tone was dry — "she treated everything as high drama. *A Card From the Dead Man's Pocket.*" He spoke in the hushed voice of the intro to an old-time radio show. Death on Demand carried CDs of the *Inner Sanctum* and *The Shadow.* Billy was a big fan. "The temptation to magnify the card must have been irresistible."

"Billy, I know Gretchen loved high drama. But she did find a card."

"Right." He was calm, a man who followed procedure. "I followed up on it. I talked to Mrs. Hathaway this morning. Since I spoke with her yesterday, she'd asked everyone in the house. No one saw a message on the telephone pad. She says someone must have thrown it away."

Annie asked quietly, "How do you know no one saw her message?"

There was a pause. "What are you suggesting?"

"Maybe the card in Everett's pocket did

matter." Annie tried to sound reasonable, sensible. "Even for Gretchen, scandal was a strong word. What if the card contained information someone couldn't afford for anyone to know? Maybe someone at the Hathaway house found the message Gretchen left and came to Better Tomorrow and made sure that Gretchen would never tell anyone what she'd seen."

"Lots of maybes there." He was dismissive. "There's no maybe about Jeremiah's fingerprints on the axe that killed her."

Annie pictured Better Tomorrow and the woodpile near the shed, clearly visible from the oyster shell parking lot. "The woodpile is easily seen. Maybe Jeremiah left the axe by that unfinished pile of wood. The killer —"

Billy interrupted. "Someone from the Hathaway house?" He was clearly skeptical.

So much for Annie's effort to build her case. But she continued determinedly, "Someone from the Hathaway house."

"What could be such a big deal about a card in a dead man's jacket?"

"Gretchen said the card explained why he took the kayak out that night. Kayaking alone at night in December wasn't usual for him, was it?" Annie hoped that Billy would let her finish, allow her to lay out the chilling scene that now seemed absolutely obvious to her. "I understand the family was surprised. No one offered an explanation as to why he might have gone out. He knew how to kayak, but he wasn't an expert. Had he ever taken a kayak out on a winter night?"

"Not so far as is known." His tone suggested there might have been instances, they simply weren't aware of them.

Annie took a deep breath. "What if someone wrote a note on a card that was guaranteed to entice Everett Hathaway to slip out of his house on a winter night and take a kayak to a cove that has only a few homes?"

"What possible difference does it make why he went out?" Billy was impatient. "We know he was in a kayak and capsized."

Annie spoke as if she were slapping an ace on a king. "If someone knew what time he was going out and where he was going, it would be easy to intercept him."

"Granted." He sounded wary.

"Let's say someone in a boat hailed him, came close, and tipped over the kayak. The water was cold. All the boater had to do was keep the kayak just out of his reach. It wouldn't take long to commit a murder that left no trace. It was too far to swim to shore, and as soon as Everett lost consciousness from hypothermia, his face smacked into

103

the water and he drowned." She kept talking over a grumbling dissent. "Maybe that's what someone is trying to hide. Maybe the card would open up lots of questions about who wrote it and what it said. Maybe the card would make everybody question whether his death was an accident."

"That seems as likely to me as the craters on Mars being man-made. You've built a case out of nothing. Maybe you need a crash course in reality. That's a pretty big leap, from a card in a man's pocket to the idea he was murdered and somebody slipped into Better Tomorrow from the Hathaway house. I can tell you for sure" — Billy was emphatic — "Everett Hathaway's death was an accident and no one will ever prove otherwise."

"It could have happened that way." Annie felt eerily confident that the dark December night had unfolded just as she imagined, a boat coming up out of the darkness, a call, the kayak pulling near as the boat idled in the water, then a hand reaching out to push and the kayak tumbling to one side, Everett struggling, submerging in the water, the shocking cold strangling the shout in his throat, the kayak caught by a gaff, the boat pulled away from the flailing victim.

"Oh, sure, and unicorns play canasta with

my dog every Saturday night. Come on, Annie" — his tone was irritated — "why would anybody kill Everett Hathaway? He was an ineffectual rich guy who quoted poetry. He got his hair cut at the same time I did every month, and every other sentence was a quote from somebody you never heard of. Look, I know you mean well" — he was trying for patience — "but I deal in facts, and I've got facts and I'm looking for a fugitive."

"That card in his pocket was a fact." Annie said hurriedly, "What if someone came from the Hathaway house to pick up the card? Gretchen would have handed it over, but I know she would have chattered. I can hear her now. *I didn't want to disturb the family. But I thought you would want to know.* She would have been quivering with excitement. It wouldn't take *a* minute for a listener to know this was a garrulous, gossipy woman who, after whispering this was so confidential, would regale people she knew with the message she found in Everett Hathaway's jacket."

"Let me get this straight." He was almost sarcastic, unusual for Billy. "One, you say Hathaway was murdered. Two, a card in his jacket contained information his murderer had to keep quiet. Three, Gretchen left a message about the card at the Hathaway house. Four, the murderer saw that message and came to Better Tomorrow. Then what?"

"On the way out" — she spoke slowly as she tried to follow a shadowy figure from the sorting room — "the killer's thinking fast. There are racks of coats, scarves. Maybe the killer stops and grabs a scarf."

"A scarf?"

"Gretchen was a small woman. If someone came up behind her, it would be easy to drop a scarf over her head and strangle her."

"She wasn't strangled." His voice was sharp.

"No." Annie tried to imagine that shadowy figure, a scarf or muffler in hand, perhaps turning back toward the hall and the sorting room and then a memory of an axe propped by chopped wood. Obviously a handyman's prints would be on the handle. A swift decision. Out to the woodpile, picking up the axe with the scarf, carrying it inside. "I think the murderer remembered the axe and decided to get it, maybe even thinking ahead that someone's fingerprints would be on the handle and if the axe were used, the workman would be suspect. Which is exactly what happened, didn't it?"

Billy was impatient. "If, if, if . . . You don't have a single fact to support your suggestions. Besides, the clincher is that Jeremiah ran away."

"He'd been in prison. He came inside and found a woman battered to death with an axe he'd used to chop wood. Let's say that instead of running, he had called you. Would he be suspect number one, especially after you heard her messages on my cell?"

"Her purse was taken." Billy's tone was dogged.

"If I'm right, this murderer thinks fast. Gretchen's purse was probably on the floor behind the sorting table. How easy would it be to grab the purse to make her murder look like a robbery gone wrong?"

"Maybe you should write some of those books in your shop." He was dismissive. "You're making something out of nothing and you ignore the facts."

Her hand tightened on the phone. "There's one fact you've ignored."

"Oh?"

"Where is the card that Gretchen found in Everett Hathaway's jacket?"

"She put it in her purse for safekeeping."

"That isn't what she said." Annie concentrated, trying to recall Gretchen's words. "She told me that she'd left a message that the card and some coins and a pocketknife were there and could be picked up anytime.

She said she put them on the table in the sorting room. What did you find on the table in the sorting room?" She heard a faint rustling of papers.

"Three quarters, two dimes, four pennies. A Buck folding pocketknife." He rattled off the model number. "Gretchen Burkholt's fingerprints overlay unidentified prints, likely those of Everett Hathaway."

"Did you find an index card?"

He blew out a spurt of air. "No."

"Until you find that card, I won't agree that Jeremiah is the only possible suspect. Will you try to find out if a car owned by someone at the Hathaway house was seen anywhere near Better Tomorrow between two fifteen and the time I called for help?"

He shrugged. "Sure, Annie. Maybe it will set your mind at rest. We'll make inquiries."

Annie called Henny's cell. She wasn't surprised when there was no answer. She had no doubt Henny's cell was with her, but she also had no doubt that Henny was intent upon avoiding Annie. A message would do. Annie glanced at her watch. "Hi, Henny. It's Annie. It's almost eleven. I'm calling because I need your help. I'm sure Jeremiah is innocent. I know he ran away, but I have good reason to think someone else was there. I'm afraid it's up to me now. Billy Cameron is convinced Jeremiah is guilty. I hope you will help me. You know everyone on the island, and I think we could find out a lot. Of course, you may not agree, but if you're willing to help, please meet me at Parotti's at noon." Annie ended the call.

She didn't want to be prideful, but if that bait didn't lure her fish, she was going to be surprised.

She gave Agatha a final caress, popped up from the table, and hurried to the back area that was part storeroom, part office. At her computer, she pulled up the *Broward's Rock Gazette,* keyed in *Everett Hathaway.* She printed out two news stories and the obituary.

ISLANDER FOUND DEAD
NEAR CAPSIZED KAYAK
by Marian Kenyon

Island businessman Everett Hathaway's body was found Saturday morning floating in Jessop Cove near his overturned kayak. Hathaway, forty-two, an island native, was the managing partner of Hathaway Advertising, a firm founded by his late brother, Edward M. Hathaway II.

Edward M. Hathaway III said his uncle was last seen at dinner Friday evening. He said the family was unaware Everett had taken the kayak out into the Sound and no alarm had been raised. It is not known when Hathaway entered the water. However, the family, after receiving notification of his death, discovered his bed had not been slept in, so the accident apparently occurred Friday night, sometime after nine P.M.

Police Chief Billy Cameron stated that an autopsy will be performed, as required by state law for an unattended death. Cameron said Hathaway's body was observed at 7:42 A.M. floating in the water about forty yards offshore by Don Thornwall, 146 Herring Gull Road. Thornwall said he was preparing for an early-morning row. Thornwall immediately notified island police, then rowed out into the cove. As he neared the body, he saw an overturned kayak. Thornwall determined that the victim was no longer living. He remained near the body to await police.

Sgt. Hyla Harrison and Sgt. Lou Pirelli arrived in the police motorboat at 8:02 A.M. The officers pulled Hathaway into the boat and determined that he was dead. Sergeant Pirelli reported there were no signs of trauma to the body and the death was assumed to be accidental.

Police revealed that Hathaway was wearing a life vest but theorized that he lost consciousness because of hypothermia, his face fell into the water, and he drowned.

Edward Hathaway III said his uncle was not a kayak enthusiast and did not kayak daily. Hathaway expressed surprise at his uncle's evening excursion and said he had not heard his uncle mention kayaking since summer.

Family members include Hathaway's widow, Nicole Nelson Hathaway, his nephew, Edward M. Hathaway III, and niece, Leslie Hathaway Griffin.

The second story was brief.

ISLANDER HATHAWAY DROWNING VICTIM
by Marian Kenyon

Police Chief Billy Cameron announced today that island businessman Everett Hathaway, forty-two, died as a result of drowning in an apparent accident while kayaking Friday night.

Although Hathaway wore a life vest, Chief Cameron said it is likely that he fell into the water and was unable to swim to shore before succumbing to hypothermia. Cameron said when Hathaway lost consciousness, his head fell forward into the water and he drowned.

Hathaway's body was found floating Saturday morning near his capsized kayak in Jessop Cove.

Cameron said autopsy results released by Medical Examiner Dr. Malcolm Burford indicated Hathaway drowned sometime Friday night. Cameron theorized that Hathaway's late-night excursion ended in tragedy because of the water's low temperature when the kayak capsized and he was unable to right the boat and was too far from shore to swim to safety. The water temperature Friday night was forty-nine degrees. The police chief said Hathaway was not especially fit. Hathaway wore cotton clothes. The chief said the sodden cloth would have offered no protection and intensified the chill. Hathaway could have lost consciousness within twenty minutes. The chief emphasized that this time of year, boaters should take all precautions, including wearing wet suits. In this instance, Chief Cameron said Hathaway's life vest kept him buoyant, but his distance from the bank was a death sentence.

An island native, Hathaway was the son of the late Edward M. and Celeste Morgan Hathaway.

At present, services are pending.

The obituary was in the next day's *Gazette*.

EVERETT MORGAN HATHAWAY

Everett Morgan Hathaway died unexpectedly Friday night. Everett was born October 13, 1970, to Edward M. and Celeste Morgan Hathaway. Everett grew up on the island. He was a graduate of the University of South Carolina with a degree in English. Following graduation, he embarked on several years of travel and study, spending two years at Warwick University near Coventry in England.

Everett treasured English literature and always aspired to the life of a gentleman and scholar. Among his favorite quotes from Joseph Addison: "For

113

whereso'er I turn my ravished eyes, Gay gilded scenes and shining prospects rise, Poetic fields encompass me around, And still I seem to tread on classic ground."

Everett met his wife, Nicole Nelson, when he was teaching as an adjunct at Chastain College on the mainland. They married in 2002.

Everett was predeceased by his parents, his older brother, Edward M. Hathaway II, and sister-in-law, Mary Kay Roberts Hathaway, and his younger sister, Kathryn Hathaway Griffin. Survivors include his wife, Nicole, nephew, Edward M. Hathaway III, and niece, Leslie Griffin.

In lieu of flowers the family suggests a memorial gift to Chastain College or to the charity of your choice. A memorial service will be held at ten A.M. Thursday at St. Mary's Episcopal Church. Officiating will be the Reverend James Cooley. Honorary pallbearers are Richard Martin, Craig Kennedy, Douglas Walker, Esteban Martinez, Bradley Milton, and John Charles Larrimore.

Annie reread the printouts and jotted notes on a small pad. She clicked off the computer and stood. She glanced at her watch. Twenty minutes to noon. She put the folded sheets and notebook in her purse, pulled on her lilac-colored L. L. Bean windbreaker.

She felt justified in her decision to keep Henny's secret. Moreover, she would craft a way to assist Henny without revealing that she knew about Jeremiah. As she did, she would not lie to Max, but she would tell the truth without compromising Henny. Telling the truth did not always entail telling everything you knew.

Now for a talk she didn't want to have.

Max Darling lined up the putt. Knees slightly bent. Relaxed stance. Watch the ball.

The head of the putter connected, the ball rolled merrily over the nylon mat of the indoor putting green that absorbed a good portion of his spacious office. He'd inserted a contour pad under the green to create a break about a foot from the lip of the cup. The ball curled over the raised portion and ran true to the cup.

Instead of a fist pump, he felt a wave of ennui. There had been a raft of cold and misty days since a last burst of warmth right before Christmas. He'd now played this little patch of phony grass until he could probably sink a putt from between his legs.

Suiting the idea to the moment, he dropped another ball, stood with his back to the cup, bent forward, and whacked one-handed between his spread-apart feet.

The ball seemed to be drawn to the hole by a magnet.

Max grinned. He knew when it was time to quit. He gathered up the balls, returned the putter to his shiny red leather golf bag in one corner, and strolled to his desk. He settled in his comfortable leather chair. The mahogany desk that had once served as a refectory table in a monastery was innocent of any evidence of work. January was a slow month at Confidential Commissions. So slow that he'd exhausted the possibilities of the indoor putting green. His Della Street–wise secretary, Barb, was tarpon fishing down in the gulf. Max looked up at the mission statement his mother had created in elegant calligraphy on yellowed parchment:

Confidential Commissions
Offers counsel and encouragement to
those buffeted by fate.
Obtains facts to clarify obscure situations.
Promises confidentiality, impartiality, and
resolution.
Reasonable fees.

He had mixed feelings about the ornate

116

presentation, but hanging the statement was the least a man could do with a Christmas gift obviously created with such . . . He frowned. Such insight? Such whimsy? Such originality?

His mother was definitely insightful, whimsical, and sometimes eerily prescient. In fact, there were those who had been known to describe Laurel Darling Roethke as just this side of certifiable. He grinned and looked at the photograph of the foremost proponent of his mother as an endearing loon. At least Annie admitted that Laurel was endearing. Exasperating? Sometimes. Entertaining? Often. Endearing? Always.

Max never tired of admiring his wife's photograph, flyaway sandy curls that spoke of sea and sand and sun, steady gray eyes that were honest and kind and eager, an open and genuine face with kissable, very kissable, lips. A winter day, a crackling fire, and Annie . . . Who needed lunch? He'd call and suggest the very best kind of rendezvous, just the two of them, the world forgotten . . .

The outer door opened and a refrain of marimba music sounded, Annie's Christmas gift to lift spirits that might sag in January. Marimba music was fine, but he would get rid of this visitor in short order. He had in mind a surefire cure for January doldrums.

"Max?" Annie's voice was tentative.

Hey, was he thinking right or what? Maybe Annie had the same cheerful plan?

She stood in his doorway.

One look and he knew afternoon delight definitely was not the reason for her visit. Her gray eyes had a telltale wideness that revealed discomfort, and her shoulders were stiff beneath her lilac windbreaker.

She took a deep breath, walked toward his desk, a beseeching look in her eyes.

"Max."

He rose, came around the desk, and pulled her into his arms. "What's wrong, honey?" She leaned against him and he knew whatever distressed her, it was not a problem between them. He cupped her chin in his hand, raised her head. "Gretchen?"

"Max." She took a deep breath. "I'm sure Jeremiah is innocent."

He felt a start of surprise. This was the last statement he would have expected. This morning she'd been withdrawn and depressed, carrying a burden of guilt despite his insistence that she was not responsible for Gretchen's death. There was a striking change in her demeanor. Now she was excited, although hesitant, and her gaze slid away from his.

"I've been thinking and I've figured out some things."

He watched. She was talking very fast, the words too glib.

She picked up steam. "I am absolutely certain" — there was no mistaking the conviction in her voice — "that Gretchen's talking about Jeremiah didn't matter. She was just being Gretchen. Oh, I suppose she'd scared herself, but that was only a little part of her calls. Mostly she was talking about the index card she found in Everett Hathaway's jacket. Max, here's what I think happened . . ."

As she sketched her dark vision of the December night when Everett Hathaway slipped from his home and paddled a kayak to his death, he listened with a growing sense of unreality.

She finished, looked at him hopefully.

He could almost be drawn into Annie's premise. Certainly Everett's death was odd, almost inexplicable. But what had prompted Annie to conclude definitively that Jeremiah was innocent? "Why are you suddenly positive the murderer can't be Jeremiah?"

Annie didn't answer. She simply looked at him.

He saw turmoil in her eyes and face,

knowledge, vulnerability, reluctance, determination, and, most of all, paramount, unmistakable, a plea. *Don't ask me. Let it go. I can't tell you.*

"I suppose" — he turned away and picked up a small jade shamrock, her gift to him one St. Pat's Day — "you thought through the facts of the day." He spoke in a reasoned tone to reassure her, a clear declaration that he was not pressing, would not press. Inside, he felt the drumbeat of worry. What did she know? She'd found out something she didn't feel free to share. "I guess Gretchen's conversations made you decide that the important fact was the index card in Everett's jacket."

"Yes." Relief buoyed her voice. "That's exactly what happened. I told Billy" — she drew a deep breath — "that someone from the Hathaway house came to Better Tomorrow to get that card and he — or she — killed Gretchen."

He leaned against his desk, carefully placed the shamrock next to the silver frame of her photograph. Luck for his Annie. Dammit, what did she know? "Well, Billy can check everything out." His gaze settled again on her face.

"Billy still thinks Jeremiah is guilty."

Max waited. He understood Billy's response.

"So" — she spoke brightly but with underlying firmness — "since I know what I know —"

He kept his expression attentive, but his mind was alive with questions. What did she know? And how could he find out?

"— I have to do something about it. I can't let a man be hunted for murder when he's innocent. I've called Henny —"

"Why Henny?"

A hint of alarm quivered in her eyes. "She hired Jeremiah."

The answer made sense, but Annie was too wary. He hurried to smooth the moment. "Oh, two minds better than one? Hey, you have a built-in partner right here, remember?"

Her smile was quick and genuine. "I was hoping you'd agree to help. I left a message for Henny to meet me at Parotti's for lunch. We'll decide what to do. You'll come?"

"You couldn't keep me away. I'll be like a hound on your heels." His tone was light, but he meant his answer on every level.

5

In summer, Parotti's Bar and Grill would have a line at noon, vacationers vying with residents for the best food on the island, hot, crisp hush puppies, succulent flounder, local shrimp. The outlanders were enchanted by the adjoining bait shop with its coolers and barrels. Regulars took the sawdust-covered floor and assortment of rods and reels for granted. When Ben Parotti had married Miss Jolene, who owned a tea shop on the mainland, and brought her to reign over his bar and grill, he'd been willing to add quiche to the menu, small vases with flowers on red-and-white-checked cloths on the tables, but he drew a line in the sawdust over the bait shop. Fishermen still carried out coolers with chunks of black bass, grouper, squid, and chicken necks. An occasional fastidious diner's nose wrinkled at the heady scent of bait mingled with the aroma of hot grease from the kitchen.

There was no line and plenty of available tables the third week in January. Usually Annie walked to their favorite wooden booth where Max, as a regular, had been free to carve a heart with their initials on the table. Today she chose instead a corner table with a good view of the front door.

When Ben arrived with menus, Annie smiled at him. "Henny's joining us." Surely she would come.

The front door opened, cool air swirled inside. Henny had changed from her informal outfit of the morning, appropriate for clambering into a boat and heading out into the Sound. Now she wore a one-button navy wool flannel blazer and cream wool slacks and low navy suede heels. She walked toward them, her expressive face pale and drawn.

Max rose to pull out a chair. "Annie asked me to join in the sleuthing." His smile was easy.

Henny slipped into the chair. She managed a smile, but it didn't reach her eyes.

Ben Parotti approached, his gnomelike face folded in lines of commiseration. "Sure sorry about the trouble at Better Tomorrow. I heard they're huntin' Jeremiah with dogs." Ben was not only one of the island's most

123

successful businessmen, owner of the restaurant, a Gas 'N' Go, the ferry, and assorted real estate, he knew everyone and was always a first source for background when the *Gazette*'s Marian Kenyon sought information about anyone on matters both public and private.

"Jeremiah's innocent." Henny was crisp and declarative.

Annie saw Max's eyes narrow in speculation.

"Glad to hear that. Brought the usual." Ben knew his customers. He plunked down ice waters, plus iced teas for Annie and Henny, a Bud Light for Max. "I hear he ran away. That boy never had a whole lot of sense, but there's not a mean bone in his body. I told the lady cop." That was his term for Sgt. Hyla Harrison. "And I told her you" — he looked at Henny — "knew folks, good and bad, and you'd never picked a loser yet. I said if you hired him, he was all right. I have to say she listened to me real nice, said she'd tell Billy."

Henny's face softened. "Thank you, Ben. You're a good friend."

Ben cleared his throat, always quick to maintain his gruff exterior, which, as they all knew, covered a kind and generous heart. "Miss Jolene's made chicken potpie today."

124

Henny and Max ordered the special, but Annie's heart belonged to the fried oyster sandwich. "And sweet potato fries."

Max looked reproachful.

Annie defended her choice. "Someday they'll find out cholesterol is good for you. Besides, everything's genetic. Anyway, chicken potpie isn't exactly dietary."

"Annie." Henny's voice was strained. "You said you had reason to think someone else came to Better Tomorrow."

Annie described the calls from Gretchen. As she described the index card in the pocket of Everett Hathaway's tweed jacket and how Gretchen linked its contents to his fatal trip in a kayak, Henny's shoulders straightened. There was heartfelt relief evident in her expression and in her posture. She'd listened to Jeremiah, taken him on faith. Now she had concrete reason to see that he might be, could be innocent.

"Don't you see?" Annie was emphatic. "The card should have been lying with the pocket change and the knife."

Max held up a hand. "Not so fast. We can worry about what happened to that card in a minute. Let's clarify what you are claiming. First, that Everett Hathaway was murdered." He ticked off the points. "Second, the card posed a threat to his murderer.

125

Third, the card was found in a tweed jacket Hathaway wore the day he died, according to what Gretchen told Annie. Fourth, the message Gretchen left at the Hathaway house was read by the murderer. Fifth, the murderer came to Better Tomorrow, took the card, decided Gretchen would never be discreet, and used Jeremiah's axe to kill her."

"Exactly." Annie met him stare for stare.

"Where" — his tone was mild — "was Jeremiah while all of this took place?"

"He'd gone —" Henny broke off.

Annie and Max looked at her.

Henny said smoothly, "I was thinking out loud. I imagine he'd gone to the back shed. That's where he did furniture repairs. Of course, I can't speak for his actions Monday, but often if he'd spent the morning chopping or lifting boxes of cans, he'd do repairs in the afternoon."

Annie visualized the shed. The small sheet metal structure stood behind some pines to the north of the house rather than in the rear. Better Tomorrow faced east. The oyster shell parking lot was between the house and the shed. "Cars make a pretty big racket on the shells. If Jeremiah heard a car sometime between two fifteen and three that would be interesting."

"If there wasn't a car" — Henny spoke

carefully — "it doesn't mean no one came."

Annie wondered if Jeremiah had told Henny in a choking voice of despair that no one had come, he hadn't heard a car, there had been only him and no one would believe him, not with his axe used as the weapon.

Henny's entire demeanor was transformed, charged with hope. "What you've told me changes everything. The Hathaways live fairly close. There's a path through the woods and a bike trail." She reached for her purse, retrieved a pen and a pad, quickly sketched, pushed the pad to the middle of the table, visible to both Annie and Max. "Better Tomorrow's on the northwest side of the island. So is the Hathaway house. I was working at Better Tomorrow when the call came for us to pick up the boxes of Everett's clothing. I looked up the address for Jeremiah."

Ben brought their plates and a bucket of hot biscuits.

Annie took a bite of her fried oyster sandwich, the onion bun heavy with Thousand Island dressing. Mmmm, succulent. She studied Henny's rough map of the lee side of the island. The main harbor with the ferry dock and downtown was toward the northwest end of the island. A big X marked a spot several inlets north of the harbor. Not far inland she'd drawn a square box that was labeled BT.

Annie touched the X.

"That's the Hathaway house." Henny sounded satisfied. She held a steaming spoonful of chicken potpie. "You can see how close it is to Better Tomorrow. It's not more than a mile at the most, and a bike would only take minutes. Oh, Annie, this should be enough to show Billy that Jeremiah could be innocent."

Annie turned her hands palms up. "I told him, but he thinks the evidence against Jeremiah is overwhelming."

Max looked bemused, his dark blue eyes skeptical. "Ladies, I hesitate to offer a discouraging word, but this entire wobbly structure is based on the assumption that Everett Hathaway was murdered. Give me one good reason why that should be true." He made an appreciative sound as he took a bite of chicken pie.

Annie spoke slowly. "I think he was murdered because there are too many peculiar aspects to his death. Why was he out in a kayak on a cold windy December night? That was always odd. He wasn't a seasoned kayaker. He hadn't taken the boat out in months. Why that night? And why at night?

Where was he going? What did he plan to do? Did he take the kayak because it made no noise, could slip up unseen and unheard? Until somebody can explain what he was doing and where he was going, the fact that he died — presumably in an accident — stinks! Especially since Gretchen found a card linked to that night." For emphasis, she jabbed a sweet potato fry into a side of Thousand Island. Ben knew what she liked.

Henny frowned. "Where was he found?"

Annie reached for her purse, pulled out several folded sheets of paper. She opened one, scanned the sheet, then handed it to Henny. As Henny read the news story about the discovery of Hathaway's body, Annie checked the island directory on her iPhone. "He was found by Don Thornwall, who lives at one forty-six Herring Gull Road. And that's" — Annie placed her finger on Henny's rough map — "in a cove that's around a headland from the Hathaway place."

Max gazed at the map, his expression unimpressed. "Okay, he took the kayak and went around the headland. So?"

"Why?" Annie's tone was sweet.

Max turned up his hands. "Who's to say? Maybe he has a girlfriend and he snuck out of the house. Maybe he had a headache and thought the cold night air would help. Maybe he'd eaten too much over the holidays and decided to start an exercise program. Maybe he got a call on his cell and his bookie wanted to meet him on the sly."

"And," Annie asked sweetly, "how likely are any of those possibilities?"

"How likely is murder?" Max countered.

"He's dead. And so is Gretchen." Annie's tone indicated she felt she'd trumped Max.

"Don't squabble." Henny's tone was impatient. "The point is that Gretchen's messages to Annie prove that there is a connection between Gretchen and the Hathaway house shortly before she was murdered. She indicated the card gave a reason for Everett taking the kayak. Annie, you have to be right. Everett Hathaway was murdered. Otherwise the card wouldn't have mattered. Now all we have to do is find out who killed him and Jeremiah will be safe."

Henny and Annie exchanged confident glances.

Max scraped crust from the side of the small baking dish. "I don't mean to quibble, but the card is gone —"

Annie broke in. "That's the point. That proves everything I've been saying."

Max ignored the interruption. "— which may mean nothing. Billy Cameron thinks

Gretchen put the note in her purse and Jeremiah took her purse."

Henny spoke hotly. "The purse was gone when —" She broke off abruptly.

Max was swift. "When Jeremiah found her?"

Annie agonized for Henny. Only fatigue would make Henny gaffe-prone. Swiftly, Annie plunged in. "I suppose Jeremiah called you last night, told you he was innocent and how he found Gretchen with his axe right there. When he saw that her purse was gone — I suppose she must have had it in the sorting room while she was working back there and he saw it there earlier — and he was afraid he'd be accused." She was aware that Max was watching with one thick blond brow raised. "I'm sure he didn't tell you where he was, so even if you'd called the police, there wasn't anything to give a hint to his location."

Henny said carefully. "I couldn't report his location."

Annie could fill in the rest of the sentence . . . *because I know he's innocent.*

Henny's face held sadness and fear. "He was terribly upset. He swore to me on his mother's grave that he was innocent, that he'd been working in the back shed. He finished gluing a broken leg on a coffee table about twenty to three. He went into the house and the first thing he saw was blood in the hall outside the sorting room. He thought Gretchen must be hurt and he hurried to the doorway and saw her lying there, but most of all, he saw the axe next to her. He recognized the axe. He'd put a notch on the handle about an inch from the top. He looked around the room and that's when he realized her purse was gone. He said he knew they'd suspect him. And he said the awful thing was, he hadn't heard a car or truck or anything. He said he turned and ran and got on his bike and rode away as fast as he could." She brushed back a length of silvered dark hair. "He told me they'd hurt him when he was in prison and he'd kill himself before he'd go back, that he'd rather die than be in jail." She looked at them gravely. "He meant what he said. If I told the police, he would kill himself. I promised him I'd do my best to find out what happened. He promised me he would hide and stay quiet. He said he would die if he saw the police coming for him. He had — He told me he had a knife." She reached out, gripped Annie's arm. "I didn't see any way forward until you called. Now I do."

Max studied Henny. "You believe Jeremiah."

"I believe him." She spoke quietly but with conviction.

"If he's innocent, someone else came to Better Tomorrow between two fifteen and Annie's arrival, killed Gretchen, and took the index card." Max picked up Henny's map. "Damned if there isn't a crazy kind of logic about it."

Annie was triumphant. "Of course there is."

Max looked from one to the other. "Finding this elusive, invisible murderer isn't going to be easy." He picked up his beer, drank it with an air of abstraction.

Annie hoped he was considering ways to investigate, not analyzing Henny's carefully chosen words. She spoke quickly. "I have a suspect list. The murderer had to have seen the message Gretchen left with the housekeeper, so we know the murderer came from the Hathaway house."

Max raised a cautionary hand. "Or someone saw the message and told someone else."

Annie nodded. "One way or another, there's a connection to the people in the house that day."

Henny's eyes narrowed in concentration. "Let's think about what Gretchen found in Everett's pocket. Gretchen's comments suggest the card explained why Everett went out in the kayak. It's reasonable to assume that the card held instructions telling him to take a kayak at a specific time after dark to the bay where he was found. Why a kayak?" She looked inquiringly at Annie and Max.

Max frowned. "No one would hear him coming."

Henny nodded approval. "He was on his way somewhere that he didn't want to be seen."

Annie concentrated. "The card was bait. Maybe the message was true or maybe not, but the whole point was to get him out in that bay after dark in a kayak. The person who wrote the card planned to intercept him, capsize the kayak, keep it out of his reach."

"So" — Henny was decisive — "we have to find out who wrote on the card."

"The place to start is at the Hathaway house." Annie picked up a printout of the obituary. "Of the home are Everett's widow, Nicole, his nephew, Edward M. Hathaway III, and his niece, Leslie Griffin."

Henny looked thoughtful. "We need to find out who Everett saw the day he died. He could have been given the card at his office as well as at home."

Annie had a nebulous sense of uneasiness. They were missing something. Yes, the card lured Everett out in a kayak. Yet why was there a card at all? Abruptly, she understood. "He didn't know!"

Max frowned. "Who didn't know what?"

Henny, too, appeared bewildered.

"Everett." Annie was impatient. Didn't they see what was obvious? "Everett received information that prompted him to take out the kayak. But why was the information written on an index card?"

Again she looked at two uncomprehending faces.

"The murderer wanted Everett out on the water at a particular time of night in a kayak. How could that be achieved?" Annie was impatient as they continued to look blank. "The murderer knew some fact, had some information that was guaranteed to lure Everett out into the night. Gretchen said it was a 'scandal.' Somebody put the slip in his bedroom or left it on his desk or placed it in the front seat of his car. But the message was *anonymous*. Otherwise Everett would have immediately collared the writer, asked for an explanation. He didn't know!"

"Oh. He didn't know . . . You mean Everett didn't know who wrote the note." Henny smiled in delight. "Mrs. North."

Annie recognized the reference. As befitted Death on Demand's most omnivorous reader, Henny was well acquainted with mystery classics. Frances and Richard Lockridge's charming heroine Pamela North nattered inconsequentially as she jumped to conclusions that befuddled her listeners.

"There is a logical progression," Annie said stiffly.

Max was quick to make peace. Sort of. "It may be another turret on a sand castle, but once you swallow the basic premise, it figures that the card in his pocket was anonymous."

Annie flipped over the obituary printout, wrote:

1. What kind of "scandal" could involve Everett? Was he engaged in a love affair? A dishonest business deal?

Max took the sheet of paper and added:

2. Who had access to Everett's bedroom Thursday night or to his car Friday morning or to his desk at the office?

Annie took the sheet back, wrote fast:

3. Who were Everett's friends? Start with pallbearers.
4. Obtain bios of family members.
5. Survey the cove where his body was found. Why there?
6. Find out if the Hathaways have a motorboat. Did anyone hear a motorboat the night he died?

Henny reached for the paper, added in her distinctive backward-slanting penmanship.

7. Who was in the Hathaway house Monday after Gretchen left the message? Include daily help and visitors.
8. Who wanted Everett dead?

Max's tone was mild. "If he turns out to have been a paragon, beloved of all, the sand castle may collapse."

Annie remembered the excitement — a hint of salaciousness? — in Gretchen's voice. Definitely something disreputable had been described on that missing card.

Max might question the reasoning behind Annie's belief that Everett had been murdered, but she was certain the pieces fit together. Moreover, someone had killed

Gretchen, and if Jeremiah was innocent, the only alternative appeared to be someone linked to Everett Hathaway.

She couldn't share with Max the clincher. So far as she was concerned, Henny's presence at Parotti's was absolute proof of Jeremiah's innocence. This morning he could easily have overpowered Henny, taken her old boat, reached the mainland. He had not. Henny trusted him. He trusted Henny. "He was murdered and we'll find out who wanted him dead and why." Annie gave a decisive nod. "Max, will you put together bios for us?" She pushed the papers to him, the printout of *Gazette* stories and the obituary, and the list of questions.

"Sure." He was agreeable. "I've been at loose ends. Confidential Commissions has been a little slow."

Annie maintained a bland expression. Confidential Commissions, to her knowledge, hadn't had a client seek help in almost six weeks.

He finished his glass of Bud Light. "A project will be a nice change."

Annie knew he wasn't taking her theories seriously, but she also knew that when he made a promise, the promise was kept. Max was a whiz at ferreting personal information from the web and adding details by talking to people.

He looked energized. "I can keep an investigation under the radar by asking people to contribute to a tribute to Everett."

Henny's intelligent face was abruptly combative. "I want to break everything wide open. We are dealing with a murderer who feels absolutely secure. There's no hint of public suspicion that Everett was murdered, right?"

Annie spoke quickly. "Billy knows what I think. Obviously he won't tell anyone. Besides, he doesn't agree."

"So the murderer is flying high." Henny looked grim.

Max frowned. "Isn't that better for us? We can nose around and ask questions without alerting a killer."

Henny shook her head. "If we had lots of time, maybe we could pick up little pieces of information that might come together to give us a pointer. We don't have time. Jeremiah doesn't have time. The weather is cold. There's always a possibility of a big nor'easter. He's being hunted. I want to shock the murderer. I want people to know we're hunting for a killer."

Max ran fingers through a thick shock of blond hair. "Billy Cameron will come down on us like a hound cornering a fox."

Henny folded her arms. "It's a free country. We have a right to our opinions. We have a right to ask people questions if they'll talk to us. If they don't talk to us, maybe that will tell us a lot right there."

Max's face furrowed. "As you say, there's no law against believing whatever we want to believe and talking to people. But we have to be careful not to imply that there is an official investigation underway."

Henny's eyes gleamed. "We won't say there is an official investigation. However, we can certainly say that the police are aware of the suspicion. That's fair, isn't it?"

Annie gave Henny a thumbs-up. "Honest. Fair. And" — her smile was approving — "a brilliant ploy."

Henny pushed away the half-eaten chicken pie. "Now that we're in agreement, let's get started. Let's rattle some cages. I know Nicole. I'll drop by to see her."

Max looked concerned. "Maybe we should find out more before you talk to her. Let me round up some information."

Henny was decisive. "I know what I need to do."

Annie felt a dart of worry. "There's a killer connected to that house. Maybe you and I should go together."

Henny was brisk. "We don't want to

140

duplicate our efforts. I'll take care of Nicole and the house. Max can get the bios. Annie, see what you can find out about the cove where Everett died." She spoke with urgency. "We need to work as fast as we can." On that she rose and turned away, hurrying toward the door.

Annie pictured the isolated wooded hammock, bathed now in a chilly mist. She jumped up. "Henny's right. Jeremiah's terribly frightened and alone. We have to find the killer in time to save him." She wasn't speaking of saving him solely from the law. Jeremiah had no intention of being taken into custody.

She saw Max's worried frown. He wasn't convinced they were right about Everett's death, but he well knew that if they were, a killer would soon take notice of their questions. "We'll be careful." She turned and hurried toward the door. She knew Max would work doubly hard now to try to keep her and Henny out of danger.

Henny Brawley slid behind the wheel of her Dodge. Anxiously she scanned the leaden sky and whitecaps tossing in the Sound. The barometer had been falling when she left the house. Low pressure off Bermuda might signal a possible storm. The hammock was only a couple of feet above sea level. A storm tide could sweep over low-lying land in a flash. She had to hurry, make things happen quickly. For now, Jeremiah had plenty of food and warm woolen blankets and a tent. Did he have hope?

She pulled her cell from her purse. Did she dare call him? She had his cell number. She'd given him her cell number. Just in case. Of course the police had Jeremiah's number as well. She didn't dare take a chance. She dropped the cell into her purse, gripped the wheel, eyes narrowed in thought. Cordgrass wavered in the wind. But a storm wasn't the only danger for Jeremiah. Much more deadly was the fear that made him determined never to go to prison again.

They had to hurry. She felt a surge of confidence. She was eager to go into the lion's den and shock a murderer.

Annie shivered, wished she'd worn her heavy wool peacoat. The wind scudded waves in the Sound, tugged at her hair, knifed through her cotton jacket. She stood on a public concrete boat ramp, her Thunderbird parked behind her on a rutted dirt road. The water beneath lowering clouds looked gray and rough as beaten pewter.

A lonely place to die. Especially at night in killingly cold water, struggling, awkward in a life vest, splashing after a kayak that remained just beyond a weakening reach, an idling motorboat spelling death, not rescue.

The next morning Everett Hathaway's lifeless body bobbed in the water, his red orange PFD a bright spot against the gray.

Annie remembered reading the story in the *Gazette,* talking across the breakfast table with Max. They had known him as they knew many people on the island, a well-known family, a successful family business, occasional gossip. "Wife much younger . . . A fussy man, kind of self-important . . . Pseudo-Brit . . ." She wished they'd been more charitable. He'd loved poetry and history, taken pleasure from elegant phrases. She remembered the quote in the obituary from Joseph Addison's *A Letter from Italy.* She recalled Everett's precise, slightly high voice. Maybe that kind of quote seemed pompous in today's heritage-dismissive world, but he recognized beauty and surely he'd had friends who enjoyed him, smiled when he walked into a room.

She stood here on a bleak misty morning because of Gretchen and Henny and Jeremiah, and now with a pang of regret, for

143

Everett, who had come here to die.

Annie carefully surveyed the small bay, similar to many that marked the lee side of the island, winter brown cordgrass intersected by channels to the open Sound. Four structures were visible, three on the north bank, one on the south. On the north bank, her eyes moved from a cabin on stilts, similar to Henny's, to a modest but well-kept white frame to a rambling one-story brick house with framing up for a room addition on one side. The house on the south side was palatial, a two-story tiled-roof Mediterranean stucco with a stone terrace. Outdoor umbrellas on white wrought-iron tables were lashed for winter. A large boathouse looked cavernous and empty.

Herring Gull Road, unpaved and rutted, served both sides of the bay. Wooden piers extended from each backyard. What drew Everett to this bay? One of the houses? The boat ramp? Was he meeting someone or looking for someone?

Many areas on the island were suitable for people to meet clandestinely late on a December Friday night, the parking lot of any church, in the pavilion at the park that overlooked the main harbor, at the lumberyard. Yet Hathaway had taken out a kayak and come to this particular bay.

If he intended to visit a house, why hadn't he driven? Was he afraid the motor would be heard? In addition, although the road that served these houses was unpaved, driveways likely were covered by oyster shells. It would be difficult to arrive surreptitiously. Parking on the road would be immediately noticeable to anyone arriving at or departing from one of the houses.

Annie pulled a note pad from her pocket. The big house to the south, 148 Herring Gull Road, belonged to Jefferson and Renee Carstairs. On the north bank, the rambling brick with bunches of pansies was 146 Herring Gull Road, home of Don Thornwall, who found the body. The small white frame house at 144 Herring Gull Road was the residence of Sheila Porter. The shabby cabin at 142 Herring Gull Road hadn't been listed in the crisscross directory.

Max Darling stared moodily at his wife's photograph. Annie was hiding something from him. He addressed her smiling picture. "I may not be the most subtle guy in the world, but you might as well have hoisted hurricane warning flags." A sudden gust of wind rattled a warped front window. The wind was picking up from the northeast. They might be in for a good blow in a day or so. "This morning you were lower than a pig's belly, sure that you could have saved Gretchen if you'd hustled to Better Tomorrow and kept her company. That was based on Jeremiah's guilt. By lunch time you were happier than Agatha with a cornered mouse. In between you learned something that convinced you of Jeremiah's innocence. But, honey" — he was skeptical — "jumping to the conclusion that Everett Hathaway was murdered is a supersized leap." He shook his head. "Okay, okay," as if in answer to an indignant rebuttal.

His face softened. Annie's mantra had always been that it never hurt to ask. Sure, the answer can be no, but sometimes the answer is yes. If you don't try, you'll never know which.

Max leaned back in his chair. If Everett Hathaway had been murdered, the crime had been cleverly devised, which indicated forethought and planning. The time, the weather, and the location precluded an accidental encounter and sudden quarrel. Premeditated murder indicated a strong motive and perhaps urgency. What had Everett done or threatened to do that resulted in his death?

Max remembered Everett as something of a poseur, certainly not a figure of strength or power. The sooner he found out every-thing possible about Everett Hathaway and the people around him, the sooner he would know if Annie's judgment was right.

If Annie was right, they were tugging at the cover of a wily and dangerous murderer.

6

The Hathaway home was oriented to the prevailing south-westerly breezes, a Beaufort-style house with a two-story verandah and double entrance stairs. Stuccoed arches supported the verandah. Ionic capitals decorated the first level of columns, Corinthian the second. Made of tabby, the exterior was a calming sage green in summer, but dull and somber beneath today's gray skies. The house had been built in 1803 by a rice planter and was on the register of historic homes. To one side at the end of a long drive sat a later-built triple garage with an upstairs apartment. At one time the apartment had been used by the family chauffeur. Those days were long gone.

Henny well remembered Eddie Hathaway's hospitality and generosity. In recent years he had made the garage apartment available at a low rent to military personnel or dependents. His father had been a marine and a lifelong supporter of the services. Eddie's wife had been a founding member of Better Tomorrow. Everett's wife, Nicole, wasn't active in island charities, but she belonged to Ladies of the Leaf, the island's most prestigious women's book club. The invitation had been made because a Hathaway had always been a member. Henny had chatted with her several times. Nicole never expressed an opinion about a book. Instead she gazed wide-eyed and parroted the reviewer's comments. Henny privately thought she was about as interested in literature as in quantum physics. In fact, Nicole once artlessly said, "Everett loves for me to come to book group. He thinks books are wonderful." She hadn't attended the luncheons the last few months.

Henny hurried up the steps, pushed the brass lion's head doorbell. Through the side window panels, the entry hall was dim. She waited for a full count of twenty, pushed again.

The door opened in midpeal. A tall, angular woman with a straight brown hair and a dour face gazed at her without expression. Her black turtleneck was frayed at the cuffs and her long gray wool skirt had an uneven hem. Sturdy black oxfords hadn't been polished in a long time. She carried a dust cloth in one hand. "May I help you?" There was no warmth in her voice.

Henny was brisk. "I'm here to see Nicole."

Oyster shells crunched behind Henny in the drive. Brakes squealed.

"Mrs. Hathaway hasn't been down." There was a flicker of interest in the housekeeper's brown eyes. "If you want to leave your name, I'll tell her you came by."

Not down . . . Henny didn't need to check her watch to know that it was almost two o'clock. Not down?

A car door slammed.

Henny opened the screen door, ignoring the surprise in the housekeeper's face. "She will see me." Henny spoke with authority. "Tell her that Henny Brawley is here from Better Tomorrow and I have information that is of great importance to her." She gave a regal nod. "I'll wait in the drawing room." She moved past the housekeeper, turned to her left into the huge and gracious room with old French furniture, a Chippendale mirror above a satinwood side table, an ornately stuccoed mantelpiece, and a faded Aubusson rug.

Quick steps rattled across the verandah. The screen door opened.

The housekeeper moved to the doorway of the drawing room. "She told me not to disturb her."

"Who doesn't want to be disturbed?" The voice was young. The teenage girl in the entryway swung free from a backpack, dropped it to the floor, and used one suede boot to shove it to the corner. "You can take it up later, Mag."

The housekeeper's face tightened, but she turned and bent to pick up the backpack. She spoke to the girl. "Mrs. Hathaway hasn't come down today. She said she was resting and didn't want to be bothered."

The girl shrugged out of a sunburst orange, high-collared fleece coat and scanned Henny with cool impudence. She tossed the coat onto a sideboard and stood with hands on her hips in a pose made provocative by a sleek sweater and tight jeans. "You don't look like a bother." She tilted her head to survey Henny. "Actually, you look like a schoolteacher. And, hey, I get out of school early because I have a job. Jay-oh-bee. I work part time at the family sweat shop. So I get to skip fifth hour. Anyway, what's up with you and Nicole?"

Henny was quite sure the girl didn't care. She was simply using the moment for a splash of attention. Henny tabbed her as a brat, but sometimes brats could be useful. The flippant teenager had offered Henny a perfect stage for a public announcement sure to be repeated within the family and guaranteed to destroy the complacency of a killer who felt free from discovery. "I'm here to see Nicole with information concerning the murder of her husband."

The girl's eyes widened. Her rosebud mouth formed an O of shock. "Murder? What are you talking about? Everett drowned." She stared at Henny, her body rigid.

Henny was firm. "A murderer flipped him out of the kayak and left him to drown. I intend to inform Nicole."

"Wait a minute. Who said so? This is nuts. Who would kill Unc?" The girl stopped and clapped her hands together. "Oh, scratch that. I guess I know some candidates. Like his merry widow or his pissed-off nephew. And me." Her tone was bright. "He was such a bore. But the last I heard, nobody ever got killed for being a bore." She shook her head. "Somebody killing Everett is kind of like a bad joke."

Henny edged her voice with steel. "Murder isn't a joke."

"Okay, lady. I get it. You're serious. But who are you and how come you claim to know something nobody else knows?" Her tone was combative.

"Henny Brawley. From Better Tomorrow. And you?"

"Leslie Griffin." A carefully penciled brow shot up. "Wait a minute. Somebody got killed at that place, right?"

"The victim, Gretchen Burkholt, found an index card in the pocket of your uncle's jacket that proved your uncle's death wasn't an accident. She called here yesterday and left a message that the card could be picked up. Someone came and killed her and the card is gone."

"Someone came . . . What the hell are you saying?" The girl scowled.

Henny was unperturbed. "Gretchen left a message here, and within an hour she was dead and the card was taken."

"Are you claiming someone from here killed a woman?" The teenager's voice wobbled.

The housekeeper's gaze slowly moved to a mahogany side table in the entryway. A white notepad lay next to a telephone.

"That appears to be the case." Henny let the silence expand and then said smoothly, "I'm sure the family will want to discover the truth. Now, I must see Nicole. Since I am connected with Better Tomorrow and learned the facts, I wanted to prepare her."

"Are the cops coming?" Leslie's eyes were huge.

"They have the information." Henny spoke carefully. "I don't know how they handle their investigations."

"Murder . . ." The girl shook her head. "That's a bummer. I guess you better go up. Her room is on the second floor. Turn right. Third door on your left."

As Henny started up the steps, Leslie scooted ahead of her. At the top of the stairs, Leslie turned to face Henny. She pushed back a strand of blond hair. "If I had a minute, I'd go with you." Her attitude was once again flip. "Not that I'm a big fan of Nicole's, but this is better than *CSI*. Non-grieving widow gets jolt; husband murdered; who's the guilty bastard? But I have to change. Cousin Trey *insists* on a skirt. If I didn't find Hathaway Advertising a tad less boring than fifth hour, I'd chuck my jay-oh-bee in a heartbeat. Plus I get credit for an internship." She glanced at her watch. "I'm running late. I can't wait to tell Cousin Trey the reason why." She whirled and hurried up the hall.

Henny watched thoughtfully as a bedroom door closed. Definitely she wanted to talk to Leslie again and learn more about the non-grieving widow and the pissed-off nephew. She wondered if the comments were as artless as they appeared, simply another indication of teenage callousness, or whether Leslie intended to embarrass Nicole and her cousin. In any event, Henny felt pleased. She'd thrown a rock into a stagnant pool and the ripples had begun.

Henny turned right, stopped at the third door on the left. The white panel was firmly shut. She knocked twice, eased the door open.

A querulous voice wavered. "Go away." Nicole slumped on a chaise longue in a rumpled pink silk robe with a coverlet drawn over her.

"Nicole, Henny Brawley."

Nicole's head twisted. She struggled to a sitting position. Her dark hair was tangled, her face pale, her blue eyes red-rimmed. She wore no makeup.

Henny stepped inside the room. "I have to talk to you." Henny felt a twist of uncertainty. Leslie didn't think Nicole was grieving, but Nicole's appearance reflected deep unhappiness. Henny knew that if she was intruding upon a widow's grief, she would soon make the pain even more scalding.

She had no choice.

Drawn velvet drapes masked the massive

windows at the front of the Mediterranean-style mansion. Annie walked up broad shallow steps. Lights glowed in several upper windows. The porch had been recently swept and was free of drifted leaves. A house such as this should have a staff, yet there was nothing but heavy silence.

Annie pushed the front bell, faintly heard deep bongs. She waited, but she was not surprised when no one came. She walked down the steps, followed a bricked walkway around the side of the house to a broad terrace. As she crossed the stones, the click of her shoes sounded inordinately loud. She looked through French doors at furniture shrouded from dust.

Not only was no one home this January afternoon, she felt certain the owners were far away on a sunny shore, possibly riding turquoise swells in the yacht that would have been kept in the massive empty boathouse she'd glimpsed earlier.

She gazed at the bay. If this house had been Everett's destination, he would have been able to meet someone very secretly indeed.

Maybe Max had found out if Everett had a reason for a secret meeting.

Or maybe she would find the answer in one of the houses across the bay.

■ ■ ■ ■

Max spread out several color prints of photographs of Everett Hathaway that he'd found online as well as some taken from the agency's Facebook site. Overlong reddish brown hair framed a long face with a thin nose, high cheekbones, and sharp chin. He favored Tommy Bahama shirts and khakis in summer, a blue Oxford cloth shirt, tweed jacket, and worsted slacks. Max had gathered some telling observations from friends and acquaintances.

His barber: "Everett only liked words most people never used. Like remiss and nubilous and lares and penates and hedonics. When you looked stupid, he was glad to explain them. He was always quoting somebody. Mostly it was dumb stuff, but recently he had one I thought was pretty good. According to Everett, somebody named Hill once said in a sermon, 'Why should the Devil have all the good tunes?' "

A fellow adjunct at Chastain College: "I always thought he was a stuffed shirt and then he surprised everybody by marrying a babe. She was in one of his classes. Nicole probably got confused when she enrolled, thought she was taking a class on antiques

157

and landed in his eighteenth-century lit course."

A golfer at the country club: "Let's just say he took life seriously. Very seriously." A pause. "The man couldn't go more than a couple of sentences without a quote. Once he was in a foursome and a player damn near had a seventeen-foot putt, but the ball hung on the lip and stayed there. Everett looked smug and came up to him, and for God's sake, quoted Henry Fielding. 'Nothing more aggravates ill success than the near approach to good.' The guy looked like he wanted to wrap his putter around his neck. Everett didn't spout a quote a day, it was a couple of quotes an hour. So maybe I shouldn't put too much stock in it. But we had a few drinks the week before he died. He was at the bar in the country club late one night. I wondered what was what. I mean, my wife was out of town and I hate the house when she's gone. Just me and the hoot of a screech owl. Anyway, I ended up talking to Everett. He'd had a little too much Scotch. Just before I left, and he wasn't speaking too distinctly then, he said, 'Ted, old buddy, Colley Cibber" — Max had later figured out the poet's name by googling the quote — " 'summed it up.' Everett's eyes were big and owlish. He was just this side of seriously drunk. Anyway, he cleared his throat and said real precisely, 'Oh, how many torments lie in the small circle of a wedding ring!' Man, I knew it was time to go home. But after he died — and that's weird as hell because he wasn't any kind of boat jock — I kind of wondered if he planned an accident."

Max shook his head. Everett didn't set out to die that night. The card in his tweed jacket clearly indicated, according to Gretchen, that there was a reason for the trip. The jaunt in the kayak had a definite purpose. But the golfer's comments prompted him to add two questions to the list.

9. Was Everett's marriage in trouble?
10. Did his widow inherit from a life-insurance policy?

After a moment's thought, he wrote:

11. What was Everett's financial situation and how does his death affect his survivors?

Max circled the last question. In much of life, the dictum to follow the money made very good sense.

After a moment's thought, he called a retired lawyer on the town council. Charles

Farnsworth played bridge for serious stakes, lived for gossip, and prided himself on knowing everything about everybody. Max easily opened the floodgates by observing a second dictum: Flattery will get you everywhere. "Hey, Charles, I'm depending on you to set me straight. You always know the ins and outs about island families" — murmurs of a modest disclaimer — "and I need some background on the Hathaways. You're always discreet" — he piously hoped this total falsehood wouldn't end up in St. Peter's ledger of transgressions — "and you know mum's the word with me. There's a question of some bills and I wondered about Everett's estate and whether there was life insurance."

Charles cleared his throat. "Substantial holdings in the family. Of course, Everett's death changes everything. As I recall, his widow will receive a nice settlement, which was determined in a prenuptial agreement, so she shouldn't have any financial concerns. No life insurance for her. There was a policy with the benefits to be used to establish a chair in his name in the English department at Chastain. The greatest changes" — a vexed noise — "and I regret that I am not certain about the details, but I believe from what I heard — one of my friends drafted the instruments — that his nephew, Trey, will now assume control of his inheritance and he will oversee the inheritance of Everett's niece, Leslie, until she reaches twenty-one. Otherwise, Trey would not have controlled his income until he was twenty-five. Trey and Leslie aren't brother and sister, you understand. Cousins. Trey is the son of Everett's late brother, Edward Hathaway II, and Leslie the daughter of his late sister, Kathryn Hathaway Griffin. Until Everett's death, the nephew and niece were to be subject to Everett's direction of their trusts until they reached the age of twenty-five. Is that what you needed?"

"That clears everything up." Max was hearty. "Thanks, Charles. I'll buy you a drink in the Men's Grill next week." As he clicked off the phone, his mind raced. Everett's death indeed transformed the financial circumstances of Nicole, Trey, and Leslie.

Max turned to his computer. One of the teenagers at the Haven, the island youth center where Max volunteered, had taught Max some useful skills to obtain information from sources that thought they were protected. He clicked to several sites, found photos, made notes.

Nicole looked young, eager, and awestruck

in a picture taken during a student trip to Europe. Max noted the rocks, pegged the beach as Nice. She was slender then, though her full figure hinted at a more voluptuous future. Sleek black hair framed a heart-shaped face with blue eyes, a faintly up-turned nose, a rounded chin. Her expression was adoring. Everett, his auburn hair stirred by the breeze, had a sunburned nose and shoulders. In a wedding picture, she looked proud and happy. A photo from an island dance last summer revealed lines of dissatisfaction and a seeking look in her gaze.

Nicole Nelson Hathaway, thirty-one, daughter of Roger and Adele Nelson of Bluffton. Roger Nelson is a bricklayer, wife an employee of elementary school cafeteria. Nicole, a B student in high school, played volleyball, interested in ceramics and woodworking. Worked in a craft store and attended Chastain College as a part-time student. Saved her money and took a college trip to Europe. Everett Hathaway, an adjunct professor, was one of the faculty sponsors. They married that fall and made their home in Chastain until Everett's brother, Edward, died two years ago. At that time, they moved to Broward's Rock, where Everett took over direction of his brother's advertising agency. Since moving to the island, she has not been employed. No children. She recently participated in a local craft show. Her entries included three wood carvings of island birds.

Information was even easier to obtain about Trey, both from the website of Hathaway Advertising and Facebook. In the agency personnel photo, he looked intelligent, intense, and impatient, a young man in a hurry. Medium-length sandy hair, the distinctive thin freckled Hathaway face with a high-bridged nose, sharp cheekbones, brown eyes, and pointed chin. On Facebook he looked equally intense on a golf green as he bent to putt. At the helm of a sailboat, the intensity remained but his smile was pure delight.

Edward Marlow Hathaway III, twenty-three. Island native. Local schools. Excelled in track and field, won state in sprints and pole vault. Majored in advertising at University of South Carolina, BA degree. Returned to the island to work at Hathaway Advertising. Single.

Has a racing catamaran. Adept at rock climbing. Postings by fraternity brothers in college: Knows how to party. Can knock out a paper in a couple of hours. Don't try to push him around or the volcano vents. A sucker for blondes.

Some of the photos of Leslie Griffin were mildly provocative — very revealing bikini shots — but that was not unusual on the web in today's flaunt-it society. In a fashion show, she was appealing in a short silk dress that emphasized the blueness of her eyes. One shot pictured her dancing cheek to cheek in the moonlight with a lean partner. They were laughing. In another shot, she held a pool cue, looked up from the table with a sexy smile.

Leslie Hathaway Griffin, seventeen. Daughter of Kathryn Hathaway Griffin, deceased, and Robert Estes Griffin, reported to be living in Majorca. Born in Atlanta. In and out of schools in LA as her mother looked for acting jobs and her father tried to sell scripts. The marriage ended when she was six. Her mother struggled with addiction and died in a car wreck when Leslie was fourteen. She came to the island to live with Eddie Hathaway and his son, Trey. Trey's mother had died with cancer some years earlier. Eddie Hathaway succumbed to cancer as well two years ago.

Max looked thoughtful. An ill-starred family. There had to be all kinds of divisions and resentments and grievances among those tangled lives.

Nicole pushed a pillow behind her, brushed back a strand of ebony hair. She looked at Henny with glazed eyes. "Maggie shouldn't have sent you up. I'm not feeling well." She didn't look well, the muscles of her face slack, her color poor.

Henny said swiftly, "I spoke with Leslie and she told me to come up."

"Oh. I suppose she's home." Nicole sounded sour. "She doesn't spend a lot of time here, which suits me fine. She's always unpleasant."

"I'm sorry you don't feel well." Henny took a step forward. "Is there anything I can do?"

Nicole made an effort to fluff her hair. "A glass of water might help."

Henny crossed to the bathroom, found a glass, brought it three-quarters full, and placed it on the table next to the chaise

165

longue. She pulled a cane-bottomed chair near the chaise longue and sat down.

Nicole picked the glass up, took a delicate sip, then a second. "It's nice of you to come."

"I'm here on an unpleasant task." Henny steeled herself to continue. Only the memory of Jeremiah's anguish forced the words. "I have bad news."

Nicole's eyes flared. Her fingers tightened on the glass. She looked stricken. "What's happened?"

"Everett's death wasn't an accident."

"Everett?" She spoke his name woodenly and sagged against the backrest, her pent-up breath a sigh of relief. "I was afraid . . ." Her voice trailed away.

Henny watched in confusion. Whatever bad news Nicole feared, it had nothing to do with Everett. Or his death. There was no anguish, no agony of grief in her tone when she spoke her late husband's name.

Henny had known loss, the death in a bombing raid of her young husband whose face was always clear in her memory, and, a lifetime later, the death of a lover who sacrificed himself to protect a wife corroded by bitterness.

Whatever sorrow had brought misery to Nicole's face, it was not grief for a man she loved. Now Henny had no qualms about her mission. "Everett was murdered."

Nicole's eyes widened. Her face registered alarm, not horror. "That's not right. Everett drowned."

Henny leaned forward, gazing deep into Nicole's reddened eyes. "An anonymous note lured Everett to the bay that night."

"I don't understand." Nicole shook her head, her dark hair rippling. "Why would anyone do that?"

Henny threw out the words, hard as stones. "To intercept him, dump over the kayak, and watch him drown."

Nicole drew in a sharp breath. She picked up a silk pillow, clutched it so hard her fingers blanched. "Oh, no. That can't be true."

"It is true." Henny was emphatic. "Yesterday Gretchen Burkholt found an index card in the tweed jacket he wore the day he died. Gretchen called here and left a message about the card."

Nicole spoke in a whisper. "Is that why the police called me? They asked about a message." Her eyes were now enormous in her pale face. "Nobody knew anything about it."

"Gretchen spoke to the housekeeper."

A reluctant nod. "Maggie said she wrote

everything down on the pad in the main hall."

"Anyone in the house could have seen the pad."

Nicole watched Henny as a rabbit might view a snake.

Henny continued, her words clipped. "Gretchen left word that the card from Everett's jacket was available at Better Tomorrow. Yesterday afternoon someone came and took the card and killed Gretchen."

Nicole stared at Henny in horror. "Are you saying someone from here killed that woman?"

"And your husband." Henny's voice was grim. "The card lured him to the bay in a kayak. The card named names. Gretchen said it was a scandal."

Nicole's face faded from pale to waxen as she listened. She licked her lips, asked in a shaky whisper, "A scandal?" Her fingers tightened like claws on the silk pillow. There was sheer panic in her eyes.

"What would take him to that bay, Nicole?"

"I don't know why he went out that night." Her voice rose. "Maybe the currents took him there." The terror in Nicole's eyes suggested she had a very good idea of what

168

had drawn Everett to the bay where he died.

Henny spoke softly. "Perhaps we can make some guesses about the information on the card."

Nicole lifted a hand to clutch at her throat.

"You can help." Henny was encouraging.

Everett's widow stiffened.

"What was he wearing when he was found?"

Nicole hesitated, perhaps inspecting the question for danger. Finally, slowly, she said, "A black turtleneck sweater, jeans, boat shoes, a leather jacket, the life vest."

Henny saw the response as utterly revealing. A woman torn by grief would have difficulty discussing the clothing worn the night a loved one died. There was no pain in Nicole's reply, merely a reluctant listing.

"That confirms my thoughts. I believe the note instructed him to wear dark clothing and to come in a kayak. He didn't normally kayak this time of year, did he?"

Nicole slowly shook her head.

"But that particular night he was in a kayak." Henny made a guess. "I imagine the card told him to arrive at a specific time. Let's say ten o'clock."

"Ten o'clock?" Nicole repeated the time, her face putty colored.

"So." Henny sounded satisfied. "We've

169

established that the card contained information that drew Everett to the bay in a stealthy manner. At this point, we have no way of knowing whether Everett thought he was going to meet someone at one of the piers" — she watched Nicole intently and saw another flash of panic in her pale blue eyes — "or whether he was going to observe some activity there."

"Observe?" It was an anguished whisper.

"However, Gretchen's murder proves that the card had a different objective. Whatever bait was used, Everett arrived in the bay at a specific time on a windy misty night. He was intercepted, possibly by someone in a motorboat —"

If possible, Nicole's face turned even paler.

"— the kayak capsized and he was left to drown. Once he was in the water, he was doomed. He was too far from shore to swim to the bank, and the kayak was pulled out of his reach." Henny leaned forward. "Who wanted Everett to die?"

Nicole began to tremble. "How should I know?"

Henny's stare was grim. "You know why he went to the bay."

"I don't know." Her voice was shrill. "I don't know anything. Leave me alone. I don't want to talk to you. Go away."

Henny rose. "I thought you would be the first to want to find out what happened to Everett. Call me if you feel that you can help."

Henny walked to the bedroom door. She opened it, stepped into the hall, closed the panel softly behind her. She looked up and down the hallway, then carefully, cautiously turned the knob until the tongue was disengaged. Her shoulders tensing, she eased the door open far enough to reveal a portion of the chaise longue. The pink coverlet was thrown back. The small silk cushion had slipped to the floor.

A frantic whisper was just audible. "I have to see you." Silence. "If you don't come, I'll call your wife. I have to talk to you about the night Everett died." Silence. "The usual place." Rapid steps sounded followed by the squeak of opened drawers.

Henny turned and moved swiftly down the hall.

Annie pushed the doorbell on the front porch of the ranch-style home that belonged to Don Thornwall. Open lime green drapes revealed a living room with comfortable chintz-covered easy chairs and a batik sofa, magazines on a coffee table, bright heart pine flooring. No expense had been spared, though if Annie had hired the architect, she would have insisted on at least a two-foot foundation in case of a storm surge. There was a reason why the older homes sat on high arches or pilings. The half-done construction on the west side was also at ground level.

The door opened and a smiling white-haired woman with warm brown eyes and a cheerful smile looked at her with gentle inquiry.

"I'm here for the Hathaway family and I'd appreciate it if I could speak to Mr. Thornwall."

"The Hathaway family?" She looked blank.

"Mr. Thornwall found his body in the bay."

"Oh, I'm terribly sorry." Her response was quick and genuine. "I didn't remember the name. We just retired here this fall. We've lived all around the world. Navy. We grew up in Bluffton and now we're finally back in the Lowcountry. We don't know many people here yet. When we talk about what happened, we think of him as that poor man in the kayak." Her brown eyes filled with compassion. "I know it was foolish of him to be out in a kayak without a wet suit, but sometimes people don't think. Finding him was such a shock to Don. I know he'd be glad to help, but he's out in his sailboat now."

"Could I possibly speak with you? Are you Mrs. Thornwall?"

The woman nodded, but her gaze was questioning.

"I'm Annie Darling. I have a shop in the marina."

"I'm Joyce Thornwall. Did you say you are here for the Hathaway family?"

Annie gambled. "It's a little complicated. I'm trying to help find out" — this time she carefully did not say she was asking on behalf of the Hathaways — "more about the time Mr. Hathaway's kayak capsized."

"Oh, Don can't help you there. We didn't know a thing about it until the next morning. Don was going out for a row and that's when he saw the body."

"Were you home that Friday night? Mr. Hathaway took the kayak out sometime after dinner. It probably took him twenty minutes to paddle around the headland. Did you hear any sounds out in the bay?" Could a motorboat have entered the bay without someone having heard the motor?

Joyce Thornwall shook her head with a smile. "Friday nights in December mean basketball, and Don makes enough noise to drown out any boat." Her smile slipped away. "That's sad to think he may have called for help. But we didn't hear a thing. There could have been a fleet of boats without our knowing."

Max flipped through several sheets, found the obituary with the list of pallbearers: Richard Martin, Craig Kennedy, Douglas Walker, Esteban Martinez, Bradley Milton, and John Charles Larrimore.

Pallbearers were chosen because of intimacy with a family.

Max knew all of the men except Richard Martin and John Charles Larrimore. Craig Kennedy ran a combination antique store and used bookshop. Doug Walker sold real estate. Esteban Martinez was the owner of the island's most prestigious art gallery. Bradley Milton was a local contractor. Max turned to his computer and Googled Richard Martin. He lived in Chastain and was a tenured professor of English at Chastain College. Larrimore was also a faculty member.

With a bit of digging, Max rounded up cell phone numbers.

"Professor Martin?" Max introduced himself and explained he was putting together a tribute to Everett for a local club and hoped the professor would provide a picture of Everett as an academic.

Martin spoke for several minutes in a dry precise fashion until his tone turned waspish. ". . . and regrettably Everett mulishly insisted that Addison authored *The Play House* and I vehemently disagree." The adjective bristled.

Max knew that academic disputes have a life and force that non-academics rarely appreciate. "Everett was a stubborn man. I'm keeping the tribute cheerful. I won't mention the troubles he'd had lately. He also managed to get crossways with some in his family. But that's another story."

"Ah, families. I'm grateful for the life of a confirmed bachelor. I told him at the time he was making a huge mistake. An affair, yes. Marriage, no. But he was always a stubborn fool. I could have told him she'd lead him a merry chase. I spoke to her after the service. I'd say she was bearing up well." The acid tone was full of meaning.

Max was thoughtful as he ended the call.

Larrimore cleared his throat upon hearing Max's request. "I can't tell you too much. Different disciplines. He was popular with students. Sometimes that just means easy As. I knew him when we lectured on a student trip to Europe. I can't say he was focusing on his topic then." A rumbling laugh. "That's when he met the buxom Nicole. The male students couldn't believe she preferred Everett to them. Testosterone-laden lads, of course. Kind of sad, really."

"Sad?"

"Just between us, she was a vulnerable girl. Seeking Galahad, you know. Everett must have seemed like a sophisticated fellow in a Noel Coward play. Not that she'd have known a Noel Coward play." The deep voice wasn't malicious. "Truth of the matter, he liked tweeds and soulful talks. She was a knockout, but I never thought a marriage would last. She was dazzled by his intellectualism. That's cold comfort on a winter night. I thought she'd wake up one morning and see him with his rounded shoulders and little vanities and have this feeling that she'd missed out and she'd fall for a fellow with some swagger."

Max wrote on his yellow pad: Swagger?

7

As Henny turned her heavy old car toward the road, Leslie Griffin ran lightly down the steps, high heels clattering. She was vivid in a red jacket and tartan skirt. She slid into a low-slung red Mini Cooper S. The sport car's motor roared. Leslie shot down the drive, leaving Henny in a cloud of dust. As the car passed, Leslie gave Henny a wary glance.

Henny drove slowly. In the rearview mirror, she saw three cars parked in front of a an old-fashioned double garage, a navy Lincoln Navigator, a small tan Corolla, and a black Lexus sedan. Likely either the Lincoln or the Lexus belonged to Nicole and the Corolla to the housekeeper.

The Hathaway drive was the last at this end of the bay road. If she stayed on the road, it would dead end on the other side of the bay. At the midway point, another road intersected and led to Sand Dollar Road.

Henny drove around a grove of pines to the next home. Nicole had no reason to look for Henny's car. Henny backed into the drive. She pulled down the driver's visor though she very much doubted Nicole would be scanning the driveways she passed. Five minutes later the dark blue Lincoln hurtled past, going fast.

Henny followed, keeping behind a cloud of dust. She too lived on the marsh side of the island and she had a good instinct for how long it took to reach Sand Dollar Road. In a moment she picked up speed. She was in time to see the Lincoln turn left. She floated the stop sign and was about twenty yards behind Nicole. There wasn't much traffic this time of year so she was able to keep the Lincoln in view as the road curved and twisted. A yellow school bus pulled onto the road. The Lincoln's taillights flared. The bus lumbered forward, then slowed. The driver flapped down the warning sign, signaling drivers to stop.

Instead of braking, the Lincoln pulled into the oncoming lane and roared past.

The school bus horn blared.

Henny coasted to a stop, waited as a half dozen kids climbed down. One darted across the road. Two teenagers followed, slouching slowly, deep in conversation.

With a rumble, the school bus moved forward.

She could go into town, cruise Main and the two smaller streets, looking for the Lincoln. But Nicole could as easily have made a left turn onto another dirt road to a destination on the marsh or in the opposite direction to the ocean or straight north to the more disreputable end of the island. *The usual place* could be anywhere, a house, an apartment, a tavern, a business. Wherever she had gone, she had carried with her anger and fear and determination. There would not be easy conversation upon her arrival. She would surely be engaged for at least twenty minutes, possibly longer.

Henny glanced at her watch. A quarter past three. Leslie had gone to the advertising agency. Possibly she worked until five, although Henny suspected the girl would chisel on the time if possible. However, both she and Nicole should be absent from the house long enough for Henny to find out what she could from Maggie.

Sheila Porter's black hair molded to her head, stiff and shiny from hair spray. Pale brown eyes looked at Annie curiously. "Who did you say you are?"

Annie introduced herself again and ex-

179

plained that she was trying to be helpful to the Hathaway family. "You can understand that they want to know as much as they can about the night he died."

Sheila looked mournful. "It's hard for families. You always wonder and worry if there's something you could have done that would have made a difference. Like the night my Sam died. He was here by himself. I'd gone to a meeting of the Daughters of the King. He'd said he wasn't feeling well. Oh, I shouldn't have gone. Maybe I could have called nine-one-one in time to save him. He had a stroke." Sorrow and guilt pulled at her face.

Annie spoke quickly. "It must have been very quick or he would have called for help."

Sheila managed a trembling smile. "I try to think so. And" — her voice grew stronger — "Sam always said to me that God would take him when it was time and for me not to grieve. It's hard not to grieve. Anyway, let me think. I was out the night Mr. Hathaway drowned." Her eyes grew wide. "I tell you that was such a shock the next morning when all the police cars came with their sirens on. But Friday night I got home a little before ten. There was one funny thing, but I don't suppose it matters."

"Yes?" Annie's voice was encouraging.

"As I came up my steps, I heard a motor-boat. That was odd."

Annie felt a rush of triumph. Billy Cameron would have to pay attention to this.

"Odd?"

Sheila gestured toward the bay. "No one on the bay has a boat now. I sold Sam's boat. Next door, Captain Thornwall has a racing shell and a sailboat. He's retired navy. The cabin" — she inclined her head to the left — "used to have one of those pontoon boats, but that was the previous family. It's rented now and they don't have a boat. Across the bay, they have a big cabin cruiser, and they've gone to Costa Rica."

Craig Kennedy's round face expressed shock. "Everett murdered? That's incredible." Craig was plump, bouncy, and usually smiling. His shop was crammed with an eclectic mixture. A portrait of Commodore Perry stared unseeing at a Korean brass-bound chest. Scattered about were Hepplewhite furniture, Japanese silk brocades, a ship's eagle from Nantucket, a griffon head harp, tables crammed with ivory statuettes, porcelain French clocks, and old pewter. A half dozen bookshelves held dusty relics of estate sales.

Max felt assailed by the familiar doubts.

Annie's insistence that Everett had been murdered was based on such tenuous, circumstantial evidence. Pursuing Everett's family and friends was going to cause a great deal of trouble and might well be an exercise in absurdity. Max chose his words carefully. He had no wish to be sued for slander. "I'm speaking to you on a confidential basis. There are some puzzling aspects to his death, which need to be explained. I know you and he were good friends. Just between the two of us, had Everett quarreled with anyone recently?"

Craig's bulbous blue eyes stared. "What are you suggesting?"

"Perhaps his death was not an accident. I have it on good authority that Everett was decoyed to the bay that night. It seems important, especially to the family, to find out exactly what happened." If Craig assumed Max was there on behalf of the family, it was his assumption, not Max's claim.

"Yeah. I can certainly understand that, but I'm afraid I don't know anything helpful. He might have been irritated with a few folks, but no big deal so far as I know. I saw him the week he died. He was a good customer. He meant well, but you have to remember that Everett was a pretty serious guy." Craig cleared his throat. "Well, between us, he was kind of a horse's ass. Everett had about as much sense of humor as that teak elephant." He pointed at a carving. "Self-righteous. Always sure he was right. He told me he was having a hard time with his niece, said she was mixed up with an undesirable guy, but he was going to put a stop to that. Then he got started on his nephew, said it was time to show him who was boss, that just because he was Eddie's son didn't mean he knew how to run the business. Between us, I think he had a grudge against Eddie and he's playing it out by deviling Trey. Then there's Brad Milton. He was big buds with Eddie. Eddie loaned him some money through the agency. I think Everett was leaning on Brad about paying up. Right after Christmas, I saw them in the parking lot of the club and it looked ugly. Poor old Brad. He's in big trouble because of the economy. He even asked me for a loan, said he had to meet a note. I figure he meant that Everett wanted the money. It shows how Everett talked out of both sides of his mouth, acting like a meet-your-obligations businessman with Brad but treating the agency like a hobby. When Trey complained, Everett claimed it was important for a business to have a soul. Whatever that meant. He had kind of a lackadaisical attitude about business, didn't want to soil his immortal soul by actually making money. I can tell you" — a quick grin — "that sure wasn't Eddie's attitude. Eddie didn't need money, either, but he had a hell of a lot of pride in doing good work and being paid good money. Not Everett. He didn't care. Most of us damn sure better make money. Now, have I told you I got in an emerald necklace — beautiful stones — in an old-fashioned gold filigree setting? Be just the thing for Annie." Craig pushed up from his chair. "Won't take a minute to get it out of the safe . . ."

As Henny expected, neither the blue Lincoln nor red Mini Cooper were in the Hathaway driveway. The Lexus, which likely had been Everett's car, and the Corolla were still parked to one side of the double garage.

Beyond the Corolla was a small open-air lean-to with a roof. She counted four bikes parked in a metal stand. Gretchen's killer definitely had access to a silent arrival at Better Tomorrow. Had a bicyclist thought ahead, decided an unheralded silent approach might be wise? Was there already a thought of murder? Why not? If Everett had been murdered, the need to avoid an investigation into his death was imperative.

Crimson streaks added a touch of flame to the lowering gray skies. Already the dusk of January shrouded the pines in dark shadows. Henny looked at her watch. A quarter to five. She'd timed her arrival to catch the housekeeper at the end of her work day. Henny moved swiftly to the steps and pressed the bell.

When the door opened, the housekeeper looked at Henny and said firmly, "Mrs. Hathaway isn't at home." The door started to close.

Once again Henny pulled open the screen door. "I came to see you. Mrs. Hathaway said you were the person who spoke with Gretchen Burkholt at Better Tomorrow. So you are the proper person to talk to."

Maggie's eyes narrowed. "Mrs. Hathaway said you should talk to me?"

Henny was bland. "She emphasized that you are the only person who has admitted direct knowledge of Gretchen's call."

Thin shoulders lifted and fell. "I suppose you'd better come in." She held the door for Henny. Obviously, she was still at work and didn't feel she could rebuff Henny.

They stood in the entryway. The heavy tick of a grandfather clock in a nook beneath the stairs was ponderous.

Maggie folded her arms, her elbows sharp.

Her face was sharp as well, deep-set eyes narrowed, thin lips pursed.

Henny tried charm. "I don't want to hold you. I know it's almost time for you to leave. That's why I hurried back. We can be quick. Just tell me about the call."

Maggie remained cool, but, finally, she nodded toward the side table. "There's a landline there. It's been there for years. And in the kitchen. And one in the upstairs hall. Mr. Hathaway" — her tone tinged on derisive — "had all the portable phones removed, said they destroyed the ambience. That meant I have to race to answer, because God forbid I shouldn't get to a call. Of course, they" — sullen emphasis — "all have cell phones." Her sense of grievance was clear. "I was doing the windows in a bay where they keep poinsettias and the phone rang. When nobody picked it up, I had to run to get it. You'd think one of them would have bothered."

"Who was here?"

"Mrs. Hathaway was in her room." She spoke without inflection. "Trey was in the study, going through his uncle's papers. There was a phone on that desk, too. But he didn't pick it up. Brad Milton was with him. Trey wanted new terrace paving installed. But" — she rolled her eyes — "Mr.

Hathaway hadn't agreed. Looks now like it will happen. Anyway, this woman said she was calling from Better Tomorrow and she'd found a card in the pocket of the tweed jacket Mr. Hathaway wore the day he died. She said the card seemed to explain why he took the kayak out that night. She said she thought Mr. Hathaway had added a name at the bottom of the card." The housekeeper paused for a moment, her eyes narrowed. "She said the handwriting at the bottom was different from the rest of the card and the handwriting was the same as on the flyleaf of some of Mr. Hathaway's books that were sent over." The housekeeper shrugged. "It sure seemed to me she was making a big deal about the thing, matching handwriting and stuff. I could have told her nobody here gave a flip about what he wrote or didn't write, but I'm just the help, so I said, 'Yes, ma'am.' She said the card and some change and a pocketknife were on the desk in the sorting room. I wrote that down on the pad next to the hall phone. That was all I had to do. Everybody knew to check the table for messages."

Everybody knew . . .

"What exactly did you write down?"

The woman spoke carefully. "I wrote: Gretchen Burkholt called from Better Tomorrow at two twelve P.M. She found a card in Mr. Hathaway's clothes that explained why he went out in the kayak. She said the message on the card was hand printed in writing different from a notation at the bottom. She said Mr. Hathaway wrote somebody's name below the message. She said the card would be on the desk in the sorting room along with a pocketknife and some change." Maggie gave a short nod. "That's what I wrote."

"Who could have seen the message?"

"Miss Leslie comes home around two thirty." There was no warmth in the housekeeper's voice.

Henny tried to sound as if this were just another question. "Did you see anyone near the table?"

Maggie looked disgusted. "I had better things to do than hang around in the front hall. It isn't up to me to tell people there are messages. They can look on the hall pad. That's what it's for. But when I carried my sponge and bucket back to the kitchen, I noticed the note was gone." Her gaze was speculative. "You think someone here took the message and went to that place and killed that woman?"

Henny did not answer directly. "Gretchen was murdered because of the card in the jacket. There's a pattern. The card Gretchen found disappeared from Better Tomorrow and the information you wrote down about the card disappeared from here."

Maggie's gaze fastened on the side table. "So the police would be interested to know who ripped off the sheet from the pad." There was a considering tone to her voice.

Henny looked at her sharply. "If you have any idea who took the message, you could be in great danger."

The grandfather clock began to boom the hour.

Maggie looked sardonic. "I'm not fool enough to go out on the bay in a kayak." Her tone was derisive. "Anyway, I've told you what I know and I'm off work now." She turned and hurried down the hall.

As Annie walked toward her Thunderbird, she heard a distant slam of a car door. She turned and looked past the modest frame house and across the bay's gunmetal dark water at the Mediterranean mansion. A dark blue Lincoln was parked to one side of the house. A woman in a peach jacket moved toward a paved walk leading to the back terrace, then stopped. She pulled back a sleeve to glance at her wrist.

Even at this distance, it was easy to see

that she was upset. She hunched her shoulders, began to pace. She kept looking back toward the road. The figure seemed familiar though it was too shadowy for Annie to make out her features. According to Sheila Porter, the owners of the house were in Costa Rica. Besides, Annie knew the Carstairs, and Renee was tall and willowy.

As she watched, a green Porsche roared into the drive.

The woman hurried toward the car as it screeched to a stop.

A stocky, well-built man slammed out of the car. His white sweater was a bright spot in the gloom.

They faced each other. He stood with his hands jammed in his trouser pockets. Every angle of his body radiated anger.

The woman was talking fast and her right hand pointed at the bay.

He stepped back, shaking his head violently.

She moved toward him, a hand held out in supplication.

After a moment, he gripped her arm and they moved onto the terrace around a corner and out of Annie's view.

They walked purposefully, which suggested they were familiar with the house. Were they guests? Perhaps they might have been at the house the night Everett drowned. Annie hurried to the T-Bird, yanked open the driver's door and slid behind the wheel.

The bell played a musical stanza as Max stepped outside. "Come on-a My House" was a nice selection for a Realtor. Doug Walker was a scratch golfer, never-met-a-stranger, curly-haired blond who'd been a linebacker with the Clemson Tigers and parlayed an easy smile into a real estate career. Despite hard financial times, he'd apparently been able to sell enough homes to — as Doug liked to put it — land on the black. He had a nice family. Annie played tennis with Janet, who was a partner in an island accounting firm.

Max hadn't been surprised to find Doug out of the office, but when he asked if Doug had gone home, his plump, cheerful secretary shook her head. "Somebody wanted to see a listing. He told me to tell Janet — she calls the office and not his cell, just in case he's out with a prospect — that he would be home in about an hour."

Max hurried down the steps of the antebellum home that housed Doug Walker Realty. When he reached his car and opened the door, he gave an admiring whistle at the jade green bloom of the sunflower propped against the passenger seat. Green? It sure was. He slid behind the wheel, smiling as he picked up a sheet of orange-colored paper with a crest of — what else? — a lime green sunflower. He read his mother's note: Seek serenity. Today affords no sunshine, but this bloom is a reminder of the color of the sea on a sunny day. "Ma" — he spoke aloud as he noted her signature with a sunflower bloom extending from the right vertical bar of an extravagantly rendered M — "sunflowers be with you, too. Thanks for a pick-me-up on a dark and dreary day."

Max checked his cell as the Maserati purred into motion. No messages from Annie or Henny. But it was cheerful to know that both were only a cell phone away. He thought for a moment, texted: *Dinner at our house. Two more stops then home. Chili and cornbread.* Thanks to the microwave, any meal was possible in a hurry. While he reheated chili, the cornbread would be baking. Max was a purist. No sugar in his cornbread and not a trace of flour, either. Sometimes he gave a nod to Annie's Texas roots and dropped in green chilies and corn.

He drove two blocks and pulled into the parking lot of a small, two-story stucco house with a red-tiled roof. Built in the thirties, the house had a Florida flavor with plenty of arched windows affording splashes of sun in good weather. Esteban Martinez had transformed the interior into an elegant gallery, which featured paintings of the Lowcountry. Max had his eye on a watercolor of a diving night hawk silhouetted against a fiery spring dawn.

Lights shone from the uncurtained front windows. A discreet Open sign hung in a side window by the entry. Max stepped inside, enjoying the warmth. A fire crackled in a massive stone fireplace to his left.

A door at the end of the hall opened. Esteban smiled a welcome. He was tall and slender with a precisely trimmed black mustache and Vandyke beard that enhanced his resemblance to a Velazquez nobleman. He gestured to a dark leather sofa a comfortable distance from the fire. "Can I offer you a hot buttered rum on such a damp evening?"

"Not this time. But thanks. I'm here because you were one of Everett Hathaway's pallbearers. I'm hoping you can tell me a bit about him."

Esteban's narrow ascetic face lost its proprietor's bonhomie, folded into suitable graveness. "Ah, a reminder that we must treasure our days. What can I tell you about

Everett?" He led the way to the sofa, settled at one end.

Max stood with his back to the fire, put his hands behind him. "Nice to be warm. I need to explain . . ." As he spoke, Esteban's hooded eyes narrowed.

"Murder." Esteban stroked his beard. "I wish I could be helpful. However, I didn't know him well. I can describe with acuity his taste in paintings. He was a good customer. On a personal basis, I would describe him as precise, serious, perhaps a little self-important. I was actually a friend of Eddie's. When Trey called and asked me to serve as a pallbearer, of course I agreed. However . . ." He shrugged.

Max was disappointed. "So you don't know if anyone was angry with him or if he had quarreled with anyone."

Esteban pulled at a long ear lobe, his face thoughtful. "Everett was punctilious about appointments. He was supposed to come by here at one o'clock that Friday to pick up a painting. When he had not come by two, I called. He answered and spoke almost roughly. He said he would come by next week, something had come up. He sounded distraught. I immediately asked if I could be of help. There was a pause and he made a kind of noise and then he said, 'You're a lucky man. You never married.' Then he hung up." Esteban looked regretful. "I can't speak to whether his comment mattered or not."

Max nodded. "It helps to have a picture of his last day. Thanks, Esteban."

The gallery owner walked to the door with Max.

Max plunged back into the darkness, the mist damp against his face, and hurried to his car. Whether important or not, Everett's words definitely required explanation. It would be interesting to see what Henny might have learned at the Hathaway house. Max continued to the edge of downtown, turned east on Marsh Tackie Road. It was a half mile to Brad Milton's construction company. He pressed the accelerator, delighted in the quick response. He loved speed. As the pines encroached nearer the road, he slowed, watching for deer. Not much farther now . . .

He came around a curve. Light spilled from the windows of the frame structure that housed Milton Construction. A bright yellow mini electric car was parked near the steps. Brad was one of the islanders who had taken advantage of the tax rebates under TARP to essentially buy the car for free. He'd sold his old Ford and instead drove the jaunty little car with a roof, windshield, seats, and not much else. He called it his gov buggy. Looming behind the office was a galvanized steel building for equipment. Two pickups were parked nearby.

The Maserati eased to a stop next to the mini car. Max parked and moved quickly across the uneven terrain, skirting a six-foot-long stack of used bricks that likely had been salvaged from a tear down. He knocked on the door and stepped inside. The two-room office was untidy. Cardboard files occupied the seat of a worn sofa near one window. Three gray metal filing cabinets and a drafting table occupied one wall. Brad Milton sat behind an old metal desk. He was Lincoln tall and ungainly. Even seated, he had a disjointed appearance, hatchet-sharp features with a down-turned mouth, one shoulder higher than the other, huge hands splayed on the desktop amid a welter of papers. He seemed to come back from a long way as he looked at his visitor.

Max knew Brad from Rotary meetings and the chamber of commerce. Brad was in his forties, older than Max and Annie. They saw him at chili cook-offs and oyster fries and charitable functions. He was recently divorced. This afternoon he looked as gray and morose as the lowering skies outside.

"Max." Brad lifted a big hand, gestured toward a straight chair that faced the desk. His demeanor brightened, a touch of animation in his deep voice. "What can I do for you? You and Annie planning on a little remodeling?" His voice lifted with hope.

Max shook his head. "I've been asked to investigate Everett Hathaway's death."

Brad looked surprised. "What's there to know? He drowned. Poor bastard." He gave a slight shudder. "They say hypothermia's a good way to go. Doesn't sound good to me. It sounds cold."

Max watched him carefully. "Someone capsized his kayak and left him to drown."

Brad's angular face looked incredulous. "You think he was dumped out of that kayak? On purpose?" He gave a slight head shake.

Max spoke slowly. "We have reason to believe he was lured out onto the bay and someone in a motorboat intercepted him and knocked him out of the kayak."

Brad placed his big hands on his desktop. "That sounds crazy to me. Are the cops checking this out?"

Max didn't answer directly. "There hasn't been a public announcement yet."

"Oh. Well, I guess you know what you're

talking about, but I can't believe anybody killed Everett." His craggy face folded in a frown. "Why come to me?"

Max's gaze was intent. "You owed him money. He wanted payment."

Brad's eyes glinted. "I don't think I like the implication." His voice was cold. "I owe a lot of people money and they are all alive and kicking. Besides that, you're way off on your facts. Everett and I had come to an agreement."

Max took a chance. Brad and Everett's confrontation in the parking lot had been angry. "You argued with him."

"Old news." Brad leaned back in his chair, his body relaxed. "We had a talk. Everything was okay."

"Since when?"

"Since I persuaded him to be reasonable." Brad's rough-hewn face looked irritated. "Look, my finances are none of your business, but I borrowed some money from the agency — Eddie was a good guy — to cover some cash-flow problems. The damn banks are sitting on capital like it's glued to their butts. Eddie would have given me an extension without any hassle. Everett had trouble seeing the forest for the trees, but I finally" — he sounded long-suffering — "got it through his thick skull that giving me more time made it a lot likelier the agency would get paid in full. If I had to go into bankruptcy, there were a bunch of creditors before the agency. Anyway, it's all been worked out. After Everett died, I explained everything to Trey, and he agreed the new plan made sense."

"So you've already talked to Trey about the loan?"

Brad's angular face looked pleased. "Trey's reasonable. I can keep the business going. I'm about to turn the corner. I've got some jobs lined up."

"When did you last see Everett?"

Brad's eyes widened. "It makes me feel kind of spooky. I talked to him the morning of the day he died. I dropped by the agency about eleven thirty. That's when we got everything worked out."

Max was sure that Brad would never have answered except he knew that his visit at the office likely would be remembered by the receptionist.

"Where were you the night Everett died?"

"Right here." Brad was brusque. "Not out drowning somebody. You can take that to the bank. Look, I don't know that much about Everett. Eddie and I were friends. I used to spend a lot of time over there, drank a lot of good whisky. Everett wasn't my kind of guy. He drank white wine. But he seems an unlikely candidate for murder. Anyway, I'm not the man to talk to and, if you don't mind, I've got a pile of work to do. For which, believe me, I'm grateful."

Max rose. "You going to compete in the bass tournament at Lake Keowee?" Brad had an island reputation as a bass angler.

Brad shook his head. "Not this year. I sold my boat in August. I got to earn back a bunch of money before I fish again. Except from a pier. Why?"

Max shrugged. "I know you like to fish."

Brad looked at Max in disbelief. "Wait a minute, are you thinking I took out a boat and dumped Everett out of that kayak?"

Max met his gaze. "Somebody dumped him out."

Brad folded his arms. "I'll believe that when somebody proves it."

"There's proof."

"Good. Then the cops can handle it. I'll read about it in the *Gazette.*"

Henny waited until the taillights of the tan Corolla were no longer visible, signaling Maggie's departure, then slipped from her car in the shadow of pines a half block from the Hathaway house. She turned up the fur-lined collar of her jacket and walked briskly, leaning a bit into the wind. She would hear any cars arriving at the house and, in the gathering dusk, could easily avoid being seen.

She passed the main house and the double garage to the winter-bare rose garden that sloped down to the marsh, her goal the wooden pier and boathouse. On the planks of the pier, her steps echoed, as lonesome a sound in the growing darkness as the cry of a mourning dove. She shivered from the onslaught of the breeze and the icy dampness of the chill mist. Cold as a witch's heart. How must Jeremiah feel, marooned on that small hump of wooded land? She must do more, faster, try to break through the seemingly impregnable fortress of a murderer's success.

She peered into a boat house at a cruiser, heard the slap of water against the hull. Here it was. A ticket to the next bay available to anyone from the house. Dimly she heard a car door slam. Quickly she turned and hurried from the pier. In the garden, she paused near a thicket of cane.

A little boy about five in a fleece jacket ran toward the steep wooden steps to the garage apartment. A woman juggled two bags of groceries, her purse, and a parcel of laundry.

"Can I have some Kool-Aid, Mama?" He raced up halfway.

"On a night like this?"

"Please, please." His high voice wheedled. He stopped on the landing and looked back at her pleadingly.

"I'll fix us something special for dessert. I'll make brownies." She reached the landing and put down her sacks to use her key. When the door closed behind them and lights flashed on, Henny waited long enough to let the groceries be put away, then hurried up the steps. She used a pocket flash for a quick glimpse of the nameplate on the post box: Hudgins.

At her knock, the door opened to reveal a woman in her thirties with honey-colored hair that needed a trim. A faded blue cotton turtleneck hung loose on her lanky frame and black jersey slacks bagged at the knees. She glanced out and said swiftly, "Ma'am, I'm sorry but I can't contribute, whatever it is. Ricky's allotment and my job just barely get us to the end of the month. I wish I could." Her smile was shy and shamefaced.

As the door started to close, Henny spoke swiftly. "I'm not collecting donations, Mrs. Hudgins. I'm seeking information about the night Mr. Hathaway's kayak capsized.

"I'm trying to determine more exactly the time of death. It will be a help to the family. And the thought was that you might be able to assist." Henny smiled. "So, if you don't mind, were you here that evening?"

She looked rueful. "That night and every night."

"Then I have just a few questions. I won't take much of your time."

The young woman nodded. The TV blared behind her. She half turned. "Make it softer, Richard." But her voice was gentle. She hesitated, then pushed the door open. "Please come in. We can talk while I fix Richard's supper."

In the small kitchen, she moved swiftly, pulling a frozen pizza and mixed vegetables from the freezer. "Richard loves pizza, but he has to eat his veggies, too. Now what about that night?"

"Did you hear the motorboat leave?" Henny gestured toward the marsh.

The young mother lifted a box of brownie mix from a cupboard and looked at her in surprise. "I haven't heard the boat in a month or more. The boat certainly didn't go out that night."

Henny felt a shock of disappointment. She'd been so confident. "Were you here all evening?"

The woman's smile was lopsided. "I'm home at nights. My husband, Ricky, is on his second tour in Afghanistan. I can't afford a sitter, but my mom lives in Bluffton. Sometimes Richard and I go over and see her for the weekends. No, ma'am, that boat didn't go out. I remember that Friday in particular. It was the night before they found Mr. Hathaway." She looked solemn. "I think I heard him leave. I was out on the balcony, maybe it was about a quarter to ten." Her eyes dropped. "I promised Ricky I'd stop smoking, but it's hard. I worry about him. But I never smoke inside. It wouldn't be good for Richard. Anyway, Richard was asleep and I slipped out on the porch. It was so cold. I heard footsteps on the pier and I saw somebody moving. I think maybe he was getting the kayak. I didn't tell anybody about it later because all I saw was this dark figure walking out there. It did seem kind of funny that someone was on the pier on such a cold night. Then I went back inside. But I'm sure nobody went out in the motorboat. The engine makes a lot of noise." She emptied the mix in a bowl. "I guess you came to ask me since nobody was home that night."

"No one?"

Francie nodded. "They all left, one, two,

three just before I stepped out on the porch. The girl's car squeals. She gets out fast. Mr. Hathaway's nephew slams his car door like he's in a big hurry. Mrs. Hathaway's car is the quietest but it makes little beeps when she unlocks it."

When a kayak slipped soundlessly across water, no one was at home at the Hathaway house.

8

Annie moved slowly across the stone terrace behind the Mediterranean home. Red bamboo shades masked the arched windows that faced the marsh. However, light gleamed between slats, marked the edges of the windows. Earlier the house had been totally dark. Annie walked through the gloom toward an oversized oak door.

At the door, she lifted her hand to knock, then saw a massive iron key in the lock. She had a quick memory of Max holding just such a key at a mid-nineteenth-century Mexican hacienda in Cuernavaca that had been transformed into a luxury hotel. A key to delight for them.

She touched the cold metal, turned, and cautiously pushed. The door slid open, silent as a snowflake. An old door such as this surely depended upon metal hinges, but doors in luxury homes never squeaked.

". . . are you out of your frigging mind?"

The man's voice was rough and furious.

"Don't talk to me like that." The woman spoke unevenly, quick breaths between her cry. "Doug, what's happened to us? I thought you loved me." There was heartbreak and despair in her broken words.

Annie eased the panel forward, just a little bit, until she could see a slice of the room. She gripped the iron handle tightly. The short peach coat had been flung across a red leather sofa. Nicole Hathaway, her face raddled, blue eyes brimming with tears, reached out a shaking hand to Doug Walker.

Annie felt sad as she looked at her friend Janet's husband. Doug was always a charmer, curly blond hair, stocky sexy build, fun-loving guy. And an unfaithful husband.

"Oh my God. You call me and make threats and insist I meet you and then you act like you think I murdered Everett. I don't know a damn thing about Everett and that fool kayak. If somebody tipped him over, it wasn't me. I was home Friday night."

"I'd called you, asked you to meet me here. I knew Janet was out of town. Why didn't you come?"

"Like I told you last week, we're history. You got to listen to me."

"I think Everett knew about us." Her voice

shook. "The way he looked at me that last night was dreadful. Did he call you? Did you work out a way to keep him quiet?"

He stared at her, his eyes glittering. "You honest to God think I'd kill him? Why the hell should I?"

"What if he called you, said he was going to divorce me for adultery? What if he said he'd tell your precious Janet?" Her tone was corrosive.

"Keep Janet out of this." He took a step toward her, his fists clenched.

"You should have thought about that before you came after me."

"Any dog will follow a bitch in heat."

She stared at him, her face crumpling. "I hate you. But" — now she was sobbing — "I don't. Doug, he's dead. I'm free."

"Great." He was sarcastic. "Good for you. Glad you're happy."

"Don't you care?" Her voice shook.

He took an exasperated breath. "You don't make a lot of sense. First you accuse me of murder and then you want to know if I love you. Listen, we had a good time." He softened his tone. "Don't ruin the memories we —"

"I don't want memories." Her voice was petulant. "I want you. That's all I've ever wanted."

"Get this and get it now." His handsome face was cold and hard. "We had a fling. That's all it was. One of those crazy-days-in-May things. It didn't mean anything. Let's leave it at that. You go your way and I'll go mine."

"I'll tell your wife."

"No." He spoke quietly but a muscle ridged in his jaw.

"You can't stop me."

He walked toward her, looked down, his round face implacable. "I don't advise that. You can't prove a thing. I'll say you've stalked me, that you're disturbed. No one has ever seen us together. I made damn sure of that. I'll make you out to be a fool and a tramp. You might also remember about the prenup you signed. We laughed about it, how if you committed adultery while married, you would inherit a grand total of one dollar from his estate. Get a grip. Trey might be very interested in your indiscretions." With that, he turned and bulled toward the terrace, his face dangerously flushed.

Annie pulled the panel shut, hoped he was too distraught to see the movement. She couldn't reach the end of the terrace before he came outside. She moved fast as far as she dared, then whirled and started toward the door.

The massive door swung in. As he yanked the key from the lock, he was silhouetted against the light.

Annie felt a moment of fear. He was big and strong and very angry. She paused. "Hello." It wasn't a brilliant beginning.

He stopped and stared, his face wary.

She came nearer. "Doug? Annie Darling. I thought I recognized your car. We have some friends who are looking for just this kind of house and I thought perhaps it might be on the market so I'd just stop and ask." As if she might be out on a jaunty drive on a road that served only four homes.

Doug Walker struggled for composure. "Hello, Annie. It's not for sale. I'm keeping an eye on the place for the Carstairs. Jeff asked me to drop by and check some measurements. He and Renee are thinking about some remodeling."

The door moved again and Nicole stepped outside, struggling to pull on her peach coat. Her face looked pasty and her hands shook. She saw Annie and stumbled to a stop.

Doug's shoulders hunched. He gave Nicole a hard, intense warning look. "Renee wanted some input on colors for some new drapes. Nicole's an old friend and Renee thought she would have some good ideas."

He patted his pocket. "I've got it written down. Light blue with some cream, I think that's what you said. Anyway, thanks for your help." His tone was formal. "I'd better lock up." He moved back to the door, reached inside. Abruptly, the golden spill of light across the flagstones was gone and they stood in the early dusk of January. He yanked the door shut and used the key. "I'm running late. Say hi to Max." With that, he strode across the terrace, his shoes loud on the stones.

Annie wished she could see Nicole's face, but now there was nothing more than a pale oval and a shadowy figure. "I'm sorry Doug is in such a hurry."

The Porsche engine roared and the headlights flicked on. The sports car jolted out of the drive.

"I'd better go." Nicole took a step forward.

"Let's talk for a minute. I haven't seen you since Everett died." In ordinary circumstances, she would have offered condolences. She did not. Instead, she appraised Nicole. She wasn't a big woman, surely not big enough to overpower Annie, especially since Annie was prepared to take flight. Annie knew she might be taking a risk, but she was willing to gamble after Doug's departure. "I've heard that someone tipped over

Everett's kayak."

Nicole's head jerked up. "It can't be true." But her whisper was almost inaudible.

"The police think Everett was coming here that night" — Annie gestured in the darkness toward the blacker mass of the bay — "because of you and Doug."

"I don't know what you're talking about." Nicole's voice shook. "I'm just here today to help Doug with the drapes."

Annie wished she had a flashlight, wished she could shine a beam unexpectedly on Nicole's face. Was there the panic of adultery revealed and the fear of a lover's complicity in murder? Or was there a quick intelligence at work, spinning out a false face of innocence? If she knew her husband suspected her of an affair, she might have decided to be rid of him before he could file for divorce. Perhaps she reasoned that if she were a widow, maybe Doug would change his mind.

"You claim you weren't here that night?"

"Of course not." She licked her lips. "I was at home." Her voice was thin, reedy, frightened. Abruptly, Nicole veered away from Annie and broke into an uneven run. She darted around the end of the house.

Annie followed slowly. The Lincoln was out of sight by the time Annie reached her car. Nicole's involvement with Doug at the Carstairs house shifted the picture of Everett's last night. Now it seemed reasonable to assume that Everett came to the bay, quietly, silently, intending to land at the Carstairs pier in response to an anonymous note informing him that his wife and a friend were lovers. Doug seemed convinced no one knew of their affair, which suggested their clandestine meetings had occurred in the Carstairs's empty home.

But someone had written the note that Gretchen found in the pocket of Everett's jacket. So far, Annie knew of only two people who were aware of their trysts, the participants themselves.

As she neared her car, she looked across the bay. She had seen Doug Walker and Nicole Hathaway at the Carstairs house when she looked out from Sheila Porter's home. Sheila or the retired navy captain and his wife or the work crew on the unfinished addition or the unknown resident of the cabin on pilings might well have noticed the Porsche or the Lincoln coming in the afternoon to the Carstairs home. Gossip spreads easily, especially in a small community. It could be that simple, a retired naval officer might have an interest in cars and would note the Porsche, and if he mentioned the car to a longtime island resident, the recognition would be immediate. There was only one Porsche on the island. The contractor building the addition to the Thornwall house certainly had a clear view of the Carstairs home. Annie hadn't noticed if there was a construction company sign posted, but it would take only a moment to find out. Or Sheila might be a bird-watcher with a handy set of binoculars. Max could check to see if there was any connection between Everett Hathaway and the residents on the north side of the bay. Doug Walker might think that the affair was hidden, but someone knew enough to write the note to Everett.

As she watched, lights came on in the cabin she had yet to visit.

Max was disappointed when he found the driveway empty at their restored antebellum home. He and Annie always left lights burning in Franklin House. The golden glow in the living room and kitchen windows made coming home in winter more cheerful. They didn't bother to draw the drapes because pines screened the old house from neighbors.

He entered from the back verandah. Dorothy L, their plump, affectionate, all-white cat with piercing blue eyes, rose on her back paws and he swept her up to his shoulder. It was a nightly ritual. Although ostensibly she was a family pet, her heart belonged to Max. "Good girl." He butted her cheek with his chin. "Good girl." She responded with a throaty purr, then wriggled free, dropped to the floor, and padded to her bowl. Max refilled the water bowl and spooned a fresh serving of cat salmon.

That duty done, he glanced at the clock. Almost six. It wouldn't take long to pop the chili in the microwave. He'd stir up the cornbread, but first he intended to seek an expert. He picked up his cell. Annie's young stepsister's number was on autodial. Rachel lived with Annie's dad, Pudge Laurance, and his wife, Sylvia, and her son, Cole. Rachel and Cole were enjoying their senior year in high school.

"Hey, Max. How's everything?" Rachel's voice was happy. Max smiled. Rachel had endured tough times, losing her mom in a dreadful way. Annie had made a huge difference in Rachel's life. Rachel burbled, "I sent Annie an e-mail. I got an A on my ancient history report. I was supposed to write about someone who made a big difference in the world, and it blew the teacher's mind that I picked St. Augustine. I ended up with a quote from him: *Love is the beauty of the soul.* Is that cool or what? Pudge knew all about St. Augustine."

"Way cool. Hey, Rachel, can you help me out about somebody at school?"

"Probably. Shoot."

"Do you know Leslie Griffin?"

"Oh, yeah." There was no fondness in her tone.

Max reached for a notepad. "What's she like?"

"Snotty. She runs with a special clique, only girls with money and looks welcome. Nobody I know cares." Rachel sounded bored. "What's she done? Caused somebody trouble, I'll bet."

Max wrote fast. He was glad Rachel's voice held genuine disdain, instead of sour envy. "It's a family matter. Have you ever heard how she got along with her uncle?"

"I don't know her that well. She just came here a couple of years ago. A bunch of us tried to be friends with her, but she blew us off pretty quick. I don't know much about her family except I think she's an orphan. I don't know what happened to her dad. Somebody told me her mother was a mess and OD'd on painkillers. But maybe she was real sick or something. Maybe that's why Leslie acts so superior, though" — and

216

Rachel spoke in a rush — "to tell the truth, she doesn't act like she's unhappy. She acts like everything's great and she's the greatest."

"Who's her bad-ass boyfriend?"

Rachel giggled. "That's a hot topic at school. Everybody knows about him. He's a couple of years older. I've seen him and he is to die for, I mean, ooooh, one sexy dude. His name's Steve something or other. He works part time at the Gas 'N' Go, hangs out the rest of the time, from what I hear. They say" — her voice dropped — "that she's spent the night with him a bunch. I'll ask around for his name if you want me to."

"No need. Ben Parotti can tell me. In fact, keep everything mum. Don't let anyone know I asked about Leslie." Just in case . . . Someone had come swiftly from the Hathaway house to make certain Gretchen Burkholt never told the contents of the card.

Henny Brawley cut a peach pie in half. She lifted out one half, double wrapped the piece in heavy-duty foil. She put a cover over the remainder. That would be a nice finale to chili and cornbread at Max and Annie's. She glanced at the clock as she poured freshly brewed coffee into a small thermos. Just past six. It wouldn't take long to go out and reassure Jeremiah. Trapped on the little hammock, the hours must pass with deadening slowness.

At the coat tree, she hesitated, chose a heavy jacket of dark gray wool and a black stocking cap. The telephone rang. Henny checked caller ID. Unknown caller. Not this evening. She heard the continuing peals as she hurried through the door and out into the night.

The warmth of wool was welcome protection from the mist-laden wind from the bay. She walked swiftly onto the pier. It took a moment to peel back the mooring cover, but she was glad she'd taken time earlier to put it in place. Otherwise the cockpit would be slick and damp. She was careful as she climbed aboard, the boat moving up and down in the choppy water. She stowed the small basket with the thermos and foil-wrapped dessert.

Familiar with the water and the currents, she handled the boat easily. The lights revealed the channel she sought. She wished she could have called Jeremiah on his cell, alerted him that she was coming. But Billy Cameron would have set up a watch for calls to and from his number. She hoped, for Jeremiah's peace of mind, that he recognized the rumble of the motor. There was always a little sputter after she accelerated. To her, each boat had a distinctive sound. But he had been alone all day and now into the night, isolated with only fear and worry and anxiety for companions.

About fifteen feet from the hammock, she lifted her voice, loud enough to be heard over the motor. "It's me, Jeremiah. I'm bringing you some coffee." As she rounded the small hump of land, came up on the Sound side, she saw him standing tensely, knee-deep in wet grasses. "It's okay, Jeremiah. I wanted to tell you what's happening." She nosed the boat close, kept it steady, and handed him the small basket.

"Miz Brawley" — there was a catch in his voice — "you shouldn't ought to come out here at night. I don't think it's safe."

"I'm fine." She was touched by his concern. "And you're going to be fine. I've learned a huge amount today. Gretchen Burkholt took Annie Darling's place Monday." Quickly, she described Annie's talks with Gretchen and the grisly discovery at Better Tomorrow. "Annie called me. She's sure you are innocent, and she and Max are looking for information, too. We believe Mrs. Burkholt was killed because of a card she found in a box of clothes."

He spoke up and his voice was eager. "I

heard her talking on the phone about something she found. She was holding a white card. I got a look at the card when I carried some stuff inside."

"Can you describe it?"

"It was one of those white cards that have lines on them."

"An index card?"

"Yeah. She was carrying on about how it was a personal note. But" — he sounded puzzled — "it didn't look personal. The words were printed in capital letters. I didn't read it except to see a word or two. I guess they caught my eye because they were underlined: *tonight* and *kayak.* Then she gave me this dirty look, like I was something smelly that a dog drug in, so I took my time going past. I got a second look at the card and there was something written underneath all those words, a little scrawl at the bottom and some question marks. I kind of think it was a name."

Henny gripped the wheel. "A name? Jeremiah, think, try to remember. What name?" Gretchen claimed the card revealed a scandal. Everett would have been shocked by the contents and he would have wondered angrily who might have sent him what he hoped was false gossip. Had Everett jotted down the name of the person he suspected of writing a nasty anonymous accusation? That would explain why Gretchen had to die. If Everett had scrawled the murderer's name beneath the inflammatory note, the murderer had no choice but to act.

There was a long silence. "Oh, ma'am, I don't know. I saw it but I didn't care. I thought it was a name."

Henny kept her voice even and encouraging. "Try to remember. Maybe tonight when you sleep, the name will come to you. Now, you better get in your tent, try to stay dry. I'll come back in the morning. I won't give up. Somehow, someway, I'll find out what happened and you will be safe."

"Miz Brawley" — there was no mistaking the emotion in his voice — "I never knew anybody'd help me like you are. I swear to God, I didn't hurt anybody ever. I was so scared when I found her. I ran away because I knew they'd say it was me. Ma'am, the police will never believe somebody from a big house came and killed her. No matter what you do. I know you are helping me, but I don't see how you can ever prove anything. I can't go back to jail." He struggled for breath. "I'll kill myself first."

"Jeremiah" — Henny spoke quietly — "promise me you'll be here for me. I know you're scared, but you can trust me. I won't let you down."

He was silent, the motor a soft rumble, the water shushing. Finally, his young voice husky, he said, "Miz Brawley, I won't let you down, either."

9

Annie slowed as she passed the Thornwall house, searching for the name of the remodeler. There it was, Milton Construction. She picked up speed and curved around a stand of pines to the last house on the bay. A rust-streaked Ford pickup nosed against a stack of old tires. The yard was littered with castoffs, a wheelbarrow missing one handle, a splintered trash barrel, a canoe with a stoved-in hull, the front seat of a car with torn upholstery, a stack of splintery weathered two-by-fours, a roofless dog house.

Annie parked and skirted the truck. The front walk was mostly hard-packed earth with a scattering of oyster shells. Drifted pine needles made the front steps slick. Hard rock music blared from inside. She knocked vigorously.

The door opened and the decibel level increased, the beat of the music an assault on hearing.

A barefoot young man in shirt sleeves and tight Levis looked out. His tawny hair was thick and curly, his eyes an arresting golden brown like honey in the sun. He was handsome and knew he was handsome. When he saw her, his sloe eyes widened with interest and his sensuous lips half parted.

She was immediately aware that she faced the kind of man who never saw a woman without envisioning her in bed.

He turned an iPhone in his palm, moved a finger, and the music stopped. "Yeah?" His voice was husky, a greeting and an invitation.

"Excuse me. Are you" — and she grasped for a name — "James Brown?"

He shook his head. "No Browns here. I'm Steve Raymond."

"Mr. Raymond, I'm looking for the owner of the cabin." She tried to sound business-like.

"Can't help you. We rent. Don't know who the hell it belongs to." His gaze moved over her.

Despite her windbreaker, Annie felt as exposed as in an airport scanner. She felt a flicker of anger, but she focused on her task and on the plural pronoun. "Is your wife home?"

"No wife, baby. Me and my dad. He's

gone. Like always. On the road. You selling something?" Again the tone said more than the words.

She ignored the question. "Are you familiar with the house across the bay, the big stucco with red roof tiles?"

His grin was sardonic. "Haven't had an invitation yet. Rich folks. Why?" His tone was easy, but his golden eyes were intent.

"The owners are out of town. Have you noticed a blue Lincoln and a green Porsche coming there in the afternoons?"

His head tilted. "You some kind of detective?" He drawled the words, but his eyes were wary.

"I am seeking information." If he wanted to assume she was a detective, that was his privilege.

"That's a hoot, but you're a couple of weeks too late. What difference does it make now if they screw out on the dock instead of going in the house? Anyway, I got better things to do than watch a middle-aged broad sneak around to meet a middle-aged dude." He was derisive in his youth and masculinity.

Annie tried to sort out what he meant. Maybe he thought she was trailing Nicole and Doug for divorce evidence and it didn't matter now that Everett was dead. "If you don't watch, how do you know how old they are?"

"Cute. Real cute. Anybody ever told you you're cute? Sometimes cute gets people in trouble. Me, I avoid trouble. I don't know about those cars or anybody over there, young, old, or in between." He stepped back and the door slammed shut.

As the boat chugged toward the pier, Henny frowned. If the murderer's name had been at the bottom of the anonymous note to Everett, Gretchen may have given the name to Maggie. Henny felt a sudden breathlessness, then reassured herself. Maggie had merely drawn a conclusion when she said the police would be interested in who took the message from the table in the Hathaway entry hall. But there had been a tone of evaluation in her voice as if she envisioned how much it might matter to someone to remain unknown to the police. She frowned and wished she had asked Maggie for her full name, but Maggie had been in no mood for a chat when they parted.

The boat drew alongside the pier. Henny automatically tied the line. As soon as she climbed the ladder, she pulled her cell from her pocket. She could check the directory, get the Hathaways' number but it might not be wise for anyone at that house to know she was interested in Maggie. Instead, she punched a familiar number.

"Yo, Henny. It's a dark and stormy night." Marian Kenyon's raspy voice sounded mellow. The island *Gazette*'s chief reporter was known to nurse a scotch and soda and watch reruns of *The Golden Girls,* and she never missed *Dancing with the Stars.* "Have you won the lottery? Eloped with a tennis pro? Sent a dead fish to the mayor?" A throaty chuckle. Henny's antipathy to Mayor Cosgrove was well known.

"Marian, you've got your laptop at home, haven't you?" Marian was as likely to be separated from her laptop as to be severed from a big toe. "Can you find a name for me?"

"Sure, sweetie." Mellow, mellow, mellow. "Ask and you shall be answered."

"Can you find out the name of the housekeeper for the Hathaways? Her first name's Maggie."

A short silence. "I got friends at the PD." Marian's tone was no longer mellow but had the quiver of a cat sighting a bird. "I understand Gretchen Burkholt left a message at the Hathaway house shortly before she was killed. However, the chief discounted any connection, and the APB is still out for the handyman. You know something different?"

"Maybe. First, help me out." Henny felt an urgency that unnerved her. "The name?"

"Just a sec. Think I've got something here," Marian muttered. "Yeah. Here it is. I did a story about her a couple of years ago. Maggie Knight. Do you remember when the winning lotto number was big, like, yeah, here it is, eighty-four mil, and the ticket was sold here on the island and everybody went nuts? Well, they never found the winner, but she had a number just one digit off. The head ran: *Still Dreaming.* Kind of a downer, really. A no-luck lady, husband killed in Iraq. She'd had breast cancer and hoped she'd beat it, but no insurance, in debt up to her eyeballs, no family. Said she still hoped her number would come in someday, and if it did, she wanted to go someplace fancy and sit on a beach and have people bring her drinks. She said she'd quit her job and never look back, that cleaning houses and being bossed around was about as much fun as being boiled in a cannibal's pot. I didn't use that quote. I didn't think it would make her job any cheerier. And here" — triumphantly — "is the phone number." She rattled off the numbers.

"Thanks, Marian."

"So what's got you excited?"

Henny took the plunge, knowing that unleashing Marian might bring Billy down on her like a ton of bricks, but Marian would dig like crazy to find out what she could. "Billy Cameron's still hunting for Jeremiah, but Annie and Max and I are sure that Gretchen died because she knew why Everett Hathaway went out in a kayak that night. We think somebody dumped him out and left him to drown. There are two murders, not one." Henny ended the connection. If she knew Marian, the reporter would scoot straight to the *Gazette* office to check out everything about Everett's death. Now she owed Henny whatever information she rounded up.

Henny hurried toward the house as she called Maggie's number. The phone rang five times before voice mail kicked in. Henny hesitated, but knew she might as well leave a message. Maggie would know Henny had called from caller ID. "Maggie, Henny Brawley. Please call me." She left her cell number. "It's important."

Max set the timer to buzz when the cornbread was done. The table was set, the chili ready to heat. Instead of margaritas, he'd fixed tropical fruit tea. Tonight he and Annie and Henny needed energy, not relaxation. He glanced at the clock. Almost six thirty. He wouldn't even think of calling Ben Parotti at this hour in the summer. But there wouldn't be a rush in the kitchen on a January night.

Max settled at the kitchen island with the phone and his notepad. "Hey, Ben, you got a minute?"

"Hey, Max. Need a carry out? Miss Jolene's special tonight is baked scallops with Dijon mustard and brandy, hot German potato salad, and steamed Brussels sprouts."

"Man, you tempt me but I have chili guaranteed to make you think you're in Texas. Listen, Ben, what can you tell me about a guy named Steve who clerks at your Gas 'N' Go?"

"Steve Raymond. He's an okay kid. Not much home life. Mom hit the road a few years back with a drummer in Savannah. Dad's a long-haul trucker. He's not on the island much. Steve does a good job for me. I've heard girls hang around when he's at work. I warned him about that a couple of times. Something wrong there?" Ben's tone was worried.

"Something else entirely, Ben. Apparently he's been going out with Everett Hathaway's niece, girl named Leslie Griffin, and

230

Everett was unhappy about that. Can you get Steve's address for me?"

"Yo. I got everything on my iPad, employee files, recipes, ferry maintenance, you name it. Hold on a minute."

Max grinned. Ben was a late convert to electronic marvels, but ever since his wife showed him the joy of apps (his favorite: a Lowcountry fishing update app), he'd embraced his iPad with fervor. "Here it is." Ben sounded as proud as if he'd landed a seven-pound black sea bass. "One forty-two Herring Gull Road."

"Thanks, Ben." As he rang off, Max reached for a file folder, flipped it open. Dorothy L jumped to the counter, placed a paw on the top sheet. Max nuzzled under her chin, gently raised her forepaws long enough to retrieve the sheets. Dorothy L always helped out when he wrote checks or looked through recipes. She was convinced that any stack of papers had been prepared to serve her as a pallet.

Max riffled through the sheets, found the printout of news stories on the discovery of Everett's body. There it was. Don Thornwall, 146 Herring Gull Road, had spotted the bobbing orange PFD on the winter gray water. So Leslie's bad-ass boyfriend lived at 142. That was a definite link between Everett and the bay where he died. Could Everett have been on his way to the bay because Steve Raymond lived there?

Dorothy L came to her feet, head lifted. She turned and dropped to the floor and padded toward the kitchen door. Max then heard the familiar purr of Annie's car.

"She's home, Dorothy L. But you knew that, didn't you?" He moved, too.

Exclamations, interjections, and deductions swirled around the table as they ate chili and cornbread. By the time they finished Henny's peach pie, there was a general air of triumph.

Henny was often a guest for dinner. Normally, the meal enjoyed, the dishes done, they settled in the library. Annie and Max shared the brown leather sofa. Dorothy L nestled on the crest against his back, her purr a rumble of contentment. Henny always chose the chintz-covered chair to one side of the fireplace. Tonight they were in their customary places, but instead of Brandy Alexanders or Tom Collinses, depending upon season, they had steaming mugs of Kona coffee. Usually conversation drifted from a new exhibit at the High in Atlanta, a jazz singer at the Johnny Mercer Theater in Savannah, or Laurel's latest enthusiasm. Not this night. Even the half dozen sunflower stalks with bicolor blooms, orange tipped with gold, in a tall beaten copper vase evoked not a single comment.

Max looked admiringly at Annie and Henny. "At lunch, I didn't think there was anything to the idea that Everett was murdered. Instead, between us, we've uncovered enough to grab Billy's attention."

Henny looked grave. "I think we should provide him with a formal report."

"Bullets are better," Annie announced, shoving one hand through a tangle of sandy hair.

Max looked bewildered. "No one's been shot."

Henny hid a smile. "Possibly Annie's thinking about presentation. Short, cogent statements."

"Oh. Sure." Max's tone was hearty. He and Henny exchanged smiles.

Annie's voice was stiff. "I am not like Pam North."

"Certainly not." Max's tone was innocent.

"Pam North always beat everyone else to the truth," Henny soothed.

"In fact, Annie's on the right track." Max was abruptly serious. "Hopefully, Billy will want expanded statements of everything we discovered, but first we sock him with the important points."

Max keystroked on his laptop as they debated how to organize a presentation. It took three drafts before they were agreed. Max printed copies for each of them.

RE: EVERETT HATHAWAY HOMICIDE

Premise: Hathaway was lured to the bay in a kayak, intercepted by a motorboat, the kayak deliberately capsized, and Everett left to drown.

Supporting evidence:
1. An index card in the jacket worn by Hathaway the day he died revealed why he took the kayak to the bay where he drowned. (See #9)
2. A resident on Herring Gull Road heard a boat in the bay around ten P.M. that night. No one living on the bay currently has a boat.
3. Gretchen Burkholt left a message in regard to the index card with Maggie Knight, the Hathaway housekeeper.
4. No one at the house admitted seeing the message. Maggie said she left the pad on the table in the entryway and that later she noticed the top sheet with the message had been removed. No trace

of the message has been found.

5. Maggie may know who took the message, though she insists she doesn't.

6. In phone messages to Annie Darling, Gretchen emphasized the index card "named names" and exposed a "scandal" and spoke of "tonight."

7. Gretchen was murdered shortly after leaving the message with the Hathaway housekeeper. The card Gretchen found in Hathaway's jacket was not found at Better Tomorrow.

8. The Hathaway family claimed not to know why Everett went to the bay.

9. Hathaway's widow habitually met Doug Walker, her lover, at the Carstairs home on the bay.

10. It is reasonable to assume Everett received a card that informed him that his wife was meeting her lover at the Carstairs home that night and suggested Everett arrive shortly after ten P.M. in a kayak to avoid notice.

11. It isn't known when Hathaway received the index card. A member of the household could have left the card in his room or car, or he may have received the card at his office Friday morning. He missed an appointment at an art gallery. When

the owner called, Hathaway seemed up-set.

12. The index card to Everett was very likely sent anonymously.

13. The card's objective was not to inform Everett. The objective was to lure Everett to the bay.

14. Leslie Griffin's boyfriend, Steve Raymond, lives in a cabin on the bay and knew about Nicole's meetings with Doug Walker.

15. Among those who could have sent the index card to Everett: Obviously either Nicole Hathaway or Doug Walker. Steve Raymond would have informed Leslie of the meetings, so both he and Leslie can be included. Brad Milton is supervising construction at the Thornwalls and would know Doug's Porsche. Was Trey Hathaway aware of his aunt's affair?

16. Possible motives for Everett's murder:
    - Nicole Hathaway — freedom from a loveless marriage in hopes of a permanent relationship with Doug Walker.
    - Doug Walker — he claims he wants to end the affair and appears desperate to protect his marriage. He might have been willing to commit murder if he feared Everett was suspicious

and might accuse Nicole of adultery in a divorce action, naming Doug as a co-respondent. Or he might be running a double bluff to obtain Nicole's freedom and possibly her substantial inheritance.

- Leslie Griffin — Everett had mentioned to friends his unhappiness over Leslie's involvement with Steve Raymond and his determination to put an end to the relationship. Leslie was flippant about motives for murder, saying she thought he was a bore but indicating Nicole was a "merry widow" and that her cousin Trey was "pissed off" at Everett.
- Trey Hathaway — apparently he was angry with Everett over the business plan of the ad agency.
- Steve Raymond — he might be determined to continue his relationship with Leslie.
- Brad Milton — faced financial ruin unless Everett extended time to repay a note. He claims Everett had agreed. There is no proof. Brad was at the advertising agency Friday morning and spoke with Everett. He left shortly before noon.

17. Appraisal of possible suspects:
   - Nicole Hathaway — emotionally vulnerable, depressed by her lover's rejection, no evidence of grief for her dead husband.
   - Doug Walker — appears focused solely on himself and his family. Beneath a Realtor's surface charm, abrasive and aggressive.
   - Leslie Griffin — immature, self-absorbed, callous.
   - Trey Hathaway — mercurial temperament, quick to anger.
   - Steve Raymond — enjoys a bad-boy image, but Ben Parotti thought he was a decent kid.
   - Brad Milton — big, tough, Eddie's friend, not Everett's.

"Number two. That's what matters." Annie was emphatic.

Paper rustled as Max and Henny checked.

"There was a boat in the bay the night Everett died!" Annie popped to her feet. At the fireplace, she grabbed a poker and thumped a log. "No one in the bay owns a motorboat." She thumped again. Embers swirled. "It was a cold and miserable winter night. Obviously no one took a boat out on a pleasure jaunt." Another thump. "When we find who drove that boat, we'll have the murderer."

Henny didn't look hopeful. "The Hathaway boat wasn't taken out that night."

Annie didn't ask if Henny was sure. Henny would be very certain before she made that statement. "Then we'll have to see if the people involved had access to another boat."

Max spoke quickly. "Brad Milton doesn't have a boat now."

Annie refused to be discouraged. "There was a boat." Her tone was stubborn. "As far as I'm concerned, a boat in the bay that night proves Everett was murdered."

"Post hoc, ergo propter hoc," Max murmured.

Annie rehung the poker with a clang. "Logic is as logic does."

Henny laughed aloud. "Ah, Pam." Before Annie could object, Henny said quickly, "We may not have a lead to the boat, but I think Maggie knows who took that message from the hall table." She frowned. "I warned her that it could be dangerous. She said she wasn't fool enough to go out in a kayak. That's the first thing I want to tell Billy tomorrow. He needs to talk to Maggie. Let's meet at the station at nine in the morning."

■ ■ ■ ■

The right wiper clacked and stuck, leaving that portion of the windshield obscured by the mist. Henny drove carefully but confidently, her headlights piercing the pitch dark of the sodden January night. Tomorrow she'd get new wipers. Maybe she'd drop by the Gas 'N' Go, see if Steve Raymond was working. Over the past few years, she'd regularly substituted at the high school, and she remembered Steve Raymond. Most women from seven to seventy would remember Steve. That observation would please him. She wasn't surprised that Leslie was infatuated or that Everett had objected. Steve moved with easy grace, athletic and masculine. There was insolence in the smooth contours of his face and a taunt in his golden eyes.

Henny curved around a pothole and turned into her drive, glad to see lights shining through her uncurtained windows. Tomorrow she'd replace the bulb on the front porch, but there was enough light to get her up the steps safely. She parked and felt a flood of contentment. A day which had begun so terribly — leaving Jeremiah marooned on that small hammock, hoping against hope that she could somehow find proof of his innocence — was ending with a sense of confidence.

She opened the door. She stepped out, then made a vexed noise. She wanted to take the folder inside. She turned and bent to reach for the folder.

A sharp crack sounded. The window in the driver's door exploded. Another crack.

Henny's ear burned. She felt a trickle of blood down her cheek, but she was moving automatically, crouching, running behind the car, away from the lighted house, plunging into darkness.

Another shot rang out.

"Miz Brawley, I'm coming." The distant shout carried over the water but sounded far away, too far to save her. "I'll be there. I'm coming, Miz Brawley, I'm coming."

Another shot. A sharp ping sounded, and Henny knew a bullet had struck the car. She was out of sight from the radiance of the porch light now. She kept running and scrambled into the pines, gasping for breath. Her ears thrummed. Was there a sound nearby? Had her attacker followed her into the woods? She couldn't be sure. She had to keep going. Where could she go? There was no road, no path . . . She stumbled, dead vines tangling her feet.

"Miz Brawley, I'm almost there." Henny heard the valiant call, knew he was trying to help but knew as well that Jeremiah could not save her. Oh, Jeremiah, you can't help me. It's too far and too cold to swim and would take too long even if you could manage. I'm alone. Someone wants to kill me. Her heart thudded. Her chest ached. She brushed through a tangle of ferns and crashed into a log and tumbled forward. As she fell, she heard Jeremiah's desperate call, deep and anguished.

"Miz Brawley, I'm coming . . ."

Annie set the dishes in the cabinet, closed the door.

Max came up behind her, slipped his arms around her. "How about a little time for us?"

Annie smiled and started to turn in his embrace. Her cell phone rang.

Max's breath was warm against her cheek, his hand slipped from her shoulder, drew the phone from the pocket of her cardigan. "New Year's resolution, never answer any phone after ten o'clock."

Annie plucked the phone from his hand. "I'd better check since it's my cell . . ." She looked down and stiffened. "Marian. She wouldn't call unless it was something important." She answered. "Marian?"

"Scanner." Marian's voice was high and excited, the connection scratchy. "On my way to Henny's house. Ten sixty-seven. Call for help. Code three. Lights and sirens." In the background was the wail of sirens. "Jeez. Three cruisers passed me like I'm standing still. Four. Something bad."

10

A police cruiser parked sideways on the rutted dirt road barred the way. Its rooftop beacons rotated. Whirling red lights from several cars flashed, ominous warning signals in the velvety darkness. Lights glowed at Henny's house and at least a half dozen harsh Maglites beamed, dotting the expanse of ground between the house and woods.

Annie braked, punched the window button.

Hyla Harrison, her face stern and set beneath her cap, strode forward, gesturing with one gloved hand. The other held a Maglite. "Clear the road. Emergency vehicles coming."

"Oh, Hyla." Ordinarily Annie was careful to address Hyla Harrison as sergeant when she was on duty. Serious and intense, Hyla was a stickler for the proprieties. Off duty, they were tentatively friendly, or as friendly as Hyla ever managed outside official police circles. Initially disdainful of mysteries, Hyla had become a faithful reader of police procedurals, especially those by Ed McBain, Dell Shannon, and Kate Ellis. "Is Henny all right?"

Hyla's pale face looked bleak. "She's missing. Everybody's looking. Nine-one-one reported gunshots, but nobody was here when we came. Stay out of the way. If you park over there" — the strong beam swerved toward her right, sweeping a patch of beaten ground near Henny's garage — "you can go as far forward as that reporter's car. She thinks she owns the world." Marian Kenyon was not a favorite of Hyla's. Hyla viewed the press as a life form slightly more elevated than bacteria.

"Max and I can help search." Annie tried to keep her voice even. Inside, she felt wave after wave of panic. Where was Henny? "We'll park and ask Billy."

Hyla nodded, stepped back.

Annie swung the car around the cruiser, drove to a spot beside Marian Kenyon's battered VW, jolted to a stop. Lights bobbed along the bank of the marsh and among the trees in dark woods on either side of Henny's road.

As she and Max slammed out of the car, Billy's voice boomed, metallic and amplified, "Flash a light. You will not be harmed. Mrs. Brawley is missing. We need your help to find her."

Annie reached out and grabbed Max's arm. The shouted words were unexpected, adding to the unreality of a disordered night.

Headlights from parked police cruisers illuminated Billy. He faced the marsh, burly, solid, and muscular, as he spoke into a megaphone. Annie also recognized Lou Pirelli, Billy's second-in-command. Henny's old Dodge was clearly visible. The driver's door was wide open, the window shattered. Bits of glass sparkled on the dusty ground. A bullet hole marred the left rear fender.

Marian Kenyon, Leica held steady, clicked photos in a frenzy.

Annie tugged on Max's arm. "Let's ask Marian." When they reached the reporter, Annie called out, "Marian —"

"Not now." She never lowered the camera. "Got to get these." Her dark hair was pulled back in a scraggly ponytail. She wore no coat. An oversized flannel shirt hung to the knees of her jeans. She'd not bothered with shoes, instead wore once fluffy house slippers.

Far out in the bay, a light flashed, once, twice, three times, then remained on, dimly visible. A distant shout warned, "Miz Brawley may be hurt." The young male voice was anguished. "There was shots. You got to find her."

Two police officers climbed into a boat at the far end of Henny's pier and chugged in the direction of the tiny spot of light.

Annie watched the boat's running lights. It seemed to take forever until the boat reached the hammock. An officer's voice was magnified by a megaphone. "Here we are. Steady. Come aboard." In the boat's lights, the hammock was a dark uneven hump on the black water. "We'll get you ashore." The officer stood in the back of the boat with the megaphone. "Chief, there's a bunch of stuff out here —"

Billy's megaphone boomed. "Not now. Bring him in." Billy handed the megaphone to another uniformed figure and he and Lou strode toward the pier. The police boat pulled alongside and tied up. In the bright beam of a Maglite, an officer climbed the ladder, turned to hold the boat steady as a young man in a brown corduroy jacket clambered onto the pier.

Marian swung toward Annie. "Who the hell's that?"

"Jeremiah Young." To Annie, it seemed as if her voice came from a long distance.

Max's head turned toward her. His eyes narrowed.

Annie looked straight ahead. There would be time for explanations, both to Max and to Billy. Henny had taken a gamble in helping Jeremiah hide. Her faith in his innocence now seemed justified, but her efforts to find out the truth behind Gretchen's murder may have come at a terrible cost. Something she'd done, something she'd said, something she'd seen today had brought a murderer here tonight.

"OmiGod. He was out there?" Marian flung an arm toward the marsh. "Okay, ladies and gents, we got a story here. He didn't get there with water wings. He doesn't have a boat. I checked on that when he went missing. First thought is always that a fugitive will boat over to the mainland. Plus, he doesn't have a car. Last mode of transport a bike. Maybe it's hidden in the woods around here." Marian practically bounced in excitement. "He didn't bike out to that hammock. Henny has a boat. My crystal ball tells me she ferried him out to the hammock, then spent the day trying to find out who killed Burkholt. But tonight how did the cops know he was out there? Last I heard there was an APB, but take a look at his welcoming committee." She gestured toward the end of the pier where Jeremiah was in deep conversation with Billy and Lou. Lou was always Billy's right-hand man in any investigation. Lou was athletic, fast-moving, and, off duty babied a nineteen eighty Chevy and loved the Braves. "Nobody's arresting Young. Looks more like he was rescued and he's part of the team."

Annie watched as directed. Marian was right. The body language of Billy Cameron and Jeremiah Young was of an older man and a younger, intent, cooperating, talking fast. Lou bent close, listening hard. On the same team, as Marian said.

Billy turned to the officer standing by the ladder, apparently gave instructions. The policeman, a bulky figure in a duffel coat, clambered down the ladder and stepped into the boat. The boat chugged back out into the channel as Billy, Lou, and Jeremiah walked fast to the shore, men in a hurry.

On the bank, Billy gestured toward Henny's car. He and Lou and Jeremiah stopped a little way from the car, about twenty feet from where Annie and Max stood with Marian. Billy pointed at the broken driver's window. "One of the shots knocked out her window."

Annie clung to Max's hand. What happened after Henny was ambushed?

In the glare of police cruiser headlights, Jeremiah looked even scruffier than usual, do-rag askew, broad face pale and unshaven, corduroy jacket streaked with dirt. "There was shots. Lots of them. I yelled after the first shot. I yelled and yelled. I called nine-one-one. I tried to sound like I was coming. I took a log and beat on the ground like somebody running. There was like five or six shots. I would of come, but I can't swim. You got to find her."

"We're looking. Did you see her at all?"

A siren sounded and an ambulance curved around the cruise car across the road and drew up near one of the parked cruise cars.

Jeremiah swung toward the road. "Has somebody found her?"

Billy shook his head. "Just in case."

Annie took a step forward, called out. "Can we help search?"

Lights in the woods winked like fireflies as searchers struggled through undergrowth.

Billy's face was sympathetic. "We got people working on a grid. Better stay where you are." Then he frowned. "How come you two are here?"

Marian lifted her sharp chin. "You can tag me for the Darlings." Her tone was combative. "I gave them a heads-up. Henny called me about seven. She wanted the phone number of Maggie Knight, the housekeeper at the Hathaway house. She and the Darlings are hunting the person who lured Everett Hathaway out in a kayak and killed him. I thought you better talk to them" — she jerked a thumb at Annie and Max — "and find out who might have come after Henny."

Billy swung toward Annie, his heavy face in a tight frown.

Annie remembered Henny's plan. The first thing the next morning, she intended to ask Billy to talk to Maggie Knight. "Henny thinks Maggie Knight saw someone take Gretchen's message. Henny called Maggie tonight. There was no answer. She asked Maggie to call back. Henny was going to ask you to talk to Maggie, see what you could find out." Annie sounded stressed. "I don't know where Maggie lives."

Marian checked her notebook, rattled off Maggie's address.

Billy unhooked his cell phone, pressed a number. "Harrison, take a run over to two eighteen Barred Owl Road. Bring Maggie Knight to the station. Explain she's needed in a missing person case. Take her into custody as a material witness if she resists." He turned back to Jeremiah. "How far out is that hammock?"

Jeremiah shrugged. "I don't know. A long way."

Billy folded his arms. "What were you doing out there?"

Jeremiah stared down at the ground. "Hiding. I was scared." His voice was tired, hopeless. "Listen, Chief" — now his voice was anguished — "I didn't hurt Miz Burkholt."

"How'd you know she was hurt?" Billy's voice was sharp.

"I had a bunch of stuff to take into the storeroom and I came in the hall and I saw blood. I looked inside the room. She was lying there and my axe was next to her. I knew everybody'd think I'd done it and I didn't." It was a cry from his heart. "I never did."

Billy stared at him, his face grim. "How'd you get to the hammock?"

Jeremiah shifted from one foot to another, looked at the ground. "Somebody brought me."

"When?"

Jeremiah's face creased in thought. Finally, he said reluctantly, "This morning."

Lou spoke quietly. "Mrs. Brawley took you out."

Jeremiah hunched his shoulders, locked his big hands together.

Billy nodded. "Had to be her."

Jeremiah looked at him pleadingly. "I don't want to get Miz Brawley in trouble."

"We can prove it when they bring all the stuff back. Her fingerprints will be on a bunch of it. Why did she take you there?"

"Last night I come here. I didn't know where to go and I was hungry. I was looking in Miz Brawley's garbage cans and she got home. She must have heard me or something and she came into that place with the garbage pails." He hunched his shoulders. "I took my coat and wrapped it around her. I was sorry to scare her. I told her I didn't have anything to do with what happened to Miz Burkholt, but she'd been hit and my axe was there beside her. I knew everybody'd blame me. I told her I'd rather die than go back to prison. She let me come inside and she fixed some bacon and eggs and we talked and she knew I didn't hurt anybody. She let me sleep on the couch and this morning she said I would be safe on the hammock and she'd find out what happened. Somehow."

Billy's gaze was thoughtful. "You knew we'd find you when you called nine-one-one."

Shots at Henny and shouts from Jeremiah. Annie imagined his panic, trapped so far from land. He'd done the best he could and

he'd called for help even though he understood the consequences to himself.

Jeremiah's face was heavy. "I had to get
help. I couldn't get to her. I couldn't let
somebody hurt her. Not after all she did for
me. I figured I had to tell you what I knew.
I owed her that. But I'd rather die than go
back to jail. They hurt me there." His voice
shook.

Lou's face squeezed in understanding.

"She was a damn fool to take you out
there." Billy looked exasperated yet excited.
"But that tells me a lot. She's smart about
people. She believed you." Billy let the
words hang in the damp air. "She could
have been wrong. If she'd been wrong, we
wouldn't be hunting her tonight. She's a
small woman, elderly. You could have overpowered her, taken her boat, got to the
mainland, dumped a body way out in the
Sound. You didn't do that. You got out of
her boat and you've been on that hammock.
All right. Run through everything again
from the time you heard her car tonight."

"She didn't come home until about ten,
but somebody was here a little before that. I
didn't think about it. I mean, I guess I
should have wondered why I didn't hear
another car. It's kind of like at Better
Tomorrow. I never heard anyone come

there, either, but when I went inside, Miz Burkholt was dead. And tonight, I was kind of watching out for Miz Brawley to come home —"

Annie felt a twist of sympathy. He'd been out on the hammock, alone, and he'd wanted to know Henny was home, not to ask for anything, not to call for her, just to know that she was there.

"— and then I saw the front door open and somebody going inside. I didn't have a good look. Just a dark figure, moving fast. I figured some friend had come over and was waiting for her. In a little while, the door opened and somebody came down the steps. It was just a quick shadow. I thought maybe her friend got tired of waiting. About twenty minutes later, her old Dodge come up the road. The motor knocks. It needs some work on the carburetor. Anyway, I felt good that she was home. I saw the head-lights as she parked. She got out and that's when the first shot came. Then two more, real quick."

"What did she do?"

Jeremiah looked miserable. "I don't know. There was light from her house windows but she didn't come that way. I guess she ran toward the woods." He gestured to his right.

Billy's head turned. He surveyed the car. "If she'd been hit, she would have fallen there. There's some blood —"

Annie felt sick. Henny had been so confident when she left. *Tomorrow at nine.*

"— but not enough for a serious wound. Likely some of the glass from the window hit her. So she knew she was a target. She'd stay away from the light and head for cover." He turned back to Jeremiah. "How many more shots?"

"Three. I was yelling the whole time —"

Billy nodded. "We got you on tape. You sure as hell were. You yelled for us to get here, too."

"— and beating with the log. I yelled and yelled. After a while I stopped and listened. I didn't hear anything except the water and the cordgrass until the sirens started."

"Right. So now —" Billy's walkie-talkie beeped. He unhooked it from his belt. "Cameron . . . Right. Yeah, might as well bring all the stuff in. He won't be going back out there." He clicked off, sheathed the mobile radio. "That hammock's a good hundred yards out. About twelve feet deep there. I'll check it out, but I figure you're telling the truth that you can't swim. You wouldn't have made it anyway. Too cold. And there's nothing out there, not a canoe, not a kayak, not a rowboat, not even a damn air mattress. You were marooned." He jerked a thumb toward the nearest cruiser. "Wait in the car."

Jeremiah stood stiff and still, shoulders hunkered forward.

"Just a place to wait until we get a break. The front seat. There's a thermos. Have some coffee."

Not the back, Annie realized, where a metal grill separated the backseat from the front and there were no handles on the doors.

"Coffee?" Jeremiah's voice shook.

"Yeah. We'll need your statement. Then you can go home."

Jeremiah's eyes widened. "You mean —"

"Right. We'll cancel the APB —" Billy's walkie-talkie buzzed. He lifted it. "You found her? I'll be right there." Billy nodded at Jeremiah. "Wait in the car." Then he gestured to the paramedics. "Time to move out."

A tall, lean man took one end of a stretcher. A burly middle-aged woman with purplish hair gripped the other. They moved toward him.

"Hurry." Billy's strong voice carried across the night. "This way. Come on, Lou." He loped toward the woods, his Maglite shining a path before him, Lou close behind.

Annie whirled to follow, felt Max's strong grip on her arm.

"Hold on, honey." He was kind but firm. "We might get in the way. What matters now is help getting to Henny as fast as possible."

Annie leaned against him. He was right. Nothing must interfere with Henny's rescue. Was she conscious? How badly was she hurt? Surely Billy's call for haste meant that she was alive, that time mattered.

The paramedics trotted past them. Officers swarmed to the edge of the woods, their lights bobbing as they ran.

Jeremiah, his head turned to follow their progress, reached the police car and opened the passenger door.

Annie stared at the dark mass of the trees, straining to see. One cluster of lights didn't move. Officers must have gathered there, shining Maglites at the spot where Henny lay.

Annie stood with her nails pressed into her palms. Max waited with his arms folded, his face grave.

"She's tough." Marian paced back and forth. "Look, if she made it into the trees, she had to be ambulatory. Right? So they're going to bring her out in a minute." Marian's husky voice was brisk but with an uncharacteristic wobble. "I guess you guys got it right about Hathaway. Listen, fill me in on what you did today."

Annie shook her head. "Not now." Her voice was flat. "Not until we know about Henny." She could see Jeremiah in Billy's cruiser, his head turned toward the lights.

All of them, waiting, hoping, praying. Minutes passed, at least five, perhaps ten. To Annie, each minute seemed interminable. What was taking so long? They'd found her. Why didn't the EMTs bring her out of the woods?

Max gave her arm a reassuring squeeze. "They'll make sure she's stabilized before they move her."

Annie found the words chilling . . . stabilize . . . Now she viewed the passage of time as an enemy. The longer it took to move Henny, the more serious her injuries might be.

Marian stopped pacing, her Édith Piaf face scrunched in worry.

Abruptly sound and motion exploded in the woods. A shout. Lights moved fast. Feet thudded as figures ran out of the woods and swept toward cruisers.

"Ohh." Annie gave a cry of despair.

Max pulled her close, his arm tight around her shoulders. Marian swore, her husky voice despairing.

Billy Cameron hurried toward his cruiser, speaking rapidly into his walkie-talkie. In the lights of the cars, his face was grim, intent, commanding. Lou reached the car ahead of him and slammed into the driver's seat as Coley Benson, the newest member of the department, opened the passenger door and yanked a thumb for Jeremiah to get out.

Car motors roared. The first of the cruisers backed and turned and drove down the drive toward the road, red lights flashing, siren squalling. Other sirens shrilled.

Bewildered, Annie shouted at Marian. "What's happening?"

Marian was already loping toward Billy's car, but the cruiser was on its way, Lou at the wheel, Billy in the passenger seat.

Coley strode toward them, obviously a man with a duty. Following close behind was Jeremiah.

Annie struggled to breathe.

"Mrs. Darling" — Coley raised his voice against the sounds of cars — "the chief wants you to go in the ambulance with Mrs. Brawley." Before she could answer, he swung to Max. "Will you drive Jeremiah Young home? We can't spare anybody to take him."

Max nodded. "Sure. I'll be glad to help."

Jeremiah appeared dazed. "They said I can go home." His voice was numb. "But I can't leave now. They're all in a hurry and they wouldn't tell me anything. I got to wait for Miz Brawley."

Annie spoke loudly to be heard as another siren squalled. "Coley, where's Henny?"

"They're bringing her." His voice was young and excited. "I got to get started. The chief said he'd be talking to you later." With that, he swung away, breaking into a run.

A breathless Marian skidded to a stop by Annie. Marian slapped her hands on her hips. "What's with the exodus?" she shouted after Coley. Her head jerked back toward the woods. "And why is it taking so long?"

"Here come some people." Jeremiah pointed toward the trees.

The EMTs came out of the woods, moving at a steady pace. Headlights flashed over them. The EMT at the back of the stretcher appeared to be chatting, her expression untroubled.

Annie felt a wild, desperate impatience. Why weren't they hurrying? Why were the police cars peeling away from Henny's house?

Her heart shifted as the stretcher came even with them and she saw the small figure

261

with a blanket drawn to her chin. "Henny." Her cry rose above the sound of motors and voices.

Henny's head turned. "Annie." Her voice was weary but clear.

Joy swept Annie. Now the relaxed pace of the EMTs was balm. Henny might be hurt, but there was no need to hurry.

Marian expelled a deep breath. "You had us going, Henny." Her raspy tone was a mixture of approbation and delight. "See you at the hospital. Exclusive to this correspondent. Now" — Marian's head lifted as Billy's cruiser roared past — "I want to know where the posse's headed." She hunched over her iPhone. "I got an app for my scanner." She brushed the screen. Her eyes widened. "Oh, hell, I'm outta here."

Annie grabbed a skinny elbow.

Marian pulled free, but over her shoulder shouted, "One eighty-seven. Two eighteen Barred Owl Road." As she wrenched open the door to her VW, she yelled. "That's homicide. Victim ID'd. Maggie Knight." The last was scarcely heard as Marian tumbled into her VW, revved the motor, and the little car wheeled and zoomed up the road.

Henny tried to struggle upright. "Maggie's been killed?"

Annie didn't want to believe what she had heard, but there was no doubt what Marian had said. "That's what Marian picked up on the scanner. That's why they left so quickly. Hyla Harrison had gone to find her. She must have called." Annie felt numb. Henny had worried that Maggie knew who took the message from the hall table. Now Henny's fears were confirmed. Obviously Maggie knew and had hoped to take advantage of her knowledge. Instead, she had summoned death. Maggie's murder made clear just how close Henny had come to death.

"I told her it was dangerous." Henny's voice shook. "I warned her."

"Rest easy, ma'am." The big woman's voice was kind but stern. "Don't want to aggravate that leg."

Annie darted to the side of the stretcher, grabbed Henny's chilled hand. "We'll find out what happened later." There was no urgency now to speak to Maggie Knight. It was forever too late. Whatever she had known, she could no longer share. "You need to rest, Henny." They were at the ambulance now and the back was open. The EMTs lifted the stretcher.

Annie said firmly, "Chief Cameron asked me to accompany her to the hospital."

The broad-faced woman pointed toward the passenger door. "You go in front. I ride with her."

Annie shifted uncomfortably in the curved plastic chair. A deserted hospital hallway late at night was a grim and burdened place. Occasionally a nurse moved quietly past with a curious glance. A twin to Annie's chair sat empty a few feet away. Officer P. K. Powell had gone to the restroom, arming Annie with a handheld air horn with instructions to push the black button if any unauthorized person attempted to gain access to Henny's room. Annie held the horn gingerly. She didn't want to accidentally unleash the unnerving *ooh-gah-ooh-gah-ooh-gah,* a warning sure to empty all the rooms and possibly precipitate heart attacks if the floor held any cardiac patients.

So far, Officer Powell had not been a cheerful companion in keeping watch at the door to Henny's room, but it was she who had found the chairs and brought them and she'd even offered Annie a portion of a Baby Ruth. She'd answered Annie's attempts at conversation politely but firmly, saying, "I'm not authorized to comment, ma'am."

Annie was both reassured and worried by

the officer's arrival. A guard certainly offered protection for Henny, but her presence indicated Billy Cameron felt Henny continued to be in danger. Still, Officer Powell's presence was a comfort, a broad Scandinavian face, pale blond hair in coronet braids, a starched uniform.

Annie felt the vibration of her cell. She retrieved it from her pocket, answered softly. "They brought her to the room about fifteen minutes ago. She waved at me, but they scooted her right in. The orderly left. A doctor and nurse are with her. There's an officer here."

"That figures." Max sounded somber. "I caught Marian on her cell. She's at the *Gazette* now, writing her story. She knows it's big. She'll do a feed to AP. Marian's pumped with enough adrenaline to power a generator. Maggie Knight was shot to death, apparently a bunch of shots. I don't think we have two separate shooters loose on the island tonight, and I'm sure Billy agrees. Shots at Henny. Maggie shot to death. So, Billy has an officer on duty."

As if on cue, Officer Powell returned, carrying a foam cup in each hand. She jerked her head toward the door, gave Annie a quick questioning look.

Annie covered the phone. "No one's been

in or out."

Powell nodded. She set the lidded cups carefully on the floor to the left of her chair, retrieved the air horn, and placed it in a pouch. To protect Henny, she would meet an intruder with a gun and a billy club. She picked up the coffees, handed one cup to Annie, and settled in her chair with the other.

Annie took a sip of scalding coffee as she listened to Max.

". . . took Jeremiah home and left him with his aunt. She was crying and holding on to him. I told her he was a hero. I don't think there's any doubt that he saved Henny's life. He raised so much ruckus the killer got spooked. Think about it, Annie. The killer's on the marsh with a gun, and it's the kind of quiet you get in a place where there's not another house within a couple of miles and the only sounds are the pine branches soughing in the offshore breeze, an owl hooting, the slap of water on the pilings. Henny pulled up and opened her car door. The killer shot at her, but it's hard to hit at a distance. Not like Maggie. She was standing in her living room and the shots came from about four feet. Whoever shot at Henny had to be fifteen or twenty feet away, or Henny would have seen someone waiting and maybe backed up and driven off. That first shot hit the window and then out of nowhere some guy started yelling that he's coming and Henny dodged out of sight. The killer fired again and again and all hell broke loose, shouts and thumps. The killer got rattled and ran."

Annie felt sick as she thought about how near to death Henny had been. "Jeremiah scared the murderer away."

"Exactly." Max was emphatic. "He's a double hero because he was on the horn to nine-one-one while the shots sounded and the cops barreled up within minutes. If he hadn't called the cops, say instead he'd called a buddy, told him where he was, asked him to get a boat and come for him, Henny wouldn't have survived. She'd fallen, the ground was wet, hypothermia would have gotten her long before she would have been missed. I told his aunt he was a good man." His voice softened. "She wanted to feed me pecan pie and send a piece for you. I finally got away by promising we'd come over for a celebration. I'm back at the house. I wanted to get our report for Billy. Also, I've made some calls. I alerted Mom and Emma. They'll set up a schedule to make sure Henny isn't alone. A team's en route to the hospital now. I'm almost there.

As soon as you see her, I'm bringing you home."

"Max, I —"

He was firm. "You need to be fresh tomorrow to help Billy."

A squeak, and the door to Henny's room was pulled open.

Annie came to her feet. "Max, the doctor's coming out." She ended the call.

A youthful but balding man whose green scrubs looked too tight stepped into the hall.

Annie looked at him eagerly. "How is she?"

The hospitalist's ruddy face was fresh and cheerful. "Resting comfortably now. Had to deal with slight hypothermia as well as an ankle with a hairline fracture. She's had pain medication. She should be up on crutches tomorrow and likely in a walking boot in about three days. Are you family?"

"Yes." As far as Annie was concerned, Henny was family and no one could prove otherwise. After all, they both had Texas roots. "I'm Annie Darling. Dr. Burford will vouch for me. Can I see her?"

At the name of the hospital director, the hospitalist became genial. "She's worried about somebody named Jeremiah. You can go in, but try to keep her calm. She needs to sleep."

Annie stepped inside the room.

A young, dark-haired nurse was checking monitors. She gave a satisfied nod, her long face calm. She exuded competence. "Everything's fine. There's the call button" — she pointed — "if she needs anything."

Annie stood beside the bed. Henny lay with her silver-streaked dark hair loose on the pillow. A small bandage covered one ear. Her face was pale, but she breathed evenly, quietly. She looked small beneath the white coverlet. Suddenly, she shivered. "Cold. So cold."

Annie pulled up a blanket from the foot of the bed, tucked it around Henny, careful not to disarrange the IV in her left hand.

Henny's eyes flickered open. She looked fuzzily at Annie, then her dark eyes focused. "Jeremiah?"

Swiftly, Annie told her. "He's safely home."

Henny's dark eyes were somber. "Jeremiah's safe, but Maggie's dead. Do you know what happened?"

Annie spoke quietly. "Hyla found her dead in her living room. She'd been shot several times."

Henny looked stricken. "I should have called Billy and told him. She must have contacted the murderer."

269

Annie was firm. "You warned her. She made a bad choice. Billy will find out what happened. And now he knows Jeremiah is innocent."

Henny gingerly touched the bandage over her ear. "I told Billy how Jeremiah shouted. He yelled right after the shots, said he was coming, but I knew he had no way to get to shore. I ran toward the trees and there were more shots. I reached the woods but I was crashing through underbrush and I knew the shooter would find me. Then I fell and couldn't get up." She took a deep breath, her dark eyes wide with remembered terror. "I laid still. I was afraid to call out. I kept thinking in a moment I'd be shot. Jeremiah was shouting and shouting." She was quiet for a moment. When she spoke again, her voice was less distinct. "By the time I caught my breath, I realized no one was in the woods with me. Then I heard sirens. There was a huge commotion, sirens, men shouting. There was so much noise I couldn't attract anyone's attention. Finally there were flashlights and I knew there was a search. I called out when some lights came close." A faint grimace of pain. "My ankle hurts." She sounded drowsy.

Annie straightened Henny's cover. "Try to relax and sleep." The pain pills were likely taking effect. "Everything will be better to-morrow."

Henny's eyelashes fluttered. Her eyes closed.

Annie stood by the bed for a moment, then walked to the window. The room was on the second floor and would be accessible only by a ladder. Satisfied, Annie turned and walked softly across the room. She opened the door. As she stepped into the hallway, she heard a murmur of voices.

Pamela Potts held out a sheet of paper to Billy Cameron. Pamela always came when people were in need, blond hair perfectly coiffed in an old-fashioned pageboy, blue eyes magnified by horn-rimmed glasses, neatly but unfashionably attired. Her earnest face kind and encouraging, she brought food for the sick, comfort to the grieving, encouragement for the fearful. Pamela was serious, intense, dependable, bewildered by repartee, but willing to join in merriment even if she didn't have a clue. Annie counted her as a cherished friend. Pamela had quickly joined Henny, Emma, and Laurel in supporting Annie and Max during those dreadful August days when Max was in peril.

". . . authorized volunteers are listed for two-hour periods. Each team is composed

271

by members who know each other. More-over, I have a duplicate sheet for the officer in the hall and the officer will require identification before permitting ingress."

Billy stood with his arms folded. The sharp lights of the hallway emphasized glints of silver in his thick blond hair, dark shadows beneath his eyes, and deep lines of fatigue at the corners of his mouth. "Excellent organization, Pamela." There might have been a tiny hint of amusement in blue eyes, but there was respect as well.

"Thank you." Pamela handed one sheet to Billy and a second to Officer Powell. "I will be joined by Rosemarie Woody. We will be on duty until two A.M." Pamela reached into the deep pocket of a baggy wool sweater. "Here is my driver's license."

Officer Powell looked a little surprised since Pamela obviously was known to Chief Cameron. She glanced at him.

He gave a slight nod.

Officer Powell, her face carefully blank, duly checked the license, returned it to Pamela.

Only then did Pamela push through the door and enter Henny's room.

Billy's broad mouth curved in a smile as the door closed behind Pamela.

Annie suspected it was the first time he'd

smiled that day.

When he turned to Annie, the moment's respite was over. His face was somber, his gaze sharp. He gestured toward the end of the hall. "I need to talk to you." For a big man, well over six feet and two hundred pounds plus, Billy moved fast.

Annie hurried to keep up.

Steps sounded behind them.

Annie looked over her shoulder, pointed at Billy's receding back.

Max nodded and walked swiftly to catch up. He came up beside her and looked down, his face creased in a worried frown. "Is Henny okay?"

"She's resting. Billy came to make sure she was safe."

Billy stood in the archway to a family waiting area.

As they stepped into the alcove, he reached for his cell phone, checked a text message, then turned to them.

Max drew several folded sheets from his jacket. "We rounded up information about Everett Hathaway."

Billy reached out, took the sheets. "Henny's copy was lying on the front seat of her car." He gestured toward faux leather chairs. As they sat, he dropped onto a sofa opposite them. His voice was heavy. "I know

what happened. You three stirred up a murderer."

The words hung in the quiet alcove.

Annie lifted her chin. "We were trying to
save Jeremiah."

Billy's heavy face wasn't hostile. "Got
that. I'm not blaming you or Max or Henny.
In fact, everything could have been handled
and two murders solved except" — and now
there was cool judgment in his voice — "for
one woman's fatal mistake. Maggie Knight
may have been greedy. She definitely was
foolish. Henny thought Maggie knew who
took the note. She warned her. Maggie
should have listened. Instead she must have
contacted the murderer. There's nothing on
her cell that's helpful, but everybody knows
cell phone records are kept. That's another
indication she intended to fly under the
radar. Maybe she went to the Gas 'N' Go
and used a pay phone. Maybe she dropped
by the killer's house. Maybe she left a note
where the murderer would be sure to find
it. We can't prove she contacted anyone. But
that's what must have happened. The attack
on Henny proves that Maggie's murder is
connected to the message from Gretchen."

"Maggie knew what happened to Gretchen." Annie wasn't convinced. "Why would
she take the terrible risk of meeting with

the murderer?"

"Oh" — he sounded weary — "she thought she was clever. All it took was a quick phone call, something like, 'I saw you take the message from the hallway.' She didn't have to be more explicit. Maybe she said, 'Henny Brawley's asking a lot of questions. If you don't want me to talk to her, tell her more, I'll be quiet. For a price.' She may have asked for a small payment, maybe a thousand dollars and asked that it be brought over at eight or nine o'clock. The murderer would have known there would be future demands."

Max folded his arms. "Why did she think she could deal with a murderer who answered one threat with an axe?"

Billy rubbed knuckles against a bristly cheek. "I suspect she used Henny for insurance, told the murderer that if anything happened to her, Henny Brawley would receive information about who took the message. Oh, yeah, she must have thought she had her bases covered. Instead" — his voice was grim — "she signed two death warrants, hers and Henny's. She was found in her living room shot approximately five times, blood everywhere. The place was ransacked. Her purse was gone. From the color and consistency of the bloodstains, the time of death is estimated at about nine o'clock. We'll know more after the autopsy. Henny arrived home a few minutes after ten. If she'd been home around nine thirty, I imagine her doorbell would have rung and she would have been gunned down without warning. Instead, the murderer had time to break in and make a search. The place is a mess. Of course, the search didn't yield anything. By this time the murderer's in a fury. The killer waited outside to ambush Henny and probably planned to search her car and take her purse as well. For the first time, the breaks went against the killer. The first shot missed and Jeremiah started yelling. Henny reacted fast and disappeared into the darkness and Jeremiah kept on yelling. I got the buzz on the nine-one-one. Any breaking crime is immediately routed to me in a dual call. I flipped on the speaker phone and the yells damn near blew my ears off."

"Jeremiah thought fast." Max was admiring. "The murderer must have thought the cavalry had arrived."

"From out of nowhere." Annie imagined the night silence broken by the crack of a gun. Glass splintered and a man's shouts came out of nowhere. "There was nothing but Henny's cabin, no neighbors, nothing to worry about, and all of sudden a guy's yelling like crazy."

For an instant, satisfaction gleamed in Billy's eyes. "I like thinking about that instant and how the killer felt gut-whacked. All hell breaking loose and nothing to do but get out. I imagine" — his eyes narrowed — "that it's been a long night. Somewhere on the island, a killer's holding a reloaded gun, waiting."

Annie's eyes widened. "Waiting?"

Billy's face was grim. "Waiting for the police to come. The murderer doesn't know what happened to Henny or whether she has the information from Maggie. The killer has to worry that we've talked to Henny. I set the guard here just in case, but we'll get word out that she'd been interviewed and has no idea of the identity of her assailant. Right now, the killer's unsure. But" — he sounded regretful — "with every minute that passes, the murderer's breathing easier. If Henny knew anything, we'd have been there immediately. By morning, the murderer's going to decide there's no danger, either Maggie was bluffing or Henny never received the message."

Annie gestured down the hall. "But you're keeping an officer at Henny's door for now?"

"For at least twenty-four hours, though I

think the danger's past now. You and the volunteers can keep her company just to be on the safe side." He pushed up from the sofa, gave them a stern look. "Leave the rest to me."

11

Dorothy L jumped over Annie, jumped back.

Annie drew the cover over her head, mumbled, "Get your cat."

Dorothy L patted the sheet near Annie's cheek.

"Go away." The order was a triumph of hope over experience. Cats never did as they were told. It must be rule number one in the cat manual. Drowsily, Annie formulated the top ten rules:

1. Ignore commands. To acquiesce would encourage foolish independence among staff, i.e., two-legged creatures.
2. Pat a cheek with claws sheathed unless provoked.
3. Claws permitted to forestall removal from chosen site, such as lap, kitchen counter, computer key-

board, top of gerbil cage, sweater, coat, jacket, pillow, mantel with antique clock.

4. If bored, stare piercingly over staff's shoulder, prompting a frenzied check of locks on windows and doors. Always amusing.
5. If hungry, nip gently at an ankle, not piercing the skin, move purposefully toward food bowl.
6. To show fondness, bring in a dead mouse or trapped bird through cat door. Staff will obligingly react with emotional intensity.
7. When staff is deep in slumber, drape over head on pillow or undulate beneath covers and settle behind bent knees. Warm bodies are intended for your comfort.
8. Take no guff from dogs. Bite the dog's butt if instructions unheeded.
9. Pens, pencils, lipsticks, earrings, any small object can be utilized in kill-the-mouse game.
10. Indicate friendliness with an erect tail. Whipping tail reserved for high dungeon and should duly alert staff to the inadvisability of proceeding on unacceptable course.

This time Dorothy L's touch was closer to a swat than a pat, and there was the tiniest hint of claws. Graceful as a ballerina, Dorothy L again jumped back and forth over Annie's recumbent form.

Annie pushed the covers away, rolled over on an elbow, reluctantly opened one eye. A distant clang indicated Max busy downstairs in the kitchen. She stared into china blue eyes. "Why aren't you down there with your bosom buddy?"

Dorothy L's tail switched. Not a good sign.

"Okay, I'm up." Annie shivered, slipped into her slippers, and reached for a Chinese red silk robe emblazoned with a dragon, a gift from Laurel one Christmas. Max had muttered, perhaps not too tactfully, that he was sure his mother had a truly positive view of the Dragon Lady and there probably wasn't a *Rebecca of Sunnybrook Farm* robe. Annie traced the dragon's flickering tongue with a finger as she gave her hair a quick comb. Actually, she was rather flattered by Laurel's choice. She'd always been convinced she could be a sultry seductress given the right circumstances.

Dorothy L pattered down the stairs ahead of her, tail cheerfully upright in approval that recalcitrant staff was finally getting a move on. In the kitchen, sunlight spread like gold through the broad windows, yesterday's clouds and mist a memory.

Annie looked toward Dorothy L's eating bowls. "You forgot her dry food, though why she had to get me up, I don't know. After all, you're down here."

Max looked harried, a smear of mustard on one hand. "New recipe. Potato and bacon pancakes. Need to get these eggs poached. And it's time to add the butter to the hollandaise sauce."

Annie came up behind him, slipped her arms around him for a brief hug and a kiss on the back of his neck, but she knew when a man had his mind on other things, and settled on a stool at the kitchen island, after, of course, filling Dorothy L's blue pottery bowl with chicken-flavored nuggets.

She poured a mug of coffee, wrinkled her nose in appreciation at the chicory flavor, soaked up sun, and rejoiced. Billy Cameron was in charge. She and Max and Henny could leave the investigation to him. They had done good work. They had proved Everett Hathaway's death was no accident. They had saved Jeremiah Young from mistaken prosecution, which might well have resulted not only in his wrongful conviction but in his death. Maggie Knight's death resulted from her own actions. Thankfully, Henny had survived the danger in which Maggie had placed her.

Annie drank a blissful sip. There had been no phone calls this morning, so all must be well with Henny or they would have been informed. She and Max were once again in their sunny world where he could concentrate on . . .

Annie sipped the hot, strong coffee. Her lips curved in a smile. She had a wide stripe of honesty in her soul that prohibited her from envisioning Max concentrating on work. Okay, not everyone was called to labor unceasingly. Max worked when necessary, but he fervently believed in the pursuit of happiness, an elastic concept that embraced her (literally) and golf and good food and hospitality. In any event, Max could play golf today and she could putter happily around Death on Demand, where murder remained on the shelves and the books celebrated good hearts that believed in a just world. She'd unpack the latest by Lisa Lutz, Dana Stabenow, Hannah Dennison, Kate Carlisle, Ed Gorman, and Steven F. Havill.

Hurried steps sounded on the back verandah, a brisk knock, and the door swung in. Marian Kenyon, wiry black curls tangled, gamin face drooping with fatigue, peered at them. "Knew you two would be up with the earthworms or whoever crawls out at this hideous hour of the morning." Her nose wrinkled. "Something smells awfully good. Of course some of us worked until the wee hours and took a snooze on the ratty sofa in the *Gazette* break room. Yeah. Break room. Break your heart, break your back, break your — Don't want to be indelicate." She drooped against the door frame in an effort to appear pitiful. She did have a woebegone appearance, still wearing last night's baggy flannel shirt and jeans. At some point she'd traded house slippers for worn leather loafers.

Max reached for another plate. "Breakfast is ready. Take a seat, Marian."

Annie and Marian settled at the white wooden table and Max brought their plates.

Marian ate a scoop of bacon-potato pancake and hollandaise-topped poached egg. She gave a sigh of contentment. "I was looking for a magic potion and this is the next best thing. Now" — she continued to eat, but her bright, dark eyes looked at them in turn — "I'll quid if you guys will quo pro."

Annie finished a delectable mouthful. "We're not looking for information now that Billy's taken over. We'll read the *Gazette* for the latest." How lovely to be free of pressure to rescue Jeremiah.

Marian's dark brows knitted. "Henny promised to fill me in on what you folks did yesterday, but the police guard at the hospital wouldn't even ask her if I could come in. Come on, guys, ante up."

Max looked at Annie. "We can give the stuff to Marian. She won't quote us. I'll get a printout."

When Max returned with the sheets, Marian just managed not to snatch them. Breakfast forgotten, she scanned the summary. "Wow. You got the goods, all right. Now, here's my skinny. Sergeant Harrison found the front door open at Maggie Knight's house. When she didn't rouse anybody, she stepped inside. Maggie was lying on her living room floor. She was shot approximately five times, including, after she fell, a contact wound to the temple. The killer wasn't taking any chances. The house is one of four on a quiet side street. One next-door neighbor was having dinner out, didn't arrive home until after the discovery. On the other side of the house, the neighbor thought she heard a car backfiring about ten minutes after nine. Knight's house was ransacked, her purse taken. I talked to a couple of neighbors. They said she kept to herself, pleasant enough, not friendly." Marian poked a fork in the remnants of the pancake. "Her dog died a few months ago. She used to walk the dog morning and night. A neighbor said she was nuts about Bitty Boo, a corgi. Everybody loves somebody." Her voice was soft.

Annie pictured a lonely woman and a beloved dog.

Marian was brisk, once more the reporter with a flip lip and attitude. "Billy's got a presser set at ten A.M. You can come —"

Annie held up both hands. "I have a date at a certain bookstore."

Max began to clear the plates. "There's a golf course calling me."

Laurel turned from arranging a bouquet of sunflowers. The gold double flowers looked like huge chrysanthemums. "Dear Annie. How lovely for you to come. I was just telling Henny and Emma that I always think of you" — she trilled the pronoun — "when I see a sunflower."

Annie closed the hospital door and looked first at Henny, who appeared relaxed and comfortable, silvered dark hair freshly brushed, in a quilted pink jacket.

Emma Clyde's sapphire blue eyes glinted as she stared at the flowers. "If you're going to be besotted with flowers, why not pick gardenias or roses? Sunflowers are tall and scraggly with petals that look like spokes around a fat black button."

Laurel, elegant in a crepe de chine blouse with loose sleeves and blue silk slacks, gave one stalk a gentle pet as if to say, *Ignore uncouth comments,* and beamed at her daughter-in-law. "Dear Annie always seeks brightness just as sunflowers stretch" — she drew out the verb — "to the sun." Her smile was kindly. "Phototropism," she murmured.

Emma rolled her eyes. "Thanks for the elucidation. Wouldn't have had a clue otherwise."

Annie moved to the bed to give Henny a hug.

Although still pale, Henny looked well rested and her dark eyes were bright. She glanced up at the TV, the sound muted. She smiled and gestured at the news alert scrolling at the bottom of the screen: Broward's Rock police announce handyman cleared in murder of volunteer. Investigation reopened.

Laurel set the vase on the windowsill. "Watch," she said complacently.

Annie had no intention of watching flowers presumably seek sunlight. She lifted a book bag, smiled at Henny. "I brought some treasures for you, some new, some old." She knew Henny had read several of the titles, but some books never lost their charm, especially Sarah Caudwell's ribald and clever Lincoln's Inn mysteries. The books were guaranteed to elicit a laugh a page.

Henny was pulling out the gifts when the cell lying on the bedside table rang. She looked up. "Annie, will you answer, say I'm resting? I'd rather not talk right now. Lots of lovely calls, but I don't want to go over and over last night." There was a flash of remembered fear.

Annie picked up the cell. "Hello . . . She's resting right now. This is Annie Darling —" Annie's face furrowed. "Arrested? But why? . . . Of course we'll help. Yes. I understand. I'll tell Henny." She clicked off the cell, looked at Henny. "That was Jeremiah's aunt. Jeremiah's been arrested."

Annie tapped Max's number. Was he already on the course with his phone turned off? The vibration would alert him. When he saw the call was from her, he would answer.

Four rings. He spoke in the hushed tones of a man on a green. "Jake's getting ready to putt." Only open heart surgery would be treated more reverentially.

"I'll talk." Annie drove with one hand, held the phone to her ear. "I'm on my way to Billy's press conference." It was a few minutes before ten. "Jeremiah's aunt called Henny. Jeremiah's been arrested. I told her we'd help. They picked him up about half an hour ago."

"Arrested? That's crazy. Find out what you can." He spoke normally. "I'll get in touch with Handler Jones." The Savannah lawyer was magic with juries. He was a youthful mid-forties with piercing blue eyes, chestnut hair lightly threaded with silver, and a matinee idol's good looks, broad forehead, strong nose, expressive mouth, firm chin.

Several cars blazoned with the logos of mainland TV stations took all the near parking spots at the police station. Cameramen and perfectly coiffed and accoutered reporters clustered at the foot of the steps.

Annie parked across the street and hurried to join a growing throng. She recognized a number of faces from town hall as well as several businessmen. She wriggled closer to the front. Marian Kenyon was on the other side of the walk, Leica in hand. She saw Annie, mouthed, "Something's up. Nobody's talking." Annie leaned toward a TV reporter with long blond hair, a sea green silk suit, and pearl choker. "Excuse me. What's going on?"

The woman checked out Annie's pink cashmere sweater set, stylish jeans, and ankle boots, and her gaze became a tad less glacial. "Special announcement to be made regarding the murder of the volunteer —" She broke off as the door opened.

Mayor Cosgrove strutted out the door, resplendent in a very expensive black pinstripe suit, which minimized his pouter pigeon shape. He was joined by Lewis Farrell, whose ill-fitting green jacket emphasized his stooped shoulders. Farrell had served as the mayor's campaign manager in the fall election. Lou Pirelli was last through the door. He stood stiffly, his face folded in tight lines.

Annie's eyes narrowed. Farrell's reddish face flushed with excitement. Why was he with the mayor? He had recently lost a race for the school board, which Annie had considered a triumph of voter intelligence. He ran a local plumbing and heating company and, surprise, was the contractor chosen for several town projects.

Most disturbing was the glum misery in Lou's face.

She craned to see. Where was Billy? Maybe he'd decided to let the mayor soak up the attention while he worked on a triple murder case.

Mayor Cosgrove cleared his throat, his porcine face pleased and satisfied. "As Mayor of Broward's Rock, it is my solemn duty to make sure that the laws are upheld and that our citizenry is safe." He looked proudly toward the cameras. "To achieve this essential goal of public safety, I am personally" — great emphasis — "taking charge of the investigation into the brutal murder of an island volunteer at Better Tomorrow, which offers help and hope for our less fortunate citizens. I have relieved Chief of Police Billy Cameron of his duties. I have suspended him, pending review by the town council, for his refusal to properly administer the department and incarcerate a felon who poses a continuing threat to island residents."

Annie pushed past the blonde TV reporter. She glared at Cosgrove. "Chief Cameron discovered that the man sought by the police was innocent."

The reporter swung toward Annie, mic outthrust. "For our viewers, you are?"

"Annie Darling. I know all about this investigation. The mayor —"

"What's your standing in this matter?"

"I'm also a volunteer at Better Tomorrow. I talked to the murder victim —"

The mayor boomed. "This is an official news conference. Interference will require removal by authorities. If necessary, I will summon officers to restore order."

Annie almost replied with a blistering attack, but if Cosgrove turned to Lou, ordered him to take her into custody for disturbing the peace, Lou would have no choice. She could create a scene, but it was more important to find out what had happened.

"Aren't press conferences open to the public?" Marian Kenyon's voice was dulcet.

The mayor's face flushed. "Upon completion of my statement to the press, I will entertain questions from accredited news correspondents." The mayor smoothed back a strand of thin hair, assumed a magisterial haughtiness. "If I may recount for you" — he looked at the TV reporters — "the sordid events that occurred Monday afternoon. Gretchen Burkholt, a fine example of the generosity of our community, was on duty at Better Tomorrow. However" — his voice dropped, took on a mournful tone — "in two recorded phone conversations, Gretchen Burkholt expressed fear" — vibrato — "of Jeremiah Young, an ex-convict employed at Better Tomorrow as a handyman. In fact, she went so far as to proclaim that she did not feel 'safe' and asked another volunteer to join her. That woman arrived too late to protect Mrs. Burkholt from an attack by Young. Proof exists: The murder weapon — an axe — bore Young's fingerprints, her purse was taken, and Young fled, hoping to escape arrest."

Marian Kenyon stepped forward, lifted her husky voice so that everyone could hear. "Last night Chief Cameron announced that Jeremiah Young was no longer a suspect, that the murder Tuesday evening of Margaret Knight and an attack on Henrietta Brawley, a Better Tomorrow board member, had been linked to the Burkholt crime, and Jeremiah Young had an iron-clad alibi for both the Knight murder and the Brawley attack."

"Spurious thinking." Cosgrove spit the words as angrily as a hissing goose. "Cooler heads have prevailed this morning. I am in charge now. As capable investigators well know, criminals follow a pattern. Since the *Gazette*'s sole reporter" — disdain dripped from his voice — "has raised the point of other crimes, I shall take this opportunity to outline the case as the facts have been presented to Circuit Solicitor Brice Posey."

Annie felt grim. Brice Posey was as pompous as the mayor and equally gifted at seizing on a muddled interpretation of facts.

Moreover, he had clashed before with Billy Cameron and would enjoy seeing Billy fired.

The mayor lifted his round chin. "Here are the facts. Monday afternoon Gretchen Burkholt said she was afraid of Jeremiah Young, an ex-convict. Shortly thereafter, another volunteer found her bludgeoned to death by an axe, which bore Young's fingerprints. Her purse was missing and Young had fled. As experienced investigators understand, criminals follow a pattern. Tuesday evening Maggie Knight was shot to death at her home and her purse" — great emphasis — "was taken. Further, shots were apparently fired at the home of island resident Henny Brawley. Jeremiah Young was found at the scene of the last attack. In an effort to appear innocent, Mr. Young claimed that he had been marooned on a hammock and that his shouts and a call to nine-one-one drove away Mrs. Brawley's attacker. Chief Cameron believed the felon's story. However, my investigation reached the reasonable conclusion that Young's story was fabricated, that he shot Mrs. Knight in the course of a robbery at her home and then ambushed the second victim, but" — he spaced the words triumphantly — "when she eluded him and disappeared into the woods, he instead concocted a story to explain away his presence."

Marian said sharply, "The police rescued Young from a hammock a hundred yards out in the marsh."

The mayor was condescending. "Young appeared to be marooned. That was essential to the success of his claims." Cosgrove waved a soft, pink hand. "Earlier in the evening, some miscreant may have brought him ashore, likely in return for payment. That person, of course, will not come forward as there would be prosecution for aiding a fugitive."

"How did Young summon a 'miscreant'? Smoke signals?" Marian's tone was scathing. "His cell phone was monitored."

"The pickup may have been arranged before he arrived on the hammock. In fact," the mayor waxed ever more confident, "it may develop that he was able to go to and from the hammock in a rubber raft. He committed the crimes, then decided after the second victim's escape to portray himself as a hero. He returned to the hammock, called nine-one-one, and set the raft adrift. The tide carried it out. Since he clearly planned ahead, he may have punctured the craft. By the time it reached the Sound, the raft took on water and sank, never to be found."

Annie's mouth opened, then closed. The mayor's thesis could be as punctured as his mythical raft, but attacking him would achieve nothing. Handler Jones as Jeremiah's lawyer would have many facts at his disposal, including Henny's testimony that she took Jeremiah to the hammock Tuesday morning and left him without any means of reaching shore. Of course, Cosgrove would then dwell on his equally mythical "miscreant," but for now, Jeremiah's arrest was likely to stand until and unless the murderer was revealed.

Annie felt a wave of panic. With the mayor in charge, no one would seek a murderer who moved silently in the night, leaving no trace.

Marian's gamin face scrunched in apparent innocent inquiry. "Mayor, please explain the connection between the Burkholt and Knight murders and the presumed accidental drowning of Everett Hathaway on" — she pretended to look at her notes — "December thirtieth."

The mayor's heavy features folded into a frown that gave him the look of an irritable bulldog. "There is no connection. Mr. Hathaway drowned in an unfortunate accident. There has been an effort to create a link between his death and completely unrelated crimes."

Marian's tone was innocent. "Mrs. Knight was the housekeeper at the Hathaway house."

"Mrs. Knight's employment is immaterial. Her house was searched, obviously for valuables, and her purse taken."

Marian continued pleasantly. "Monday at Better Tomorrow Mrs. Burkholt discovered an index card in the pocket of Everett Hathaway's donated jacket. According to Mrs. Burkholt, the card revealed that Hathaway was lured to his death in the bay. Mrs. Burkholt left word about the card with Mrs. Knight. Mrs. Burkholt was killed shortly thereafter. Mrs. Knight appeared to have knowledge of the person who took the message she had written down. Evidence therefore links the Burkholt and Knight homicides to Everett Hathaway's drowning."

Both of the mayor's plump pink hands fluttered as if shooing away a dragonfly. "There has been quite a bit of loose talk, but I can assure our citizenry" — he looked at the TV cameras — "that there is no foundation in fact for these conjectures. There is no proof that a card found in Mr. Hathaway's jacket posed a threat to anyone. Further, Mrs. Knight's connection is tenuous and again unproven, merely the imaginings of misguided individuals attempting to divert attention from Mr. Young. We deal in real evidence. Moreover, it is necessary only to charge Mr. Young with Mrs. Burkholt's murder where there is substantial physical evidence of his guilt. The circuit solicitor is drawing up charges. I am pleased to report that Mr. Young is now in custody and being held in Beaufort. I intend to make sure that the Broward's Rock Police Department properly functions, and with that end in view, I am appointing as temporary chief an island resident with a long involvement in civic affairs, Mr. Lewis Farrell. Mr. Farrell will monitor the investigation of the homicide cases, reporting directly to me. Now, if members of the press have questions . . ."

The mood in Henny's hospital room was in stark contrast to Annie's earlier visit. Anger and despair had replaced confidence and hope. Henny pushed aside a lunch tray, the meal untouched. "Jeremiah was on the hammock and there was no rubber raft." She gestured at the TV screen, silent but with the continuing Alert scroll at the bottom of the screen, now reading: Island mayor suspends police chief. Ex-convict arrested in island murders.

Annie felt entangled in a web of untruths

298

that should be easy to refute, but weren't. "We can't prove he didn't have a raft. How do you prove a negative?"

Emma's square face ridged in outrage. "The police rescued him."

Annie shook her head. "The mayor has an answer for everything."

"We heard the news conference." Henny moved restlessly. "I'm stuck here and we need to get busy."

Annie remembered the happy beginning to her day when she was certain that Billy Cameron understood what had happened and would find out the truth of Everett's last night. Instead, Jeremiah was in jail and there would be no investigation into Everett's death. She turned toward the bed. "Henny, I know it's hard, but try to remember everything about last night. The murderer was there, waiting for you. Did you see anything to give us a hint of who may have come? And how?"

Henny's dark eyes narrowed in thought. "Everything was just as always. It was very dark —"

Annie nodded. There were no lights on the narrow road that led to Henny's solitary house.

"— as I drove on the road. There's no room to park on the road. The woods come right up on both sides. When I turned into my drive" — she paused, seeking remembrance of the split instant when her headlights illuminated the open space around her house and near her garage and dock — "I would have seen a car. There's simply no place to hide one. It's dark enough under the house, but there's not room for a car between the pilings."

Henny's face furrowed. "It was the same at Better Tomorrow. Jeremiah didn't hear a car, yet someone came and killed Gretchen."

Annie recalled her sobering talk with Billy in the quiet hospital waiting room. "Last night Billy said no car was heard at Maggie's house, either."

Emma declaimed. "A bicycle. That's the only answer."

"We can find out who had access to a bicycle." Then Annie shrugged. "Who wouldn't be able to get a bike? Most people we know have bikes. That's not a good lead."

Emma was gruff. "Dismiss wild goose chases. Bikes are everywhere. Focus the mind." A pause clearly heralded a pronouncement. "Where were they" — emphasis — "last night?" Emma gave the sentence the flavor of a radio melodrama.

Three sets of eyes turned to Emma.

Always pleased to take center stage, Emma looked superlatively confident. "As Marigold Rembrandt always instructs Inspector Houlihan, pinpoint the suspects during the critical period."

If Annie had been Emma's hapless fictional inspector, she would long ago have dropped Marigold down the nearest black hole.

Emma was on a roll. "This morning Henny shared the information that she compiled with Annie and Max." The author's spiky hair, a bright mixture of white tipped by violet, nodded approvingly. "I knew at once it was time to heed Marigold's sage advice. Here is what we need to discover. When Maggie was killed and Henny ambushed, where were Everett's widow, Nicole Hathaway, and her lover, Doug Walker, nephew, Trey Hathaway, niece, Leslie Griffin, and her boyfriend, Steve Raymond, and Brad Milton?"

Laurel beamed at the author. "So cogent. So telling. So utterly essential. However" — Laurel touched a sunflower stalk as if for luck — "the difficulty" — her husky voice was thoughtful — "is that those with a motive to kill Everett Hathaway can in no way be compelled to speak to any of us."

"I'd make them talk if I wasn't trapped in

this bed." Henny was forceful.

Annie understood Henny's frustration, but even if Henny were able to confront those in the Hathaway house, she would be doomed to failure. As Laurel rightly pointed out, none of them had official standing. No one had to talk to them, but perhaps guile might succeed. Slowly Annie began to smile. "There's more than one way for the fox to get into the hen house." Quickly she described a plan. "So we can —"

There was a knock. The door opened and Billy Cameron walked in.

12

Cosgrove's an idiot, Billy." Emma's deep voice throbbed with condemnation.

Laurel's smile was encouraging. "We will do everything possible to help you. We'll hold a rally when the town council meets. Everyone will come."

Henny looked forlorn. "I feel responsible. If I hadn't taken Jeremiah out to the hammock —"

"If you hadn't taken Jeremiah to the hammock" — the suspended police chief's face was somber — "you wouldn't be alive now. That's why I'm here."

Annie was struck by the weariness evident in his broad face. He was Billy, big, brawny, and muscular, but Billy without his customary equanimity. Tight lines marked the corners of his eyes, bracketed his generous mouth. Instead of a jacket and slacks or a suit, his usual dress for work, he wore a navy pullover and jeans. His blue eyes had a lost

303

look. "I know you support me, but that isn't what matters at this point. There's a dangerous killer out there who will remove anyone seen as a threat. Right now Henny is safe. Jeremiah's arrest will reassure the killer that she doesn't know enough to be a danger. As for the rest of you" — he looked at Annie, Emma, and Laurel in turn — "don't even think of trying to investigate."

Annie felt a deep twist of disappointment. "Jeremiah's innocent!"

"I believe that's true. Right now he's in a tough spot, but there are too many holes in the case for it to get far. This morning I was out early. I got some interesting stuff before I got the call from the mayor. Everything I learned is in the file. If the case goes to trial, I'll testify. I can demolish Cosgrove's theory. He's persuaded the circuit solicitor that Jeremiah killed Mrs. Burkholt because she caught him stealing her purse and that the Knight murder was a homicide committed during a robbery and that the attack on Henny was part of a break-in at her cottage, a fugitive stealing purses for access to cash and credit cards." Billy's expression matched a tomcat viewing a canary. "Sometimes ordinary police work turns up a fact that can't be ignored. Last night about half an hour after shots were fired at Henny,

304

Gretchen Burkholt's Visa was used over the payphone at the Gas 'N' Go to order a sweater from L. L. Bean to be shipped to Jeremiah's address. Now, all the circuit solicitor has to do is prove how Jeremiah used that card when he was at that exact moment sitting in the front seat of a police cruiser."

"That won't stop Brice Posey." Annie's tone was bitter. "The mayor's already saying maybe someone picked Jeremiah up off the hammock in time for him to shoot Maggie. He'll say Jeremiah paid him off with a credit card."

"Somewhere along the line" — Billy was decided — "the prosecution has to bring up facts, not theories. Why would Jeremiah give the Burkholt credit card to anyone else if he committed murder to get it? He would have paid off somebody with cash taken from the purses. Moreover, who is this mythical somebody? Why would a conspirator order a sweater for Jeremiah? The killer was just a tad too clever. The prosecution can throw out theories all day. Where are the facts? There are plenty of facts, and they all prove Jeremiah's innocence. I'll testify that I was talking to Jeremiah and I heard shots. He wasn't holding a gun out to one side and firing. I know the difference between gunfire at four feet and gunfire at a hundred yards. The testimony will clear Jeremiah."

Emma's face corrugated in a tight frown. "Maybe. Maybe not. Conviction of the innocent isn't a rarity. Besides, how cold will the trail be if we have to wait weeks or months to see an investigation of Everett's drowning? What happens if the mayor succeeds in putting in a crony as police chief?"

Billy suddenly looked older, grimmer. "I don't know. But" — and his deep voice was steely — "you three" — and he looked again at Annie and Laurel and Emma — "keep out of it. No investigating."

There was a silence.

Annie saw Emma's sapphire blue eyes narrow.

Before Emma could attack, Annie spoke loudly. "Billy, just before you came, we all agreed that we have no official standing. There is no way we can question people about Everett's death."

After an instant's thought, Laurel's eyes widened. Her quick glance at her daughter-in-law was approving. She joined in, her smooth, husky voice tinged with sadness. "Annie puts everything so well. We have no way to question those connected to Everett about motives for his murder."

Emma spoke judiciously. "It is chastening

to admit that we are barred from pursuing facts regarding the deliberate capsizing of his kayak." A heavy sigh. "We shall work toward your restitution as chief of police. That is the ultimate solution."

Billy had the appearance of a man who had expected to battle hard for his position and instead finds himself victorious without a struggle. "Yeah." He sounded wary. "Do I have your sworn promise to back off?"

Annie sighed heavily. "Billy, we know when we're licked. None of us will approach anyone about Everett's murder."

He gave her a hard stare. "How about the Knight homicide and the attack on Henny?"

Annie spread her hands, palms up, assumed an air of reluctant acquiescence. "I think we all agree that both Maggie's death and the shots at Henny resulted from our questions yesterday about Everett's death. In fact, I think we found out as much as we could, and further investigation will require official inquiries."

Billy looked satisfied. "I'm glad you agree. I'll feel a lot better knowing that none of you will be at risk." He turned to the bed. "Don't worry about Jeremiah. I understand Max has hired Handler Jones. Even if the case comes to trial, Jones will get him off."

"If only I could walk." Henny sounded

despairing. "I can't do anything to help him."

Annie wondered if Billy was whistling "Dixie" in an effort to derail them from finding out what they could. He knew better than anyone that judges had their own biases and juries could be swayed. They could not take the chance that Jeremiah be tried. They had to do what they could, but they would be wily, mask their intentions, be careful not to alert the murderer that information was being gathered. Every word each of them had said to Billy was true . . . as far as it went. Annie maintained her appearance of forlorn resignation, a woman accepting the reality that she was precluded from actively investigating the circumstances of Everett's death.

Emma sat with her head lowered, redoubtable face creased in morose lines.

Laurel, her smooth golden hair perfectly coiffed, her aristocratic features sorrowful, reached for a sunflower from the vase, sped lightly across the floor. "Dear Billy, take a bit of sunshine with you to remind you that we are always loyal friends and true."

He looked down at her, his face softening. "Thanks, Laurel. You guys —" He broke off, pressed his lips together.

Annie knew that he wasn't confident of

the future for Jeremiah or for himself. But he wanted them to be safe.

"Well, thanks for the flower. Kind of big, isn't it? Anyway, things will come right." But his tone was hollow. He turned away, pulled the door to step into the hall.

The door closed behind him.

Laurel said gently, "What a dear, sweet lamb. So trusting."

Jeremiah was pale and unshaven, his dingy brown hair lank. He sat on the other side of the wired screen, hunched in a too-big orange jumpsuit. His voice was scarcely audible. "I don't have no money, Mr. Jones."

Max spoke up quickly. "Don't worry about money, Jeremiah. I've retained Handler to defend you."

Jeremiah lifted his gaze, his face uncertain. "You don't hardly know me."

"Henny Brawley is as near an aunt as either my wife or I will ever have. You saved Henny's life." Max spoke quietly, but there was no mistaking the emotion behind his words.

Jeremiah jammed his fingers together. "She helped me. I had to help her. Mister" — he turned toward the lawyer — "they're gonna ask for the death sentence, aren't they?" His eyes were huge and sick and scared. "I should of walked into that water when I heard the sirens. I wouldn't be here now. They couldn't hurt me any more."

Max's face was grim. "Nobody's going to hurt you here. We'll make sure of that. We'll let them know we'll be on them like a wild boar on a deer."

Handler Jones spoke quietly. "Don't be scared. We're with you, Jeremiah, all the way." The lawyer had an invincible aura, thick chestnut hair, chiseled features, a piercing gaze. He exuded power even when seated, immaculate in a dark gray Oxford suit, pale cream Hamilton dress shirt, navy tie dotted with yellow palmetto palms. His smooth tenor voice was confident. "This is a detention facility, not a prison. You are safe. Right now, you are being held as a person of interest. That gives me time before the arraignment to marshal the facts." He tapped a green folder. "Mrs. Brawley and Mr. and Mrs. Darling collected an impressive amount of information. Now let's talk about everything that's happened." He was encouraging, calm, reassuring.

Max listened and tried to remain impassive. He knew much of what Jeremiah recounted, but he realized for the first time the enormous fear that had gripped Jeremiah when he was alone on the hammock, isolated, marooned, and waiting. ". . . so bad now to think how glad I was when I heard Mrs. Brawley's car. It made me feel better to know she was coming home, and then the shots come. I almost couldn't breathe I was so scared, but I yelled and yelled."

Handler looked up from his notes on a legal pad. "You didn't hear a car before Mrs. Brawley arrived?"

Jeremiah shook his head. "Like I told Mr. Darling, I saw somebody on her steps, but there never was a car. I would of heard the motor."

"You shouted, called nine-one-one." Handler looked thoughtful. "There were two shots, then about three more. When did you think the shooter was gone?"

Jeremiah's face squeezed in thought. "I don't know. Just, there was shots and I made a lot of noise and then more shots and then pretty soon it was quiet. It took the police about ten minutes to come."

Handler reached into the folder, pulled out a map of the island. He spread it open. There were several Xs. He pointed at each in turn. "X number one — the Hathaway house; X number two — the bay where Everett drowned, which is around a headland from his home; X number three — the

311

Carstairs house where the lovers met; X number four — the cabin where Steve Raymond lives; X number five — the home of Maggie Knight; X number six — Henny Brawley's cabin on the marsh. Now" — the lawyer leaned back in his chair, clearly the master of his facts — "the Knight house on Barred Owl Road is inland a half mile from the Hathaway house, the Brawley cabin is on a narrow dirt road that dead ends at the marsh. A bike path connects Maggie Knight's street to Henny's road. About a mile and a half distance between the two."

Jeremiah listened, his eyes wide.

Handler looked satisfied. "The murderer could easily have traveled on a bike. That almost has to be the case since Jeremiah didn't hear a car. Max, find out who among the suspects had access to a bike."

Max replied quickly, "According to Henny, there's a shed with several bikes on the Hathaway property."

"Ah, yes, the Hathaway family." Handler looked toward Max. "In the report compiled by you and your wife and Mrs. Brawley, several facts stand out. All members of the Hathaway household departed in cars the evening Everett drowned. The Hathaway boat was not heard by the renter in the garage apartment. Brad Milton claims to have sold his boat. Steve Raymond doesn't have a boat." He looked at Max. "Does Nicole's lover have a boat?"

Max squinted in thought, then pulled out his cell. In a moment, "Hey, Doug, Max Darling. I'm looking for some help in a fishing tournament at the Haven next month. Do you have a boat? . . . Oh, sure. Makes sense this time of year. Yeah. Well, thanks." He clicked off. "His boat's down in Florida at his brother's house."

Just for an instant, Handler's face creased in a frown. "That's critical. We have to find out where the murderer obtained a boat. Max, see what you can come up with. On a positive note, an excellent source informed me — before the police chief was relieved of his command — that vital information was obtained this morning concerning the whereabouts of family members the night Everett drowned."

Max had no doubt that Billy Cameron was Handler Jones's source.

Handler continued, "Mrs. Hathaway claims she was at home, but we know she was at the Carstairs house waiting for Mr. Walker, who never arrived. Leslie Griffin says she followed Mrs. Hathaway and was watching the Carstairs house in hopes of getting photographs of Everett's wife and her lover. Leslie confirms that Mr. Walker didn't come. Trey Hathaway insists he was at his office, trying to straighten out a campaign that Everett had botched. We already knew from the inquiries you and Annie and Henny made yesterday that Doug Walker says he was home, Steve Raymond was at the cabin, and Brad Milton was at his office. No one has an alibi unless we think Leslie Griffin corroborates Nicole's claim. However, Leslie knew about the affair and could easily say she was watching the Carstairs place and instead have been en route to kill her uncle." Handler smiled at Jeremiah. "We've found out a great deal. We will find out more." Handler stood.

In a moment, Handler and Max walked down the corridor outside the visiting area. His face grave, Handler looked at Max. "We'll do what we can. Judge Brown is a tough old bird. Doesn't like ex-cons. Jeremiah'll be arraigned on first-degree murder unless we work a miracle."

Laurel added the tiniest dollop of Notorious behind each ear, smoothed her white cashmere sweater, gave a last check in the car visor mirror at perfectly shaped brows, Nordic blue eyes, gardenia-smooth skin with no recourse to cosmetic surgery, thank you. She added a touch of pale rose lip gloss, nodded approval, and slipped from the driver's seat.

Fog wreathed the live oaks, swirled above the gray water of the bay, obscured the tops of the pines behind her. She noted the disarray in the cabin yard, the splintery wood on the second step, a discolored foam cooler lying on its side on the porch. Through the thin walls, rock music blasted. Laurel pressed the bell, held it.

The door opened.

Her eyes widened in genuine appreciation. Mucho hombre. She was reminded fleetingly of a matador she'd once known well, the same languid grace and heavy-lidded gaze and full sensuous lips. Of course, she was merely admiring his muscular physique, apparent in a pullover sweater and tight jeans.

"Hello." Her husky voice was, she well knew, seductive. She beamed. "What a relief you are."

He was smiling in return and his gaze was equally admiring. "So how come I'm a relief?"

"You're young!" Her delight was evident. "The other houses had nothing to offer. I'm doing a survey for Island Hospitality." She spoke as if the nonexistent group would, of course, be familiar to him. "The hope is to discover what island residents do for pleasure on an ordinary week night. The playhouse? Eating out? Card games? Hot tubs? Movies? Of course, with Netflix, who ever goes to a movie now? In fact, I'll bet you and your girlfriend watch movies from Netflix all the time. But, I won't take too much of your time and I must make many more stops." She pulled a small notebook from her pocket, lifted a pen. "Please, if you don't mind, what were you" — her tone made the pronoun warm and intimate — "doing last night between" — she glanced at the pad — "nine and eleven P.M.?"

"Last night?" An odd look flickered across his face.

The fleeting expression came and went so quickly Laurel couldn't decipher its meaning.

"Last night." She spoke with cheer.

"Yeah. Well, I guess I was here and there." He jerked a thumb over his shoulder. "TV sucks most of the time, and I don't watch movies by myself. I guess I was restless. Anyway, I drove around, got home about eleven."

Laurel waggled her pencil. "The survey is especially interested in purchases. Pizza?

Beer? The Gas 'N' Go?" How would he respond if she asked if he'd used a dead woman's credit card to order a sweater?

"Nah. I didn't spend anything. Sorry."

"I'm surprised you didn't go see a girl-friend." She kept her tone playful.

His gaze was suddenly brooding. "That wasn't in the cards." A muscle ridged in his jaw.

The door closed.

Emma Clyde looked out at the bay, though fog limited visibility. The mystery writer sat in her maroon Rolls Royce, blunt fingers firm on the steering wheel, the motor of the luxury vehicle scarcely audible. It was her first glimpse of the choppy water where Everett Hathaway had drowned.

The view was indistinguishable from many other marshes and bays bordering the Sound, remarkable only because a man had been done to death as he sought to prove — or disprove — his wife's faithfulness.

Emma found damp air bracing. The front windows were down, though moisture was beginning to bead the fine leather interior. However, her chauffeur would hasten to dry the interior as soon as she returned home. For now, she took a deep breath. A fine afternoon for adventure. Marigold was especially fond of fog, rather like a Patricia Wentworth heroine in a London pea-souper. Faintly Emma heard the whack of hammers on wood. Brad Milton had not been in his office. Hopefully, he was at the Thornwall addition or the foreman could direct her to him.

She was in no hurry. Her head swiveled toward the Mediterranean mansion, which looked ghostly in the fog. No lights shone. Annie's confrontation yesterday with Nicole Hathaway had been fruitful. Nicole apparently feared that her lover had killed Everett. Or perhaps she was playing the innocent. Perhaps she was guilty and feared that Doug might suspect her. Perhaps she thought her best defense was to accuse him, thereby underlining her innocence.

As a writer, Emma played variations on that theme: Nicole killed Everett, Doug killed Everett, Nicole and Doug planned the crime together. The scene might have been a rehearsal to practice an apparent estrangement. A clever camouflage. She poked a hole in the reasoning. Conspirators when alone would not be likely to maintain a false position. More likely was the guilt of one or the other acting alone.

Emma turned the wheel and the majestic car glided, the superior suspension over-com-

318

ing the ruts. She stopped at one side of the Thornwall home, noted the small yellow open-air electric car tucked between two palmettos. The Rolls dwarfed the little vehicle. As she walked toward the construction crew, she easily picked out Brad Milton, tall and angular in a well-worn leather jacket, jeans tucked into brown leather work boots. Obviously in charge, he gestured to a man with a wheelbarrow.

Emma strode up to him. "Mr. Milton."

He turned, his Jack Palance face alert. His eyes scanned her, flicked to the Rolls. "Ma'am?" His voice was deep, his expression abruptly genial though his slate blue eyes were cold.

Emma summed him up, about as huggable as a grizzly but voraciously hungry for work. She thrust out a strong, stubby hand, saw him note the luster of her huge ruby ring and her ornate antique garnet gold bracelet, a trifle she'd picked up on her last visit to Harrods. "Emma Clyde. I live on Bayberry." She had his attention. Bayberry was one of the most exclusive and expensive roads on the island, home only to mansions. "I write mysteries."

His expression was blank.

She maintained a pleasant attitude. Clod. However, she wasn't selling books, though as a hangover from her early unknown days, she never passed up an opportunity to promote her titles. She added automatically, "The bestselling Marigold Rembrandt series. In fact, I'm here because of my current book. I have a few questions about contracting and I've tracked you down." Her smile was arch. "A good detective always gets her man." She was satisfied to see his broad mouth curl down in disdain. Being catalogued as a fool gave her an advantage. He would not see her as a threat. "And I am looking for a general contractor both for the book and for a project I have in mind. I overheard some ladies at bridge the other day, and they spoke very positively about you. Let me see, was it Ellen?" Her tone was vague. "Or could it have been Joan? Possibly Muriel. No matter. I'm hopeless with names. They go right in my head and out again. Now, where was I? Oh, yes, the new pool house. Could you come by around four o'clock a week from tomorrow? Three Bayberry. I chose the address when my house was built. It's three thousand square feet. I might have you add a mosaic surround to the pool —"

His eyes were alive with calculating the profit on a pool house mosaic paving.

"— with threes in red against an azure

background. Three," she confided, "is considered a lucky number by the Chinese. The word sounds similar to alive. Don't you think that's cunning?"

His expression was stolid. "Thursday a week. I'll be there." He reached in his pocket, pulled out a card. "It's got my office number as well as my cell."

Emma took the card, holding the edges between thumb and forefinger. "Now, while I have you here I'll steal just a moment more of your time. In my new book, I have a character who runs a construction company. I need to have a sense of what the owner does in an ordinary day. For example, please describe yesterday."

He rocked back on his heels. "I met a couple of crews at the office, got my foremen to take them out. I worked on two bids, attended a Rotary lunch. In the afternoon, I went to the lumber yard, picked up some shingles. Later, I checked on the work sites, got back to the office about six."

"And last night, were you home with your family, a well-earned rest?"

"No family." His voice was cold.

"Then the pleasures of a brew with convivial friends, perhaps?"

His bony face was unreadable. "I picked up a burger at Parotti's, took it to the office. I had some stuff to do. I got home about eleven."

"My" — her tone was admiring — "you work long hours." She widened her blue eyes. "What do you enjoy most in your job?"

He looked sardonic. "Stamping 'Paid in Full' on a bill."

The live oak trees appeared festooned with cobwebs as the fog thickened, suitable for a Charles Addams drawing. Annie stopped and parked a block from the Hathaway house. Stepping out of the snug car, she pulled her jacket close. When she reached the Hathaway drive, she paused and slipped behind a cluster of palmettos. Light seeped from around the edges of drawn drapes in the living room. She slipped in the shadows of pines until she reached the double garage. With a swift look to be sure she wasn't observed, she crossed to a roofed open-air shed.

Four bicycles were slotted into the steel stand, one eight-speed, the rest the usual upright bikes without cross bars common on island paths. She looked at each in turn, a scarlet eight-speed and three standard bikes, one green, one red, one yellow. The green and red bikes had baskets. The eight-speed was unadorned. The red bike had a flat front tire. The yellow bike's chain was loose. She felt foolish. She was hardly going to find a sign reading: Last ridden by a murderer. She was turning away when she noticed a clump of mud caked on the right pedal of the green bike. She knelt, delicately touched the mud on the pedal of the green bike. Still damp. Perhaps there wasn't a printed sign, but fresh mud indicated the green bike had been used within the last day or so. She squeezed the tires and found both of them firm.

If only Billy Cameron were chief. She could call and Billy could send a crime tech, check for matching tire indentations near the Knight house and at Henny's cabin.

Annie yanked her cell from her purse. It wasn't much, might not be useful at all, but she took a half dozen pictures of the green bike and one of the pedal. The cell would register the time the photos were taken.

She was thoughtful as she walked swiftly to the porch. Maybe that bike could be tied to one of the murder sites. At least it was only fog now, not rain, but if any tire prints existed at Better Tomorrow or Maggie's or Henny's, rain would wash them out sooner rather than later. Maybe tomorrow Handler Jones could send someone from the mainland with the equipment to make a search for tread prints.

On the porch, she took a deep breath. No more thoughts of bikes or tire prints. She pulled a notepad from her jacket, held a pen, and pushed the bell.

Light spilled onto the porch as Nicole Hathaway opened the door, her heart-shaped face sagging. She looked haggard, eyes bleary, skin blotched. A red cashmere sweater fit too snugly, emphasizing her full breasts. Matching red wool slacks appeared uncomfortably tight. Tiny silver bells decorated high-heeled black patent pumps. She lifted a hand to her throat when she saw Annie. With a look of panic, she started to close the door.

Quickly, Annie flashed a warm smile. "Nicole, I know you'll help out. I'm doing a survey for the League for Women's Protection. You remember how everyone was talking about it at the last Ladies of the Leaf meeting."

Nicole's face registered surprise, relief, and, to Annie's discomfiture, pathetic gratitude.

Annie maintained her bright smile. Nicole assumed that Annie was blandly ignoring their encounter on the Carstairs terrace. "The survey will only take a few minutes and it will be such a help to the league's planning." Without waiting for an invitation, Annie opened the screen door.

Nicole stepped back, gestured toward the living room.

Hurried steps sounded on the stairway. Leslie Griffin in a tan blouse, long brown and black plaid skirt, and ankle-high boots rushed into the hallway. "All hail the agency." She sounded aggrieved. "Got to hurry. Trey expects me to *work*. What a crock. I think I'll see if I can switch to a study hall."

"Annie, this is Leslie, Everett's niece."

Annie stood between Leslie and the door. "I'm Annie Darling. For the Women's Protection League. I'm glad I caught both you and Nicole. That will give me two women in one house for our survey." She sounded triumphant. "The objective is to ascertain whether women feel safe after dark on the island and one measure is their activities. We are focusing our research on last night. When we finish, we'll know exactly how most women on the island spent Tuesday evening and you can see" — her tone was portentous — "how important this will be. Leslie, since you are leaving, let's do you first." Annie flipped open her notebook. "Please describe your activities last night between the hours of nine and eleven P.M." Annie looked at her expectantly, pen poised to write.

"Last night?" After an instant's hesitation, Leslie laughed. "This'll show how statistics don't mean a thing. I once had a math class, the only one that ever made any sense to me, and I learned that statistics prove anything you want to prove. Believe me, I'm not afraid to go out at night, but I just so happened to be home last night. I was watching a soccer match in Brazil. Men in shorts. Doesn't get any better than that. Now I got to go." And she darted around Annie and out the door.

Annie turned toward Nicole, who looked after Leslie with a puzzled stare.

Another bright smile. "And you, Nicole?"

The widow turned her attention to Annie, though she glanced toward the door as the muted roar of the Mini Cooper sounded. "Actually, I was here last night. I don't have any plans now." There was a forlorn quality to her voice. "I was reading some magazines."

Annie was hearty. "I suppose it was nice to have Leslie's company."

"Leslie's company?" Nicole sounded blank. Then her lips twisted. "Oh, Leslie has her own suite. She never has anything to do with the rest of us."

Annie ostentatiously made several notes. She was profuse in her thanks. Her last glimpse of Nicole was of a woman deep in thought.

13

Max placed a golf ball on the indoor putting green. He assumed a putting stance, waggled the club head. He tapped and the ball rolled over undulations to the hole. His eyes widened in surprise. He'd scarcely been aware of the putt. His thoughts were running like a gerbil on a wheel, trying to find some avenue to help Jeremiah.

He hated to face the truth. He and Annie and Henny had pointed the way, but what was needed now was police authority to question and probe and discover. No matter how much more they might discover, Jeremiah's fate ultimately hinged on the Broward's Rock Police Department.

Maybe it was time to try a different tack.

Max left the ball in the cup, tossed the putter in his bag, and settled at his desk. After a moment's thought, he turned on the speaker phone and punched the number. "Hey, Charles, Max Darling here. I wondered when the next town council meeting is scheduled." He pictured Charles Farnsworth home from an afternoon of cards at the club, likely in his library with a book on birds. Charles was tall and loose-jointed and reminded Max of a blue heron.

Charles's precise voice was pleasant. "The second week in February."

Max frowned. "Is there a way to call a meeting to consider an emergency matter?"

"Billy Cameron?" Charles, of course, certainly was aware of Billy's suspension. "I told the mayor I felt his action was hasty. Unfortunately, we need a quorum to meet and three of our members are out of town. I'm afraid nothing can be done now, Max. Certainly the story in this afternoon's *Gazette* raises a number of questions."

Laurel shifted the armload of cinnamon-colored sunflowers with chocolate centers in their loose wrapping of pink tissue. The blooms were gorgeous, but the stalks were scratchy. She retrieved a key to the bookstore from her purse. Though she wasn't an employee, she was always willing to help out at Death on Demand if needed. She was sure Annie and Emma would be along soon. It would be interesting to know if any of the suspects had alibis for last night. Steve Raymond had readily admitted that he was out in his car. Was that an indication of innocence? Laurel rather hoped so. He was an appealing young man.

She turned on the lights and gazed happily about the bookstore. She took a deep breath, savoring the smell of books overlain with the delectable scent of coffee and a hint of wood smoke. She had never realized how much she would come to love both her charming, though rather earnest daughter-in-law, and the books that delighted her.

Tissue crinkled.

Laurel looked down as Agatha snaked a paw at the bunched paper. "Agatha, as always" — Laurel's throaty voice was warm — "you exhibit exquisite taste. But for a cat of your stature, that is only proper." Laurel bent, smoothed sleek fur. "The sunflower is a symbol of adoration and it is very appropriate that you should lay claim because everyone adores you."

Agatha rubbed her cheek against the tips of Laurel's fingers.

"Come now, we'll make a beautiful bouquet and wait for Annie and Emma."

The cat followed her down the aisle.

Laurel rested the half dozen sunflowers atop the coffee bar and darted into the storeroom. She returned with two vases, one a lovely cobalt pottery, the other an art deco square column in aluminum. She hummed as she pondered which vase to choose. Possibly the blue put the cinnamon color of the leaves to better advantage. She lifted the stalks and the phone rang. She noted caller ID as she answered. "Death on Demand, the finest mystery bookstore north of Delray Beach."

"Is Annie Darling there?" The man's tenor voice was hard edged.

Laurel raised an eyebrow. Obviously the caller knew Annie's voice. Once a young man had compared Laurel's voice to velvet at midnight. Her daughter-in-law always sounded so wholesome. Laurel heartily approved of wholesomeness — for Annie. "Annie's out just now. She is expected soon. May I take a message?"

But there was only emptiness on the line.

Laurel frowned. She replaced the receiver, picked it up, dialed. Annie didn't answer her cell. Laurel left a crisp message: "A man called from Walker Morrison Realty, asked for you, left no name. He sounded" — Laurel thought for an instant — "disagreeable."

The Rolls slowed as Emma glided to a stop behind a green Porsche parked near the garages of the Mediterranean mansion. Yesterday from the conversation Annie overheard between Doug Walker and Nicole Hathaway, Doug had made clear his lack of interest in meeting Nicole. So why was he here?

Emma parked and retrieved her cell phone. Her butler answered. "Miguel, I will have the connection open in the event that I need to call for help. Remain on the line. Thank you." Miguel was a treasure, never evincing surprise at her instructions, which sometimes were unusual. Recently she had sent him to Atlanta to make notes of surveillance cameras at a museum. He had returned with precise measurements as well as the make of the cameras.

Emma held the phone in her left hand as she walked across the terrace. As she approached the French windows, a door swung out. Doug Walker, his round face in a tight frown, stepped onto the tiles. He carried a chamois in a gloved hand.

"Hello, Doug." He had contacted her last year to be among local sponsors of a golf tournament. She had made a substantial donation.

He looked startled. "Emma."

Her gaze dropped to the chamois and conclusions clicked tight as lock tumblers.

"An interesting choice for a cleaning cloth. Were you removing fingerprints from a particular bedroom?"

He walked toward her, face taut, shoulders bunched.

Emma held up the phone. "I am connected to the police dispatcher. Stop where you are, Doug Walker."

He jolted to a stop, an odd figure for melodrama with his tight blond curls and smooth-shaven face and expensive cashmere pullover and gray dress slacks. "Turn that damn thing off."

Her crusty voice was untroubled. "When we finish."

"We are finished. Look, you can write mysteries, but don't try to put me in the middle of one. Did Annie Darling send you to spy on me? I know what's going on. I talked to the mayor. He told me all the lies about Everett are coming from Annie and that jerk she's married to. That's where the *Gazette* got all that stuff about Everett Hathaway being murdered. After I read that tripe, I called the bookstore. I'm going to tell her she better not mention my name to anybody if she knows what's good for her."

"It isn't 'stuff' in the *Gazette*." Obviously Marian Kenyon had used the report put together by Henny and Annie and Max for a story in this afternoon's *Gazette* and Doug Walker was making sure nobody could link him to an upstairs bedroom tryst with Nicole. "Marian's a careful reporter." Careful and clever. Emma was sure that Marian would be alert to slander or libel, but using the old reliable *confidential sources,* it would be easy to suggest Everett Hathaway had been lured to his death and to include hints about the note in his jacket pocket.

"Nobody's proved anything. And Annie Darling better keep her mouth shut."

Emma raised an eyebrow, held up the phone. "Are you threatening Annie?"

He glared. "With libel. The mayor says there's no proof a note to Everett ever existed."

Emma spoke quietly. "The woman who found the note was battered to death."

"They got the guy who did it. He stole her purse." Doug's tone was triumphant. "So there's no scandal, nothing to any of that."

"But you came here with a chamois." Emma was derisive. "And you insist there's no scandal?"

His face twisted in a smile. He waggled the supple leather. "No scandal at all, Emma." His smile was arrogant and satisfied as he moved past her, strode to the elegant car.

Hathaway Advertising occupied a Victorian house two blocks from Main Street. Turreted and gabled, it had recently been painted and the white shone even on a foggy afternoon. The heavy oak door boasted two inset art glass panels, a listening stag on a mountainside and a peacock flaunting a magnificent train of iridescent blue green plumage, as well as a collectible bronze doorknob and an ornate bronze letter drop.

Annie opened the door and stepped into a hallway with a grandfather clock, an elegant ormolu mirror above a teak table, and a collection of silver pitchers in a breakfront. A distant silver bell chimed. Quick footsteps sounded.

A petite middle-aged woman with shingled gray hair and wire-rim glasses smiled in welcome. "Hi, Annie." Dolores Wright was a volunteer at Better Tomorrow on the weekends. "What can I do for you?"

"I'm here for the Animal Welfare League today. Do you think I could see Trey Hathaway? I'm on the hunt for a missing dog." Annie didn't know Trey Hathaway. He hadn't been back on the island long. She checked her image in the mirror, dusty blond hair, open and frank face, cream silk blouse, pearl necklace, and long gray skirt. Did she look respectable or what? "A cocker spaniel named Betsy. Someone thought they saw him in the area and I wanted to check and see if he might have seen her."

"Let me check. Everything's a little hectic since Everett died. Trey's taking care of a bunch of estate stuff for Nicole." Dolores's low heels tapped on the heart pine flooring as she hurried down the hall.

In a moment, she returned. "He'll see you." She looked puzzled, almost spoke, then said simply, "The last door on the left."

The door was ajar. Annie pushed the panel and stepped inside.

Trey Hathaway stood behind his desk, arms folded. He looked like a successful young professional in a blue blazer, sandy hair trimmed short, brown eyes alert. His distinctive Hathaway face — large forehead, high-bridged nose, high cheekbones, and pointed chin — was cold and unsmiling.

The smile on Annie's face slipped away.

"Missing cocker?" His tone was sardonic.

Annie felt kinship with a boater who hears the roar of falls ahead. But she might as well try. "Last night someone thought they saw you on a block where an elderly dog escaped from her pen. About nine o'clock."

"What block would that be?

The current was running fast. Disaster loomed. "Barred Owl Road."

His brown eyes glittered. "Good try. But I wasn't on Maggie Knight's street last night." He came around the desk, strode close to Annie, glared down. "Leslie told me all about the lady who came Tuesday and claimed someone knocked over Everett's kayak. And a little while ago you showed up there with a survey. You didn't get much, did you? Leslie and Nicole were home. And now this preposterous" — he jerked his thumb toward the *Gazette* lying spread out on his desk — "stuff about Maggie Knight seeing somebody take a message from our hall table. The story makes it sound like the arrest of the ex-con might be a mistake. I can tell you who's making a mistake and that's anyone who says somebody killed Everett."

Annie looked at him curiously. "It doesn't bother you that your uncle was murdered?"

For an instant uncertainty flickered in his eyes, then his face stiffened. "It bothers me that people are making stuff up."

Annie shrugged. "The woman killed at Better Tomorrow wasn't making up the index card in Everett's pocket. I know about that. I talked to her just a little while before

337

she was killed. She described that card to me."

He wasn't impressed. "So there was a card. Nobody knows what was in it."

"The card informed Everett that Nicole and Doug were meeting at the Carstairs house. It talked about a 'scandal' and 'naming names.' " Annie knew she was expanding on Gretchen's words, but she had no doubt that she was correct.

He made a dismissive gesture. "I don't care about an index card. The cops have arrested the guy who killed that woman."

Annie lifted her chin. "Since you are certain that Jeremiah Young is guilty of two murders, I'm sure you won't mind saying where you were last night and the night your uncle died."

"Why not? Not that it's any of your business. I work for a living. I was here both nights."

She turned to leave, then paused, said quickly, "You knew about Nicole and Doug."

He shrugged. "I didn't personally see them there."

Annie was certain that Leslie had delighted in telling him. Trey knew about Nicole and Doug. "You could have written the message on the index card, telling Everett to take a kayak to the bay."

Abruptly, he glanced at his watch. "I've got a meeting. You can show yourself out."

As she stepped into the hall, he added sardonically, "Good luck finding that cocker."

Emma looked up at the watercolors over the mantel. "I know that third book, but I can't quite place it."

Annie was well aware that if the artist had depicted another main character, both Emmy and Henny would have identified the title at once. When the answers were revealed, she might face bitter complaints. But fair was fair. Henny and Emma were contest hogs. Almost always one of them solved the watercolors before any other readers. Neither had paid for a cup of coffee in a very long time.

With a dreamy look, Laurel sipped her coffee, a concoction possibly unique in the annals of indulgence. "The grated maraschino cherries and chunks of Perugia chocolate make all the difference."

Annie drew the line at fruit floating in coffee.

Emma stood with her back to the fire, mug firmly grasped. She looked like an analytical bulldog, square face squeezed in thought. "As Marigold brilliantly points out, 'Murderers reveal themselves by apparently meaningless facts. Finally, when the strands are gathered, the hangman's noose will dangle from the scaffold.' " Blue eyes steely, she gazed at Annie, then Laurel.

Annie would have been more impressed, but the quote was verbatim from the finale of Emma's most recent book, *The Case of the Daring Dandelion.*

Confident that she'd mesmerized her audience, Emma proceeded to pontificate. "Of course, we must always, as Marigold —"

Annie tried hard to maintain an attitude of intense interest even though she found Marigold Rembrandt about as charming as House in the TV series that was her least favorite.

"— always emphasizes, remember that murderers lie — and so do the innocent!" Her tone was triumphant.

Her smile angelic, Laurel murmured, *"The Case of the Malingering Malamute."*

Emma's glance at Laurel was sharp.

Laurel's classically beautiful face was unmarred by even a hint of sarcasm. Indeed, her gaze was one of utter admiration.

Mollified, Emma ticked off, "No alibis Tuesday night for Steve Raymond, Brad

Milton, Nicole Hathaway, Leslie Griffin, Doug Walker, or Trey Hathaway."

"Right." Annie felt glum. Emma could put the best face possible on the conclusion, but as a matter of fact, their efforts had put them no nearer a solution to the murder of Maggie Knight and the attack on Henny.

Laurel clapped her hands together. "However, Annie's visit to the Hathaway house resulted in a possibly critical piece of information. A chunk of damp mud indicated the green bike had been recently ridden."

Annie appreciated Laurel's effort to find a ray of sunshine in a bleak landscape. But a chunk of mud didn't name the rider.

Laurel reached out to pat Annie's hand, her blue eyes empathetic. "Never despair, my dear. Possibly tomorrow something may occur. Tonight we'll think sunflower thoughts."

Emma reached for the huge mink coat she'd tossed carelessly over a chair. "Laurel has the right idea. Tomorrow one of us may have a brilliant insight."

Max added a log to the fire in the library. Flames danced.

Annie watched with pleasure. As he knelt, lean and muscular in navy flannel pajamas, he was Joe Hardy handsome, blond, blue-eyed, strong featured. And hers. Even though this particular night was filled with worry, his presence made everything better.

He turned, looked at her, smiled. "We'll make something happen tomorrow."

She smiled in return. "That's what Laurel said. Sort of." Annie's tone was dry. "Although I don't know that 'sunflower thoughts' will be helpful."

"Sunflower thoughts," Max mused. "As in, pluck petals and murmur, 'He did it, she did it, he —"

The phone rang.

Annie reached for the mobile. As always she noted the caller ID: Nicole Hathaway. An eyebrow rose. She pointed at the desk. "Catch the extension."

She waited until Max held the receiver. "Hello."

"Annie?" Nicole's voice was soft.

"Yes." She made her tone warm and welcoming.

"This is Nicole."

Annie strained to hear.

"I saw the story in this afternoon's *Gazette.*" There was a quiver of shock in the whispered words.

The newspaper lay on the coffee table in front of the sofa. Most readers would come away from Marian's story convinced there was an ongoing mystery behind the murders of Gretchen Burkholt and Maggie Knight, and grave suspicion about Everett Hathaway's death. Annie was sure that His Honor the Mayor was not pleased.

"Trey said you weren't really doing a survey. He said you were trying to find out where all of us were when Maggie was shot. Maggie shot . . . It's so dreadful. I can't think about Maggie without feeling sick. And she was shot last night . . . I thought you should know" — she took a quick breath — "Leslie wasn't here last night. Wait. I think I hear —"

Silence.

Max cupped his hand over the receiver. "Annie, grab your cell. We might need to call nine-one —"

A relieved sigh came through the night. "It's okay. Leslie's gone. I hear her car when it leaves. Last night I never heard her car" — Nicole sounded puzzled — "but about a quarter to nine Leslie's dog barked. Crystal scratches the door when she wants to go out. If nobody comes, she barks. I heard Crystal and I thought it was funny, because if she was in Leslie's room, Leslie should let her out. Sometimes Leslie forgets and shuts her in the room and someone else has to go get her. She barked again. I went out into the hall and sure enough Leslie's door was closed. I knocked and Crystal really barked. I opened the door. Leslie wasn't there. I went downstairs to let Crystal out. Leslie wasn't anywhere. It was so odd. Her car was in the drive yet I couldn't find her in the house. It wasn't" — her voice dropped to a whisper — "a good night for walking. And she never walks . . . Oh, I don't know what I'm thinking. I'm so confused. Trey says it's that handyman. That has to be right. They've arrested him."

The connection ended.

There was no trace of the pale winter sun this morning. Instead, fog hung thick in the live oaks, made a dense cloud at the foot of their garden, hiding the pond. Max held her car door open. He spoke as if they hadn't wrangled at breakfast over what to do. "Catching Leslie in a lie about Tuesday night may be as important as you think. But let's sit on it for now. The arraignment's tomorrow afternoon. Let me see if I can round up a quorum of the town council and set up a Skype call. If I can get the votes, Billy will be back on the job. We need him to follow up on Leslie."

Annie almost retorted that the chances of

seeing Billy reinstated seemed slimmer than Laurel taking vows of — She broke off. Some comparisons were better left not only unvoiced but unthought. Max was remarkably intuitive.

"That would be great." She wondered if she sounded as hollow as she felt.

"Then you'll be at the store." He sounded relieved.

Annie offered a cheery smile. "That's where I work."

"Annie —"

She spoke quietly. "I am going to the store." She tapped the folder in her left hand. "I am going to look over everything again. Maybe something will come to me. Maybe I'll tear petals off of sunflowers."

He looked alarmed.

"I wouldn't," she reassured him. The majestic flowers were living creatures to Laurel.

Annie spooned fresh-minced chicken into Agatha's bowl and looked at the magnificent bouquet of sunflowers in the blue vase near the fireplace. Laurel had suggested sunflower thoughts. There was nothing sunny about envisioning a brash teenager as a killer. But Leslie was almost-eighteen-going-on-thirty-five. She wasn't too young to make dreadful decisions. Annie's thoughts swung back to the green bicycle and the fresh clump of mud on the pedal.

With Agatha eating and purring, Annie poured a cappuccino. She reached for the folder she'd brought from home.

The shocking creak of rusted hinges marked the opening of the front door. Annie had loved the *Inner Sanctum* sound when first installed, but on a foggy January morning, the hollow rasping was a little too scary for pleasure.

However, it would be lovely if an actual customer had arrived, rare as that was in January. Annie put down her mug and started up the central aisle.

Hyla Harrison strode toward Annie. Instead of her khaki uniform, she wore a plaid flannel shirt, brown corduroy slacks, and brown leather loafers. Her dark red hair was drawn back in a tight bun. Her pale face was intense. Hyla always appeared intense. Hyla dropped into the store once or twice a week, always interested in police procedurals. Annie had a sheaf of critiques written in Hyla's small, tight handwriting. Often the comments were scathing. Hyla had no tolerance for inaccuracies.

She stopped in front of Annie. "I'm off

duty." It was a grim, purposeful announcement.

Annie knew this wasn't the moment to mention the new Liam Campbell mystery though Dana Stabenow was one of Hyla's favorite authors. Instead, she waited with a sense that something big was happening.

There was a pulse of uncertainty and anguish in Hyla's face, then she said gruffly, "I've always done everything by the book." She gazed at the bookshelves. "Not those kind of books."

Annie understood that no slight was intended. "I know."

"That plumber's shut us down. The case is finished, he said." Her words were clipped, her eyes hot with anger. "That doesn't mean I couldn't study the files. The chief —"

She meant Billy Cameron.

"— had decided Hathaway was a homicide, that somebody intercepted him in a boat, dumped him out of the kayak. The chief was going to wring out the family." She gave a decided nod. "That's always the place to start. There's more money and more murder inside a family than out. The family has a boat, but apparently it didn't go out that night. But" — she leaned forward — "we got a call Saturday morning, an abandoned boat on Treasure Creek. A bird-watcher found it. Could've been there for weeks otherwise."

Annie waited, scarcely daring to breathe.

"I went out." Hyla drew a sheet of paper from her pocket, unfolded it, and handed it to Annie. "That creek threads off a marsh around a headland from the bay where Everett drowned. Isolated spot. No houses. Boat belonged to Gordon Sanders. It turned out they always left the keys in it. Somebody took the boat Friday night. They don't know when. In fact they didn't know it was gone until I got the registration number and called them. So the boat was stolen. I looked it over pretty carefully. Nothing trashed, no whisky bottles, no food wrappers. That didn't look like kids out on a joy ride. And who steals a boat on a cold winter night? I had my evidence kit with me. I decided to check the wheel for prints." Hyla's pale green eyes glittered. "Clean as a polished mirror. That gave me a funny feeling. How come? It was cold that night. You'd think anybody would have worn gloves. But what if a glove got wet?"

Annie was puzzled. "Wet?"

Hyla's pale eyes gleamed. "Boat lights pick up the kayaker. Maybe there's a call. Maybe not. Maybe the boat just slides up to the kayak and the driver leans out with a gaff, pokes. Hathaway flips out. Water splashes up. Hathaway's churning in the water. More splashes. The gaff's pulled back, but the glove's drenched. It's too cold to keep on a wet glove. Everett tries to reach the kayak. The gaff again. This time the hook pulls the kayak out of his reach. Pretty soon Hathaway's weakening. Time to get rid of the boat. But the thief takes off that wet glove and that's how prints got on the wheel and the wheel had to be polished. That's my take." Her eyes narrowed. "One other funny thing. After I didn't find prints on the wheel, I went over that boat real carefully. On the back starboard rail, I found a scrape that looked fresh. Speckles of green paint. I lifted them." She looked thoughtful. "I figured the thief had something stowed in the back and gashed the rail when hauling it out. There are no lights on Treasure Creek. It would've been dark as a cavern. But" — she sounded regretful — "the mark wasn't real noticeable. I took some pics, just in case. I also found some threads snagged on the railing. I figured somebody left in a hurry and a sweater or jacket got caught on the railing. I took the material into evidence, too. Anyway" — she took a deep breath — "I figure if it comes to it" — she was deliberately obscure — "that lawyer —"

Annie wasn't surprised that Hyla knew Handler Jones had been hired by Max to defend Jeremiah.

"— might want some testimony about a boat one of these days. I did some follow-up work this morning. The names are all in the file, the people the chief intended to check out, the widow and her lover, the nephew, the niece, her boyfriend, and Brad Milton. I called Mrs. Sanders, told her I needed to run some names by her, that we had some fingerprints from the boat theft and we needed to eliminate people who had been out with them. Turns out that Doug Walker had never been on the boat or, of course, Leslie Hathaway's boyfriend, Steve Raymond. However, Nicole Hathaway, Trey Hathaway, Leslie Griffin, and Brad Milton were familiar with the boat and could know that the Sanders never took out the keys. Of course, Nicole could have told Doug Walker and Leslie could have told Steve Raymond. So" — the thin taut woman turned her hands palms up — "I didn't prove anything except" — her jaw jutted — "any one of them might have taken the boat. That's all I know for now. Since the station's dead as a belly-up mackerel, I'm taking a few days off. Maybe things will get better." She swung about and marched toward the door, her shoulders stiff beneath the plaid wool shirt.

As the creak of rusty hinges signaled Hyla's departure, Annie walked slowly back to the coffee bar. She stepped behind the counter, poured out the cold cappuccino. She felt a flicker of excitement. Everything Hyla had discovered made it likely that the stolen boat had been used the night Everett drowned.

Annie retrieved the island directory from the back office. The Sanders house was within the island's gated community. There would be so little traffic on a late December night that nonresident cars would be noticeable. Moreover, she pictured the address. She knew that area. Residents put up their cars in three- and four-car garages. There wouldn't be any place to park that might not be noticed. How did the murderer get to the boat?

Green paint . . .

Annie's eyes widened. Maybe, just maybe . . . She hesitated, should she call Max, tell him? No, it wouldn't hurt to look first. Then there would be more to go on. Abruptly, Annie whirled, grabbed her jacket and purse, and, at the last minute, the folder with their point-by-point summary of what they knew, and hurried through the store. In the parking lot, she opened the driver's door. Four sunflowers with fuzzy-appearing leaves fluffed around a pale green center were propped in the passenger seat. As Annie slid behind the wheel, she smiled and reached out to touch the head of the nearest bloom.

Max read the text from town council member Roland Dubois somewhere in the Galapagos: *Hm nxt wk — no Skyp avlbl — dmn big trtls —*

Max leaned back in his big leather chair. Dubois hadn't committed to supporting Billy Cameron. Did Dubois have some business dealings with the mayor? Max frowned. Billy Cameron needed Dubois's vote. Max turned to his computer, clicked a half dozen times, brought up the contributor list for the mayor's last campaign. Roland Dubois was a heavy hitter, ponying up twenty-five hundred dollars.

Dubois was the swing vote.

Something had to break before the town council meeting. Max pushed up from his chair, headed for the door.

Annie drove slowly in the fog. She passed the Hathaway house. The only car in the drive was the black Lexus, which very likely had belonged to Everett. Apparently no one was at home. Trey should be at work and Leslie at school. Nicole could be anywhere from the grocery to the beauty shop.

Annie parked around a curve, out of sight from the Hathaway house. Though grateful for the patchy fog, she still felt as if a spotlight were trained on her. She now better appreciated the challenge faced by the murderer in attempting to remain invisible. Strange cars in quiet neighborhoods were as noticeable as blinking neon. She walked swiftly around the curve.

The dead man's Lexus was a powerful reminder of danger. Annie was sure that Everett had no sense that the hours of his life were dwindling down when he parked the car for the last time.

Annie kept to the edge of a pine grove, at the last minute slipped across the drive to the bike shed. Fog shrouded the house. She moved close to the green bike. She glanced at the ten-speed. It would have been faster but it takes some skill and familiarity to ride a ten-speed. Of the three remaining bikes, only the green bike was in riding shape. Hyla had lifted green paint flakes from the railing of a stolen motorboat. Annie had found a clump of damp mud on a pedal of the green bike. Annie slipped nearer. After a swift glance to be sure she was unobserved, she started at the front of the bike, looking inch by inch at the frame.

She almost missed the shallow scrape on the rear wheel fender. The mark flared like an open fan. The paint chips could be compared. That would prove a connection between the Hathaway house and the stolen boat. She frowned in thought, tried to imagine the murderer's actions the Friday night that Everett died. A bicycle was useful for traveling unnoticed because bike paths usually cut through woods. But that night Leslie, Trey, and Nicole each had driven away from the house shortly after Everett walked out on the dock.

Did any of the cars have a bike rack? If not, it was easy enough to slip a bike into the back of a Mini Cooper or the trunk of a sedan. Then the murderer's car could be left where it would not be noticed, perhaps in the parking area that served as a hub for many of the bike trails at this end of the island. Hop on the bike, ride into the gated area on a trail, avoiding the checkpoints, take the motorboat. The bike was swung into the back of the boat. Annie abruptly understood. There was no intention, obviously, of returning the boat, but the craft had to be left somewhere. At that point, the murderer needed a way to get back to a parked car.

Annie visualized lifting the bike over the boat rail. The scrape could have occurred either at the beginning or end of the journey. It was much more likely at the end. The boat had been abandoned in a remote area with no lights. It would be easy to bang the railing with the rear fender.

The bike was ridden to a vehicle, once again carried back to the Hathaway house, returned to the bike rack.

When the shocking call came from Better Tomorrow, how easy to hop on the bike for the short trip through the woods. No cars had been heard at Better Tomorrow or Maggie Knight's house or Henny's cabin. A bike was the perfect explanation for the murderer's silent arrival.

Who rode the bike?

Either Leslie Griffin or Nicole Hathaway had lied about Tuesday night. It was also possible that Trey had not been at his office or Brad Milton at his construction firm or Steve Raymond driving aimlessly around the island or Doug Walker at home.

Annie felt a twist of disappointment. All she had was the bike. She never doubted that paint flecks lifted by Hyla Harrison would match the scrape. Proving the bike had been in the stolen boat bolstered the claim that Everett had been murdered, but it didn't give a lead to a definite suspect.

A crow cawed. She looked up. A half dozen silky black, hawk-sized birds roosted in a live oak. The raucous caw came again, but she couldn't discern which crow warned her, just as she had no link to a silent, elusive killer.

She walked away, fog twisting around her. Visibility was decreasing. Soon it would be a challenge to drive. But she knew the roads and would find her way.

Somehow she had to find the road that led to a killer.

The crow's caw followed her into the mist.

14

Marian Kenyon dribbled peanuts into her Pepsi can. Her eyes shone. She glanced at her steno pad and neat block-letter notes. "Ten thou. That might shake loose some info."

Max held a mug of coffee. "A reward seems like our only hope now."

Marian's dark eyes gleamed with satisfaction. "If it helps to poke a beehive, yesterday's story has 'em buzzing. I've even had a couple of calls from Brice Posey. He may be as stuffed as a moose head above a fireplace, but even he can see there may be chinks in the case. However, the mayor's doubling down. He's scheduling another news conference at four, and my sources tell me it will be an attack on 'the infamous local scandal sheet and its scurrilous exploitation of tragic events.' In case you don't make the connection, that's the *Gazette* and I am the equivalent of Axis Sally." She gazed at Max as she drank Pepsi and chewed peanuts, a Southern skill. "In case ditto, Axis Sally broadcast propaganda over Radio Berlin during World War II. Too bad hizzoner can't tell the difference between in-depth reporting and propaganda. I was scrupulous to attribute information to confidential sources, which tells any savvy reader that somebody had an axe to grind and the assertions may or may not be true. No damn opinions in my stories. I got a great quote from Handler Jones emphasizing that serious allegations had been made about the course of the investigation and there appeared to be information that should be considered a matter of interest to authorities." She was complacent as a Persian cat licking cream from its lips. "Which, when sanity returns to our golden isle, will certainly be true." She glanced up at the clock on the dingy plaster wall of the *Gazette* break room, finished the Pepsi, grabbed the half-empty Planters bag and notebook. "I better get back to work. A boxed story about a ten thousand dollar reward for information leading to an arrest in the murders of Everett Hathaway, Gretchen Burkholt, and Maggie Knight will probably run above the fold. Maybe next to a picture of the mayor." She gave Max a thumbs-up before she turned away.

Annie sat behind the wheel, stared unseeing at eddying fog. She'd discovered something important, but the bike wasn't enough to help Jeremiah, even if its presence in the stolen boat was confirmed. Somehow the murderer had to be flushed.

Her lips curved in an ironic smile. Oh, sure. That was easy, wasn't it? Okay, maybe not easy, but nobody ever won by giving up. She picked up the folder from the passenger seat. Maybe if she looked at what they knew one more time . . .

Annie read each point thoughtfully, weighing whether there was anything else that could be discovered. With that criteria, her eyes widened as she read, then reread numbers six and eleven: number six — In phone messages to Annie Darling, Gretchen emphasized the card "named names" and exposed a "scandal" and spoke of "tonight." Number eleven — It isn't known when Hathaway received the index card. A member of the household could have left the card in his room or car, or he may have received the card at his office Friday morning. He missed an appointment at an art gallery. When the owner called, Hathaway seemed upset.

The note spoke of "tonight." That implied that the note had been written on Friday, that the decision to lure Everett out into the bay vulnerable in a kayak had been reached that very day.

Had Everett received the index card that morning at the house? If not, it was reasonable to conclude the card reached him at the office.

Annie knew she might be so desperate for a way forward that she was foreseeing a tantalizing possibility that might not exist. Yet, if she could determine where and when the card arrived, if there was a particular moment in time that the card reached Everett, it meant the murderer, unseen, had been present. Of course, the card could have been slipped under his bedroom door or left in the front seat of his car. If that was the case, the delivery could have been unseen by anyone. But if he received the card at his office when others were around, someone might have seen someone nearby. Everything depended upon when and where Everett received the card. He had been upset at the office, forgetting an appointment that mattered to him, so sometime after breakfast and before his appointment, the card had come.

Annie plucked her cell from her purse. As

always she knew the quickest route to information. She tapped a familiar number.

"Yo, Annie." Marian Kenyon's raspy voice sounded bright and eager. "You just missed your best chum. He's offering a ten thou reward for information regarding the homicides so he'll be busy fending off nutcases. But maybe the chaff will hold some wheat. What's up?"

"I'll fill you in later. Right now, what's Nicole Hathaway's cell number?"

"Hold on." A rustle. "Here it is."

Annie wrote down the number. "Thanks, Marian. Got —"

"Not so fast. Give me a heads-up."

"— to go. Nothing solid yet. You'll be the first to know." As soon as the line cleared, she tapped the number.

"Hello." Nicole's voice was cautious.

Annie said quickly, "Nicole, you've been a great help in trying to figure everything out. My question is really simple. Did you see Everett that Friday morning before he went to the office?"

"Yes." Nicole sounded as if she stood at the edge of a yawning pit filled with crocodiles.

"Was he in a good mood?"

"Oh." Nicole's relief was palpable. "Actually, he was happy. He was looking forward to picking up a painting from Esteban. That's what he talked about. The painter was some California artist. I don't remember the name. He enjoyed his breakfast and he told Maggie how good the cheese grits were." A pause. "I'm glad. I like to remember him that way. A long time ago, that's how he was. He was whistling when he went out to his car. But when he came home that afternoon, he slammed into the house without a word to me. Dinner was awful. He never looked at me, didn't say a word. He and Leslie quarreled. I've never seen anyone as angry as she was." There was a pause. "But she's only a teenager." The last was scarcely audible.

It was as if Nicole faced a dreadful thought and pushed it away.

Annie knew that Nicole was thinking of Tuesday night and the barking dog, Leslie's car in the drive and Maggie dead.

"Oh, I hate what's happened to us." The connection ended.

Annie had a sudden vision of a slim young figure, pedaling fast. She shivered. Could someone as young as Leslie commit three murders?

Nicole's description of her husband at his last breakfast seemed uncontrived, open, even heartfelt. Annie believed Nicole had spoken the truth. Moreover, Annie couldn't imagine Nicole stealing a boat, intercepting the kayak, and dumping Everett into the water, or riding a bike through the night to shoot and shoot and shoot again. If Nicole was telling the truth about Everett's last morning, it seemed even likelier she had told the truth about Leslie leaving the house Tuesday night.

If Leslie committed the murders, she sent the index card to Everett about his wife and her lover. When Everett left the house Friday morning, he had not yet received the card that lured him to the bay that night. Sometime between his departure and late morning, the card reached Everett. Annie knew she was one step closer to pinpointing the arrival of the card.

Now she must find out about Everett's last morning at Hathaway Advertising. Unfortunately, Trey Hathaway refused to believe that his uncle had been murdered. He wouldn't talk to her. Annie's thoughts darted. If she could have ten minutes with Dolores, she might find out everything she needed to know. If Trey saw Annie, he'd send her away. She had to talk with Dolores without Trey's knowledge . . .

Her eyes settled on the quartet of sunflowers.

Her lips curved in a sudden smile. Lucky flowers, indeed.

She pulled out her cell, touched a familiar number.

"Dearest Annie." The warmth was genuine.

Annie felt a huge lift. She wasn't surprised when Laurel answered her cell, because there was scarcely ever a call Laurel didn't answer. As her mother-in-law always said, "Of course I answer all my calls. One never knows . . . Once the most darling young man was in a poetry class I was taking and he called me with a question about dactylic metre. His name was Giuseppe and he danced divinely."

"Laurel, I need your help. I want to find out what happened at Everett Hathaway's office the day he died. You're my ticket inside Hathaway Advertising. Here's what we can do . . ."

As the taillights of Annie's Thunderbird, faint red beacons, diminished in the fog, an old but scrupulously maintained yellow motor scooter rolled from behind a weeping willow and set out in pursuit.

A clump of bamboo screened Annie from Hathaway Advertising.

Laurel carried a huge bouquet of sunflowers, big double flowers that looked like chrysanthemums. She was gorgeous, white gold hair in a chignon, patrician features assured, stylish navy silk suit a perfect fit. On the porch of the Victorian house, she waggled her left hand in a signal of reassurance, opened the oak door, and disappeared inside.

Five minutes later, Annie opened the door and stepped into the elegant hall.

Quick steps clicked on the parquet flooring. Dolores Wright stepped into the hallway. She looked surprised and dismayed.

Annie understood. Trey Hathaway had very likely announced in grim terms that Annie Darling was to be turned away.

"Annie, I'm sorry, but Trey has a client. I think he's going to be engaged for quite a while."

Annie had no doubt that Trey Hathaway would be fully and completely engaged and, unknown to him, firmly in place in his office for at least another twenty minutes. He would certainly recognize Laurel from her island activities and know quite well that she had the money to spend freely on her enthusiasms. He would be very interested as she elaborated on her plan to launch a campaign to have the sunflower named the official blossom of Broward's Rock and how a full-scale advertising campaign in print, radio, television, Twitter, and Facebook might achieve that goal.

"If you want to leave a message, I'll be sure that he gets it."

"I'm not here to see him." Annie was pleasant but definite. "I want to talk to you."

Dolores's eyes widened. "Me?"

Annie didn't respond directly. Instead, she spoke gravely. "Have you read yesterday afternoon's *Gazette?*"

Dolores nodded, her eyes wide.

"So you know there's excellent reason to believe Everett Hathaway was murdered."

Dolores's face drew down in a worried frown. "Trey says it's all nonsense."

Annie held her gaze. "If Everett was murdered, the wrong man is in jail. Even worse, a killer is loose on the island. What happened here that Friday morning could help solve three murders. And" — her smile was reassuring — "my questions are easy to answer and they don't have anything to do with anyone in the office" — Annie didn't consider Leslie Griffin a true member of the agency staff — "and there is no reason Trey would object to your answering them."

The tension drained from Dolores's kindly face. "In that case, I'll be glad to help."

"Were you here when Everett arrived?"

"Oh, yes. He usually came in around nine thirty. Trey was already here. He was in a conference call with a client in Columbia."

"How did Everett appear?"

The receptionist looked surprised. "Natty. He had on one of his favorite jackets." Her smile was confiding. "You can always tell when someone loves what they're wearing, can't you? A blue-checked tweed with blue leather buttons. I know how he felt. I have a white wool jacket with this little fleur-de-lis design and I feel like I have springs in my shoes every time I put it on."

"Did you talk to him?"

"Just good morning and that sort of thing and then in a little while I took in his coffee, double cream and two spoonfuls of sugar. He looked on top of the world."

Annie felt as triumphant as Secretariat draped with a garland of flowers. Everett was happy that morning. He had not yet received the note accusing his wife of adultery.

A faint frown drew Dolores's eyebrows down. "Something upset him later. I think it had to do with the letter that someone put through the slot." She looked beyond Annie, pointing at the rectangular bronze opening in the center of the old door.

Annie half turned, saw the slot.

Dolores was amused. "We don't have our mailed delivered like that, of course. We have a post office box. I pick up the mail about two every afternoon. But that day someone pushed through an envelope. I heard the clank of the back plate. It's funny. I knew what it was. It's a distinctive sound. I finished an e-mail and came out into the hall. An envelope lying on the throw rug. I picked it up and I didn't know what to think. Everett's name was printed in all capitals and right underneath, underlined three times, it said, *Personal and Confidential.* It didn't have a stamp on it, but it was sealed and addressed to Everett."

"What time did the letter come?"

"About a quarter to twelve. It was getting close to lunch time. I heard steps in the living room." She pointed at the opposite archway. "Brad Milton came to the archway, then looked back and gave a thumbs-up. Everett's office is in the old library behind the living room." Annie knew the living room now served as a waiting room. "I realized Brad's meeting with Everett was done. Brad said good-bye and hurried outside."

Annie sorted out the timing in her mind. The clank of the mail slot back plate, Dolores picking up the letter, Brad heading into the hall.

And outside someone moving quickly away.

"Did Brad go directly outside?"

Dolores looked surprised. "He saw me and smiled and walked out."

Brad just might have been in time to see someone — Leslie? — hurrying away from the house. High school students had the option of eating out. Leslie could easily have been downtown around noon. She could have parked several blocks away. If she wore a hoodie and jeans, there would be nothing noticeable in her appearance.

"Did you take the letter to Everett?"

Dolores nodded. "He asked me how the letter came and I told him. He was opening it as I left the library. I didn't see him again until after lunch and that's when I knew he was upset. He looked like he'd had bad news. He told me he wasn't taking any calls, that he had to work on a special project and not to interrupt him. He left about three. He walked out without a word. That's the last time I saw him."

Annie carried two thoughts out into the fog: The letter came through the mail slot and Brad Milton may have seen Everett's murderer.

Once again the driver of the scooter, unseen in the fog, followed the faint red blobs of Annie's taillights.

Annie gripped the wheel of her Thunderbird, strained to see. The car crept forward. On her map, the graveled road snaked perhaps a half mile to the isolated location of Brad's construction company. Fog altered her perception of reality. She couldn't see the woods. She knew trees and shrubs and vines were there, pressing up to the road, affording no shoulder. She had the suffocating feel of being submerged in silt-laden water. Her first intimation that she had reached the clearing was a glimpse of diffused light and, looming directly, stacked used bricks.

Annie jammed on the brakes. Brad Milton wouldn't have been pleased if she'd crashed into the bricks. She switched off her motor. A harrowing drive. She stepped out of her car, skirted the stacked bricks, and walked toward the lighted window.

No sound penetrated the fog. Silence lay like a heavy weight over the clearing. There was no activity. He'd probably dismissed his crews for the day.

Annie hurried to the steps. The door opened with a slight squeak. She stepped inside and welcomed the warmth from an electric heater.

Brad Milton sat behind a large gray metal desk, a calculator in hand. He looked up in surprise, placed the calculator next to an open folder, and slowly came to his feet.

Annie realized he was a bigger man than she remembered, probably six foot three or four, tall and angular with long arms and legs.

"Hi, Annie." His craggy face held a mixture of surprise and wariness. He looked past her, possibly seeking Max.

Annie plunged ahead, hoping against hope. "Brad, you may have the answer to who killed Everett and Gretchen and Maggie."

His big face was abruptly still. "Yeah?"

"Everything depends upon what happened at Everett's office that Friday. I need to know what you saw when you walked outside."

"Outside?" He sounded puzzled. Then he waved toward a shabby brown sofa. He waited until she was seated before he lowered himself into his chair. His deep-set eyes gazed at her intently.

Annie sat on the edge of a lumpy cushion. "You were at Hathaway Advertising the Friday Everett died."

"Right. We'd worked out a business matter. Why are you asking?" He folded his arms.

She leaned forward. "Please think back to when you left. It was a few minutes before noon."

"Yeah. That's about right." He nodded. "I went over to Parotti's. I had a bowl of chili."

"When you stepped out on the porch, what did you see?" Annie watched him, scarcely daring to hope.

His heavy brows crinkled. "I don't think I understand. I mean, what is there to see on Harbor Street? Some old houses. A couple of vacant yards. I don't think it's changed much in twenty years, maybe fifty years."

"On the sidewalk." Her lips felt stiff. "Did you see anyone at all walking away from the house?"

He looked bemused. "To tell you the truth, I was thinking about lunch. I don't know. There may have been somebody. I wasn't paying any attention."

Annie sighed and pushed up from the sofa. "If you remember anything, a car, a glimpse of someone, please call me. It's important."

Brad stood, came around the desk. "I saw the *Gazette* story. I figured you and Max were stoking the fire, all this stuff about somebody drowning Everett. I don't think there's anything to it, but if you two want to bait the mayor, I'm all in favor." He came up beside her and reached for the door handle. "He's a crooked snake. A couple of times I definitely submitted the low bid, but the jobs always go to somebody who's helped his campaign."

Annie stepped out onto the porch. The fog was even worse.

Brad remained on the threshold, the door open.

Annie welcomed the light but felt daunted by the heavy quiet. Not a sound filtered through the thick mist. She came down the steps and felt as though she was in an alien place, remote, isolated, far removed. What was the poem? The fog coming in on little cat feet . . . Silent as death. Death had come silently . . .

She was absorbed in her thoughts and realized just in time that she was about to stumble into Brad's minicar. She reached out, touched damp metal. Electric cars could be a hazard to pedestrians, arriving without a sound . . .

Annie jolted to a stop. Her hand gripped

the stanchion that supported the top. She held to the moist cold bar, thoughts tumbling . . . Silence . . . Electric cars made no sound . . . The minicar could easily be hidden behind shrubbery or a willow or a stand of cane . . . A bike could be slipped into the back . . . He'd often been at the house when Eddie was alive . . . The bike shed was close to the driveway . . . He'd used the bike to go from the beached boat to the mini car . . . He was at the house talking with Trey when Gretchen Burkholt called . . . He took the message from the hall table, drove the minicar to Better Tomorrow . . . Tuesday night the minicar slipped into the shadows behind Maggie's house and then between the pilings that supported Henny's cabin . . . Of course Brad was at Hathaway Advertising when the letter came . . . Clever . . . He'd left Everett, gone out on the porch, pushed the prepared envelope through the slot, then hurried back inside to pretend — if anyone ever asked — that he had been coming out of Everett's office when the note came and could not possibly have delivered it . . . but Everett connected the arrival of the letter with Brad's departure . . . He must have written Brad's name followed by a question mark at the bottom of the index card . . .

Almost as if pulled by an irresistible force, she slowly turned to look up at the tall man standing on the porch, a big man with long arms and legs, looming huge against the light behind him.

Annie ran.

"Hey." Brad's shout was harsh.

She plunged around the minicar. Her car was about ten feet farther, but even if she reached the Thunderbird and locked herself inside, she would have to fumble for her keys in her purse, start the car. He would move fast, as desperate as he had been the day he saw the message on the hall table at the Hathaway house. He would break through a window, reach for her, and then she would die.

He pounded down the stairs.

Annie veered away from the car, fled into the fog. She fell and scrambled up, hands and knees scratched, terrified, heart thudding. Over the ragged whistle of her breathing, she listened for his running steps.

Nothing. Only the sound of her frantic breaths.

A screech. Was the rending sound the rasp of metal scraping against concrete?

Silence.

Terror plucked at her mind. Silence. That's how death came.

She shuddered. She'd told Max she would be at the store. Instead, she was within yards of a murderer who did not intend that she should live to tell what she knew. She listened with every fiber of her being. He was listening, too. That's why there was no movement. He was waiting for her to reveal her presence.

Annie strained to see through the fog. Was he coming near? She had to move. But she was disoriented. She had no sense of where he was. The fog was opaque, wrapping her in a heavy grayness. If she could reach the woods, maybe she could hide. But if she moved, he would hear. Yet at this moment he might be edging silently toward her, one long softly placed step after another. Perhaps he had figured out how far she might have gone when she ran from the electric car.

His voice came eerily through the fog with a horrible attempt at geniality. "What's going on? Something scare you? Sometimes I see a cougar. Look, come on out, I'll see you safely to your car."

He sounded so reasonable, so measured.

Annie bent down. Her hand swept the ground. She found a knob of wood. Not heavy enough. Gently, she placed the piece on the ground and again spread her fingers, seeking, seeking. Her fingertips touched a rough remnant of brick half buried in the sandy soil. She scratched and scraped with her nails until the piece came free.

"Annie, I'll bet you're lost. Give a call. I'll try to find you." A grotesque attempt at normalcy.

Annie held the portion of brick tightly. Slowly she stood and cautiously turned. She thought she faced the area where she'd parked. Her hands shook. She had to do something, find out where he was. Maybe this was a mistake. But she couldn't bear to wait and wait and wait and have him creep toward her out of the fog, big and powerful and deadly.

Using all her strength, Annie threw the clump of brick as hard as she could. She felt a flash of triumph at a loud metallic clatter.

The shots came swiftly, one, two, three, flashes of brightness no more than twenty feet away.

Hyla Harrison held her cell close to her lips. "Ten thirty. Milton Construction. Ten seventy-five. Ten eighty-four. Ten forty-three." She moved silent as a wraith through the swirling fog, repeating her call. She'd left her shoes near her scooter. Her feet were wet and cold, but she stepped quietly, lightly as a feather falls. "Ten thirty. Milton Construction. Ten seventy-five. Ten eighty-four. Ten forty-three." The warnings were explicit: danger/caution, location, shooting, crime in progress, urgent/use lights and sirens. It was only when she was sure the message had been received loud and clear, Lou Pirelli barking, "Ten ninety-three, ten ninety-three," that she added, "Assailant armed and dangerous. Shots at Annie Darling. Stalking Annie Darling with gun. Officer off-duty, unarmed."

Lou's voice was shocked. "Unarmed? Wait for us."

Hyla didn't answer. She couldn't be sure of the location of the shots, but she felt if she kept going slightly to her left, she would find him. How many bullets did he have left? Did he have an extended magazine? Or a supply in his pocket? One step, two, three . . .

"Hey, Annie. I got a deal for you." There was a burble of panic in Brad Milton's deep voice.

Hyla stiffened. Over there. She moved cautiously from behind a tree.

The fog shifted. Brad Milton stood hunched in a tight posture only a few feet from Annie's Thunderbird, his head swiveling back and forth, back and forth. Perhaps he heard the crackle of a twig near him. He turned, saw her.

Hyla lunged for cover, shouted, "Police. Hands up. You're surrounded. Police. Throw down your weapon."

He raised his arm. Rapid gunshots, harsh, cracking like a whip.

Max hummed as he placed the ball behind an especially challenging curl in the indoor carpet, worthy of a Pete Dye course. His cell rang. He tapped the ball, which promptly veered off onto the floor. That was probably about as well as he would do on an actual Pete Dye course. He leaned over his desk and retrieved the phone. He noted the caller ID. "Hey, Mari—"

The reporter's raspy voice was an octave high. "Scanner. Shots. Brad Milton Construction. Annie's there. Oh, God, Max, he's shooting at her."

Shots. Hyla's shouts. Thrashing in the underbrush.

Annie knelt behind a wheelbarrow. Hyla was off duty. Annie felt a welter of conflicting emotion, gratitude that Hyla was there, guilt that she was in danger. Annie understood what must have happened. Hyla had followed Annie, dogged her path from the Hathaway house to the agency to this isolated place of terror. How like Hyla, so stiff and serious, wanting to help Billy, trying to think how, offering what she knew to Annie. Hyla pondering that decision in her careful way and deciding she might have set more in motion than she had intended. Hyla out of uniform. Unarmed. Trying now to save Annie.

The fog seemed to press down on Annie, a living entity, heavy, dark, unrelenting.

Annie blinked back tears. Hyla had done her best, yelling that the police were here. But they weren't. In this mist-heavy, forsaken place, three of them were frozen in time, Hyla and Annie and Death.

Max gunned the Maserati, his hands clenched on the wheel. Despite the fog, he careened around curves, picked up speed on straight stretches, plummeted through the swath of gray, watching, ready to brake, willing anything and everything out of his way. Annie. He had to get to Annie. Brad Milton. That out-of-the-way, remote clearing. Max felt numb. He should have known. Brad had been glib, quick to claim that he and Everett had ironed everything out. Why would Everett have backed off? Everett was small natured, petty. There had been no agreement. Brad faced financial devastation. So he killed Everett and then Gretchen and Maggie, and now Annie was in dreadful danger. The police were on their way. But Brad had a gun. The Maserati jolted in the ruts leading to Brad's buildings. Ahead of him, Max heard the wail of sirens. He ached inside.

Shots rattled. Annie covered her ears. She trembled. She wanted to run for the woods, plunge into the trees, slam to earth behind a fat-trunked live oak, escape from a man who was ready to blindly kill and kill again. He must be hoping that Hyla lied, that once again he would be safe if only he killed some more. There was no sound from Hyla. Had bullets ripped into her flesh, stained the plaid shirt?

A branch crackled nearby.

Annie's heart lurched. He must be very near. If she could find anything to serve as a weapon . . . She swept her hands inside the rough interior of the wheelbarrow. Nothing. She hated to leave the spurious sense of safety from the wheelbarrow, but she had to find a weapon. She moved in a crouch, one step after another. There — straight ahead — a greater darkness in the fog, the waist-high stack of used bricks. She reached out, hefted a brick. She was not strong enough to throw the five-pound weight very far. Perhaps ten or twelve feet. That might bring Brad close enough to see her.

Hyla had called and shouted to help Annie. Then the terrible crack of gunfire and awful silence.

Annie took a deep breath, whirled like a shot putter. The brick arced away toward the woods, opposite where she'd last heard Hyla, and thudded heavily to the ground.

Heavy running steps sounded near, so near.

Annie grabbed another brick.

Here he came. Breathing heavily, Brad pounded out of the fog only a foot or so away.

Brush crashed off to one side. Hyla's voice rose in a brusque commanding shout. "Police. Drop your weapon. Police."

Brad swung toward the sound of Hyla's voice. He looked huge, head butted forward, big shoulders hunched. His hand rose, lifting the gun, pointing the barrel toward Hyla.

Annie scrambled toward him. He was too big, too strong for her to bring down, but she had to stop him from firing. Hyla had come after her . . .

His breath came in huge rasps, masking her approach.

Desperately, she lifted the brick, crashed it down on his right hand.

The gun spun from his hand as he grunted in pain.

Hyla exploded out of the mist, running toward them, her feet pounding on the hard ground.

Brad flung a long arm toward Annie, knocking her away. She fell backward, rolled to one side, tried to get up.

Shouting, Brad started for her, then stopped, chest heaving. He swung away in search of the gun, swearing in a harsh monotone.

Red lights whirling, cars squealed into the clearing, men erupted, lights shone. "Police. Hands up. Police. Drop your weapons. Police."

Brad was down on one knee, reaching for the gun.

Without hesitation, Hyla propelled herself forward, dropped a thick strand of vine around his neck, and yanked as she slammed a knee into his back.

Maddened as a pricked bull, he twisted and bucked, heaving Hyla to one side.

Lou Pirelli, stocky and strong, and Coley

Benson, young and tough, slammed Brad to the ground and held him until he was shackled.

"I'll sue the police." Brad's voice was hoarse and his eyes wild. "I try to deal with a trespasser and I get attacked. I don't know what's going on . . ."

15

Milton can play any tune he wants to, but we got him for attempted murder and that's enough until we prove the rest of the case. But" — a sigh — "I have to get the so-call chief involved." He clicked the phone. "Mr. Farrell." Lou Pirelli was polite even though his face registered disgust. "We've solved a triple murder case and now must arrange for the release of a man arrested in error."

"Listen, I got busted pipes to deal with." Farrell's querulous voice blasted over the speaker phone in the station break room. "If you got questions, ask the mayor. He said there wasn't nothing for me to do. Or handle it yourself."

Lou's face brightened. "Sure thing, sir. We have everything under control." He was crisp, forceful. "With your approval, we'll provide the mayor with an update at the appropriate time."

"Yeah. That's the way to handle it.

Thanks." The call ended.

Lou clicked off the phone. His look of satisfaction slowly seeped away. "Okay, we charge Milton, start rounding up evidence, enough that even the circuit solicitor will agree. But Billy's still out in the cold. You know what will happen" — he looked at Annie and Max on the other side of the long green table — "the mayor will take credit and conveniently forget he insisted on charging Jeremiah. He won't reinstate Billy."

Annie finished a last bite of a golden hot glazed donut, welcomed a pulse of energy and, yes, the lift might be a temporary sugar high, but she needed all the bolstering she could get. It would be a long time before she forgot the fog and the fear. She would never forget the debt she owed to Sgt. Hyla Harrison, one arm now in a sling to ease the discomfort of the shoulder bruised when Brad shook her off. And, of course, there was Max. She slid a tentative glance toward him. He was pale, his face set in tight lines, his dark blue eyes haunted. As soon as they left the station, he would be very explicit about the foolishness of walking into a lion's den.

She reached out, touched his arm. "I was sure it was Leslie."

His gaze was grim. "You should have

called me."

"I would have called, I swear, if I'd had any idea I'd stumbled close to the truth. Honestly, it never occurred to me that Brad was the murderer." She took a deep breath. "I know I'm lucky." Her voice was small.

His face softened. "It wasn't just luck. If Hyla didn't respect you, she would never have told you about the boat. And, being Hyla, she realized she had to be sure you didn't do something dumb."

Annie didn't think Max was excelling at tact. But whatever Hyla's motivation, Annie was grateful. However, she knew that Hyla would simply shake her head and mutter that she'd just been doing her duty.

Annie was quite willing to pay respect where respect was due. "Thanks to Hyla, Brad Milton's under arrest for assault with a deadly weapon. I'll bet they find tire prints from his electric car at Better Tomorrow and at Henny's and Maggie's and somewhere near the Hathaway house. His fingerprints may be on the green bike he used the night he killed Everett. If the bullets that killed Maggie match the gun he shot at Hyla and me, that's all the proof anyone needs."

"Yeah, we got him." Lou sounded confident. "We'll fill in the chinks. But that won't get Billy his job back." He heaved a sigh.

"Now I got to call the mayor and tell him what's happened. He'll prance like a peacock."

Annie sat up straight, her expression eager. It might be the sugar but she had an idea. "That's the answer. Achilles' heel."

Lou looked worried. "You feeling okay? Maybe you should go home and rest."

"Attention." Annie beamed at her husband and the stocky police sergeant. "The mayor has a news conference scheduled at four o'clock. He'll want to look good, right? Here's what we can do." She talked fast.

When she finished, Max gave a fist pump. "It's a great idea. But Annie and I can't make the pitch. Cosgrove loathes both of us."

Annie looked thoughtful. "Laurel?" Men from nine to ninety responded to her beauty and charm.

Max slowly shook his head. "He knows she's my mother."

Annie was reluctant to pass over Laurel. But Max was probably right. "Okay, we need someone with a strong personality who is well known on the island, preferably rich. Cosgrove loves rich. Someone who is impossible to divert once started. A friend of Billy's . . . Oh, yes. Yes!" She reached for her cell. "The mayor won't know what hit him."

Blue sky and a balmy afternoon reminded Annie anew why a South Carolina barrier island was undoubtedly the most glorious place in the universe to live. The morning's fog and chill were just a memory. She nosed the Thunderbird into a parking slot a couple of blocks from the station. Cars lined the curbs on either side of the station. The lot at the park across the street was full. She picked up oversized sunglasses, slipped them on, and turned to Max. "Would you recognize me?" She wore a straw hat from last spring with daffodil yellow ribbons tied beneath her chin.

Max grinned. "Sweetie, I'd know you in a burlap bag. Especially a short burlap bag."

She laughed. "Would the mayor recognize me?"

He tilted his head. "Most men —"

"Max." Her tone was warning.

His gaze was innocent. "If you want a primer on what men look for, I'm your guy. Actually, Cosgrove will only have eyes for the TV camera, so you're probably safe enough. How about me?" He tapped the brim of his baseball cap. A paint-splashed blue cotton shirt hung untucked over aged white jeans. He'd burrowed in the hall closet and found an old pair of cowboy boots.

"No one should pay any attention to us." She glanced at her watch. "Five minutes to four." She felt a flutter of anxiety. Everything was set in motion, but she and Max had to remain in the background. She gave him a jaunty salute. "Let's go."

A half dozen TV cameras ranged in front of the police station. Annie thought it likely that news crews had arrived on the ferry from as far away as Savannah and Charleston. Lou Pirelli had sent out bulletins to all the coastal stations, alerting them that the solution to a triple murder would be announced at the mayor's four o'clock news conference on the front steps of the Broward's Rock police station.

The front door opened at precisely four o'clock. By this time a crowd of perhaps fifty had gathered, including many downtown shop owners who had put out Back Soon signs, boat captains with no charters that foggy morning, retirees glad for a break from dominos, and high school students attracted by the television crews. Annie and Max stood behind a group of twittering girls.

Mayor Cosgrove, natty in a gray pinstripe, lavender shirt, and yellow tie, bustled outside. Lou Pirelli, freshly shaved, his curly dark hair neatly brushed, looked impressively muscular in his crisp khaki uniform. His eyes skittered around the crowd. He saw Annie, made a quick thumbs-up.

Annie grabbed Max's arm. "Everything's set."

Cosgrove cleared his throat. "Ladies and gentlemen." He lifted his rounded face, beamed at the cameras. "I am pleased to announce —"

A horn powerful as a sub's klaxon boomed as a maroon Rolls Royce slid to a stop in the middle of the street. A chauffeur in matching purple livery came from the driver's side to open the rear door.

Emma Clyde, bristly hair bright silver today, stepped out. Her lavender caftan with dashes of gold swirled as she swept toward the front door. Stubby fingers clutched four rolls of parchment. She nodded regally in passing as the crowd drew back, affording her passage.

The TV cameras swung toward her.

The mayor's face drew down in a petulant frown. "Here now . . ." His voice was drowned out by rising murmur from the onlookers.

"Mayor Cosgrove." Emma might have been greeting a royal personage. She reached the end of the walk. Without hesitation, she climbed the steps, turned to face the cameras, standing beside him. In her eye-catching dress, her square face serene and imperious, she was the focus of every gaze.

"Excuse me," the mayor sputtered.

Emma held up a stubby hand and a ruby ring glittered in the sunlight. "Your Honor, it is my pleasure as the director of the Broward's Rock Good Government League to present you with a special award to recognize your achievement and that of Broward Rock's exemplary police chief, Billy Cameron —" She paused, lifted her head, looked around. "Chief Cameron? We need Chief Cameron."

Billy Cameron, in the navy suit that he wore to funerals, walked forward. Big and impressive, his broad face looked hesitant.

The mayor stared in shock.

Emma turned toward Cosgrove, her blue eyes steely though her face formed in a smile. "Don't be modest, Mayor Cosgrove. Your accomplishment for the island of Broward's Rock shall stand through the years, a moment marked by triumph. Now, now,

now, let me finish. As one of the myriad vot-
ers —"

Cosgrove stiffened, his plump face
abruptly intent.

"— on our lovely island, I hope you will
enjoy your moment in the sun. And" — she
gestured toward Billy — "come up here,
Chief Cameron. Without your excellent
work behind the scenes, justice could not
have triumphed."

Once again she faced the cameras, a big
woman with an aura of command. "The
League wishes to thank Mayor Cosgrove
and Chief Cameron for today's apprehen-
sion of Bradley Milton, a suspect in the
murders of island residents Everett Hathaway, Gretchen Burkholt, and Maggie
Knight." Emma unrolled one of the parch-
ments, held it up to obscure the amazement
on the face of the porcine mayor. "Whereas,
Mayor Cosgrove cooperated with Chief
Cameron in a plan to convince Bradley
Milton that the police thought another
suspect guilty, thereby making it possible
for investigation to proceed sub rosa, the
League presents a certificate of honor to
Mayor Cosgrove." She thrust the certificate
at him.

Cosgrove's lips made guppy movements.

The color of his face rivaled an island sunset.

Emma faced the cameras. "Our mayor is overcome by modesty. But that is what we would expect. Always, his first thought is to do what is right for the community. Moreover, he is eager for Chief Cameron to receive his certificate." She nodded at Billy, whose face held an interesting mixture of amazement and incredulity. "Our chief is also a modest public servant." She cleared her throat, unrolled the second parchment. "Whereas Chief Cameron cooperated in pretending that he had been relieved of his command and thereby made it possible for Sgt. Hyla Harrison to pursue her inquiries, which led to the capture of a dangerous criminal, this certificate of honor shall be presented by the mayor as he officially reinstates Chief Cameron to his position. Now, Mayor Cosgrove, repeat after me. I, Mayor Cosgrove, take great pleasure —"

Cosgrove's eyes flickered toward the cameras and the excited audience. "I, Mayor Cosgrove, take great pleasure —"

"— in publicly reinstating Chief of Police Billy Cameron to his post —"

Cosgrove hesitated for a fraction until he saw Emma's steely gaze. "— in publicly reinstating Chief of Police Billy Cameron to his post —"

Emma nodded in satisfaction. "— and personally presenting this glorious certificate of honor to Chief Cameron." Ceremoniously she handed the certificate to the mayor.

The mayor took the parchment and thrust it at Billy.

"Thank you, Mayor Cosgrove and Chief Cameron." Emma held up the third roll. "It is also a pleasure to recognize Jeremiah Young, who exhibited great personal courage when he summoned help and saved island resident Henny Brawley from a murderous assault. Moreover, Jeremiah endured false arrest, making it possible for the investigation to successfully capture Bradley Milton. The mayor's office will" — she turned to the mayor and spoke emphatically — "submit papers requesting that Jeremiah be granted a pardon, erasing his previous conviction for a car theft. Jeremiah Young and Henny Brawley?"

Without a do-rag and freshly shaved, Jeremiah moved hesitantly forward, the TV cameras turning toward him. He walked slowly, a hand on Henny's elbow as she used her cane to limp toward the steps. Henny took the scroll from Emma and tucked it in Jeremiah's hand, then turned to the cameras. "Jeremiah saved my life. Jeremiah is not only brave and kind, he is dependable and a hard worker. His ambition is to open a repair store, and we know island residents will welcome him into the business community. Thank you."

Emma nodded agreement. "Finally, it is a great honor for the League to recognize the bravery of Sgt. Hyla Harrison, who saved island resident Annie Darling from an attack by Bradley Milton. Sergeant Harrison was subsequently injured while subduing the suspect. Sergeant Harrison?"

Hyla Harrison approached reluctantly. As always, her uniform was immaculate, but her right arm was in a sling. Her thin face was pink with embarrassment. She stopped at the foot of the steps, looked up at Billy.

Emma handed the fourth scroll to Billy. "As police chief, it is appropriate that you shall present the certificate." She smiled at Cosgrove. "Isn't that right, Your Honor?"

The mayor managed a smile. "Absolutely. Proper channels and all that."

Billy stepped toward Hyla. "Good work, Sergeant Harrison."

Hyla took the parchment and fled into the crowd, her cheeks bright red.

Billy addressed the cameras. "Sergeant Harrison is an outstanding police officer who follows procedure. The evidence she found in an abandoned boat, a paint streak that links a bicycle to a homicide and several fibers, which match a jacket belonging to the accused Bradley Milton, came as a result of her exceedingly thorough investigation. Thank you, Sergeant."

Emma was like a big cat with a cornered mouse as she beamed at Cosgrove. "Now, Your Honor, some pictures with you and our chief of police . . ."

16

It was after hours at Death on Demand. Max turned the cork in a magnum of champagne.

Emma sat at the center table in the coffee area. Tonight's caftan was an improbable swirl of yellow, red, and purple. She accepted her flute with a gracious nod.

"Emma, you were wonderful." Annie lifted a glass.

Max's hand rose. "Magnificent."

Emma's square face was receptive.

Annie squashed the uncharitable thought that Emma was as hungry for applause as the mayor. But Emma had taken time from her writing — she was only a chapter from the end of the manuscript, a time of intense and harried effort when nothing short of a cataclysm could draw her from her computer — to win back Billy's job, and that was as generous a move as she could ever make. "Emma, you're the best."

Emma nodded in agreement, her sapphire blue eyes approving.

Henny burbled with laughter. "I loved the way the mayor had to shake hands with Billy and pose for pictures between Billy and Hyla."

Max raised an eyebrow. "The only downer is you can bet he'll use those shots in his next campaign."

"Oh well." Annie was feeling generous. "What matters is Billy. And Jeremiah." She raised the glass. "To Emma. To Billy. To Jeremiah. To Hyla —"

Voices joined in a chorus. "— to Henny. To Annie. To Max. To Handler."

Flutes were upended.

The phone rang.

Annie checked caller ID. She answered, clicking on the speaker phone. "Hey, Hyla."

"I did a little more checking." The officer's voice was matter-of-fact.

Annie raised an eyebrow. "Checking?"

Hyla cleared her throat. "You were convinced that Leslie Hathaway was guilty because you thought she went out on her bike that Tuesday night."

"She didn't take her car." Annie felt defensive. She'd put herself and Hyla in grave danger because she had been sure of Leslie's guilt. "And we were hunting for a killer who arrived without making any noise and that bike definitely had fresh mud on it."

"Yes." Hyla's tone was just this side of patronizing, implying that a careful investigator would have kept digging and not jumped to hasty conclusions. "I called Leslie and explained that the bike was part of evidence in the murder case and would she please explain her use of it on Tuesday evening. She did not take the bike Tuesday evening. The explanation is simple." Hyla's brisk voice held a tiny hint of empathy. "Her boyfriend wasn't returning her calls and she was afraid he was interested in someone else. She didn't want to take her car in case he saw her. She said, 'I'd rather die than have him think I was spying on him.' Which, of course, she was. In any event, she didn't take the bike. She took a canoe from the boat house and lurked in the water near his cabin. He came home alone. She watched for a while, but no one came so she went home." A pause. "Poor girl. She thought he was guilty and he thought she was, but they've worked everything out. He's taken the GED and saved his money and enrolled in Armstrong State. She said she was going to go to school, too. Possibly she's grown up a bit."

"Hyla, thank you for everything. If it hadn't been for you —"

Hyla was gruff. "Just doing my job." The call ended.

Henny sat with her walking boot elevated on a small stool. "Another toast. To Hyla."

They lifted their glasses.

Laurel darted to the blue vase by the fireplace, selected a sunflower stalk, and held it out to Emma. Laurel's husky voice was soft but clear. "Nothing speaks of loyalty and generosity better than a sunflower and" — she raised her glass — "a toast. To Emma, Queen of Crime and Restorer of Integrity to our island's police department."

"Hear, hear." Henny drank from the flute. Despite the lines of pain and lack of color in her face, her vivid brown eyes sparkled. She looked up at the paintings above the fireplace, then slid her eyes toward Emma, whose square face was abruptly creased with hostility. "In order, *The Jasmine Moon Murder* by Laura Childs, *Death and the Lit Chick* by G. M. Malliet, *The Mamo Murders* by Juanita Sheridan, *The Darling Dahlias and the Cucumber Tree* by Susan Wittig Albert, and *The Mamur Zapt and the Return of the Carpet* by Michael Pearce."

Emma's sapphire eyes narrowed. She glared at the third painting. "It scarcely seems sporting to include a book written in the nineteen fifties. That, of course, threw me off. Moreover, Juanita Sheridan's books are important because Lily Wu was the first female Asian detective along with her Anglo friend Janice Cameron. A more representative scene featuring Lily and Janice could have been chosen. However" — she managed an almost gracious smile — "if dear Henny found thoughts of the paintings comforting while she was in the hospital, I am certainly pleased for her."

Annie felt a surge of sheer delight, the fire flickering in the fireplace, Henny and Emma dueling for mystery superiority, lovely Laurel with her unquenchable spirit, and Max, a grown-up Joe Hardy and sexy as hell. Slightly giddy from the champagne, Annie looked at each in turn — wonderful, handsome Max; elegant, enchanting Laurel; brave, generous Henny; crusty, brilliant Emma — and raised her glass. "Forward Faithful Five, friends forever."

ABOUT THE AUTHOR

Carolyn Hart is the author of the Death on Demand and Henrie O series. Her books have won the Agatha, the Anthony and Macavity awards. She was a founding member and is a former president of Sisters in Crime. This is the twenty-second Death on Demand title.

The employees of Thorndike Press hope you have enjoyed this Large Print book. All our Thorndike, Wheeler, and Kennebec Large Print titles are designed for easy reading, and all our books are made to last. Other Thorndike Press Large Print books are available at your library, through selected bookstores, or directly from us.

For information about titles, please call:
(800) 223-1244

or visit our Web site at:
http://gale.cengage.com/thorndike

To share your comments, please write:
Publisher
Thorndike Press
10 Water St., Suite 310
Waterville, ME 04901